THROW

LIKE A

GIRL

THROW LIKE A GIRL

SARAH HENNING

POPPY

LITTLE, BROWN AND COMPANY

New York Boston

Poppy
Hachette Book Group
1290 Avenue of the Americas, New York, NY 10104
Visit us at LBYR.com

Originally published in hardcover and ebook by
Little, Brown and Company in January 2020
First Trade Paperback Edition: July 2021

Poppy is an imprint of Little, Brown and Company. The Poppy name and logo are trademarks of Hachette Book Group, Inc.

The publisher is not responsible for websites (or their content) that are not owned by the publisher.

The Library of Congress has cataloged the hardcover
edition as follows:
Names: Henning, Sarah, author.
Title: Throw like a girl / Sarah Henning.
Description: First edition. | New York ; Boston : Little, Brown and Company, 2020. | Summary: "When high school junior Liv Rodinsky is kicked off her private school's softball team and loses her scholarship she must join her new school's football team to prove she can be a team player, all while falling for the star quarterback"— Provided by publisher.
Identifiers: LCCN 2018050934 | ISBN 9780316529501 (hardcover) | ISBN 9780316529518 (ebook) | ISBN 9780316529532 (library edition ebook)
Subjects: | CYAC: Teamwork (Sports)—Fiction. | Football—Fiction. | Sex role—Fiction. | Family life—Fiction. | Dating (Social customs)—Fiction. | High schools—Fiction. | Schools—Fiction.
Classification: LCC PZ7.1.H4642 Thr 2020 | DDC [Fic]—dc23
LC record available at https://lccn.loc.gov/2018050934

ISBNs: 978-0-316-52949-5 (pbk.),
978-0-316-52951-8 (ebook)

Printed in the United States of America

LSC-C

Printing 1, 2021

To Amalia and all the other girls who
keep up with the boys—pass 'em.

1

IN EVERY BASEBALL MOVIE EVER, IT'S THE SAME.

Bottom of the ninth. Bases loaded. Two out.

The crowd breathless at the batter's back. The players in the dugout on their feet. The opposing pitcher staring daggers from the mound with steam pouring from flared nostrils.

At the plate: the team's star, bat pointed toward the wall, challenge clear.

In real life—in softball—it doesn't exactly work out that way.

It's close.

But not as if penned by a writer's hand.

It's the bottom of the seventh—there aren't nine innings

in high school softball. But the bases *are* loaded. And there *are* two out.

The crowd is breathless, the players in the dugout are on their feet, and the opposing pitcher has got the raging-bull thing going on from the mound.

But the team's star isn't at the plate.

She's *on* it.

Wilted in the dirt after taking a sixty-mile-per-hour fastball to the back. Motionless. Eyes stunned open. All senses on pause, a rolling clap of pain drowning out everything else.

As the crowd holds its collective breath, I search for mine. My lungs don't seem to be working, and the catcher and umpire both loom over me, outlines blurry with the same fuzzy energy as a 3-D movie left to the naked eye.

I blink a few times. First at the lights. Then at the catcher and ump. And, finally, at the upside-down EAGLES name scrawled across my chest, willing my rib cage to nudge my lungs into action.

Up. Down. Up. Down. In. Out. In. Out.

The sound comes flooding in as my chest finally rises. The shouts of my teammates, the sweet girls of Windsor Prep, will me up. My coach's voice—my sister's voice—above them all.

"Stand, Liv! Stand!"

I make it to my feet, back hot and lungs still warming up.

Brows pulled together, I shoot my game-day glare at

the mound. Kelly Cleary's red hair clashes horribly with her stupid orange-and-white uniform; her cat-eye liquid liner is so thick it hides the fact that she has actual eyes. And they must not be able to see worth a crap, because she just hit a batter with the bases loaded and one down.

Which means that if I can walk over to first base, everyone advances and we score a run to tie it. Not exactly the walk-off grand slam of my dreams, but it's one way to move out of this round and into the Kansas state championship game.

Or at least get one run from doing that.

Again, another true-life technicality.

Both sides of the crowd are clapping, because that's just what you do when someone gets hit by a pitch. My parents, brother, and Heather are on their feet. My teammates are a rowdy block of purple, crowding the dugout rail, ribbons and ponytails kissing their cheeks in the breeze, clapping me to first.

"Nice job, O-Rod!" There's my best friend, Addie, cheering even though she's about to bat.

My sister, Danielle, has her arms crossed over the EAGLES scrawled on her chest, the wedding ring Heather gave her two years ago glinting in the stadium lights. She does her stern-coach nod. It's a look I first saw at age three, when she was twelve and egging me on as I threw her the ball for the millionth time. She was a hell of a player, but she's always—*always*—been a coach.

On the other end of the stadium, I spy my boyfriend, Jake. Dreads to his shoulders, he's dressed out in his orange football jersey, number thirty-two, clapping along with a few teammates in Northland's section of the crowd. Wearing their jerseys out of season to big games is a tradition, or so he says. But while he looks the part of a good, supportive student-athlete from the rival school, I know that even though we've only been dating since the Spring Prep Preview photo shoot at the *Kansas City Star* in February, he's totally here for me.

Below the Northland section is its dugout where the Tigers' veteran coach, Trudi Kitterage, observes from the steps. Coach Kitt looks like the burnt-bacon version of a head cheerleader—all hard curves and tan lines. But her talent is real. And her team is good. Too good for Kelly's mistake. Meaning, if I sawed Kelly in half with my own glare, Coach Kitt's stare is roasting the pieces of her in a bonfire of why-the-hell-did-you-do-that.

Because in ten of my shuffling steps, we'll be tied.

Eight more steps. Six. Four. Two.

And then I'm on the bag at first, squeezing in next to Stacey Sanderson. Who, up until a minute ago, was my least favorite player on the Northland team.

She can hit. She can run. And she's Jake's gorgeous ex-girlfriend.

From, like, two years ago. Or something. Whatever. I'm not sure—but there's a history there. And she's been reminding me of it the whole game. Giving me side-mouthed sass every time I've gotten on base. Which, let's be honest, has been a lot.

This time, I strike first. Shaking my head as I clap home our third-base runner, Rosemary, for the tying score. "One away, Sanderson. All because your girl Cleary can't hit the broad side of a barn."

The corners of Stacey's mouth quirk up but her eyes stay at home, where Addie is settling into her mega-erect stance. The girl can dunk and hit the three, but she's a praying mantis in cleats. "I'd say she hit the broad side of something, all right."

I snort and roll my eyes. "Jake loves my curves."

"Jake also runs headfirst into a pack of bodies for three months a year. Brain cells aren't his forte, Rodinsky."

"Whatever, Skeletor."

Addie dusts Kelly's curveball, but it falls straight into the catcher's mitt. Strike one.

Come on, McAndry. Just a base hit. No extra innings. Just a straight seven-inning pass to the championship.

Stacey sniffs. "I have a lot of admirers of my ass, *thankyouverymuch.*"

I don't even miss a beat. "They're just trying to figure out how you sit comfortably on something so flat."

Addie squares her shoulders and waits for another pitch, looking very badass. Kelly is taking *forfreakingever,* and I *so* want to inch off the base and away from Stacey's fish lips—too bad it's not allowed. But then Cleary actually does something right and rips a strong fastball. I lead off base, sure Addie will connect, but McAndry hesitates—strike. Shit. I dive back in just as the catcher whips the ball to first. I hit the dirt just in time, fingertips grazing the base before Stacey gets the tag.

Called safe, I stand, not bothering to wipe off the dust streaking across my chest and the Eagles logo.

"Nice skunk streaks, Rodinsky."

Whatever. I keep watching Addie, willing her to mow down whatever-the-hell pitch Cleary comes out with next.

"I think they highlight my assets much better than my uniform on its own," I shoot back.

"I'm not so sure about that"—here comes the pitch, fast and straight, and square in the batter's box—"better ask your sister."

Addie's bat rockets forward and connects, sending the ball straight into the gap between second and third, dropping short of the outfielder at left.

My body knows it's supposed to run—it's been trained to run at the crack of the bat for the past thirteen years— but my mind is reeling. Did she just imply what I think she implied?

Stunned, I stutter-step, weighed down by her voice in my ears. Somehow, I move forward enough to make it to second, giving Addie room at first so Christy can score the walk-off run. But my brain is back at first. Where Stacey is standing, punching her free hand into her glove, pissed that Northland's state run is now officially over. She's a senior, so it's really the end of her road. We've won and she's ended her high school career with a loss.

I should smile. Collapse in relief. Cheer about going to the championship game. But I can't—not until I respond. I have to. I can't just let her say something like that and then go home like it didn't happen.

Sanderson is moping at first, so I jog back down the first-to-second line. My teammates are all celebrating at home base with Christy, but there's no way I can go straight there. I drop in next to Stacey, now walking in the direction of her dugout.

"What did you say?" My voice is clipped.

She doesn't even look in my direction. "Nothing."

"No, I think you did. And I think you meant something very specific."

Stacey's eyes roll my way. They're a muddy shade of brown, made worse by the fact that her eyebrows are on the endangered species list. "Doesn't it bother you? Your sister being paid to check out your teammates?"

"Excuse me?"

She purses her lips and says, slowly, "You heard me. Your sister. Is paid. To check out. Your teammates."

The knuckles of my right hand smack her straight across the ski jump of her obnoxiously pert nose, and we tumble to the infield dirt. I have her pinned, my butt across her kidneys, knees on either side of her squirming stomach.

"Don't talk about my sister like that!"

At the taste of infield, she bucks wildly and we both land on our sides. She scrambles on top of me but I get her hard across the nose again. She yelps, blood leaking onto her lips.

"You owe me a new nose!"

Her right hand goes back, fingers pulled into a fist. I see a heavy caking of dirt across her knuckles before she misses my nose and lands a blow square to my right eye.

Tears immediately begin to pool at my lash line. We're upended again, and I'm on top of her long enough to score one more open palm to her cheekbone before I'm finally yanked away by at least two teammates. Maybe three or four.

I vaguely hear Addie's voice. "Be cool, O-Rod! Cool! *Liv.* OLIVE."

It seems to come almost from the inside of my head rather than outside, where the crowd has gone for a collective gasp.

Her words and hands carry me—I'm tall, but Addie's taller and stronger, using all her leverage to pull me away. More hands come. More voices, too. Above the din, I hear Danielle, her coach voice turned up to eleven. "Hey, hey, hey! Stop! *Stop!*"

Three of Stacey's teammates have a hold on her—two at her shoulders, Kelly Cleary at her waist. The girl's still swinging, though, blood dripping down her chin and onto the stylized Tigers logo scrawled across her boobs.

Coach Kitt strolls over and calmly fills Sanderson's line of sight just as I'm wrenched in the opposite direction of Stacey and right into the arms of Danielle, who can't quit it with the *"Hey, stop!"*

She hooks one of her arms around my shoulders and hauls me toward the dugout. The move effectively turns both our backs on the celebration happening at home plate, delayed initially when everyone stopped to watch us fight. On Danielle's word, the assistant coaches run out to get our team set to shake hands with Northland. My good eye tries to look up at her, but all I see is her lips quiver.

When she speaks, it's at a disappointed whisper—one I hear over the crowd, over my teammates hesitantly going back to celebrating our state championship berth, over the pounding of my heart that's doing a drum solo for my ears.

"Olive Rodinsky, *how could you.*"

2

DANIELLE YANKS ME INTO THE STADIUM'S FAMILY REST-room and slams the door so hard that it bounces back open. But she doesn't even care. Doesn't even close it, because even though I don't know who will address me—sister Danielle or Coach Rodinsky-Simpson—that person is *pissed*.

To my horror, a tear slides out of her right eye. I have never, *ever* in my life seen my sister cry—even on her wedding day to Heather; even when Mom was diagnosed with cancer—and suddenly I'm so scared I think I might pass out.

"Olive Marie Rodinsky," she starts, my full name a weapon as her voice rises an octave, that tear rolling down her suntanned face. "You are supposed to be a leader. Not just a star. Not just the coach's sister. A leader. And the crock of crap you pulled out there? That's not leading. That's minor-league rat shit. That's stuff drunk suburban dads pull when the rec league trash talk spanks a nerve. That's not something a girl with a résumé like yours does. You think the college scouts out there didn't notice that? They're here to see you!" The volume of her voice drops, and it's somehow even worse. "And that is not something a Rodinsky pulls. Not now. Not ever."

Another tear escapes, bringing a whole new level of terrifying to the hard line of her glower. Her index finger whips out and jabs me hard enough in the sternum that my breath hitches.

"You disappointed your teammates, made a fool of yourself, and hurt another human being."

The words are right there on my lips. About what this supposed human said and why I slugged her. But they stay stuck in my windpipe, blocked by the fear that repeating Stacey's words would make things worse.

"I'm your coach. Everything my team does is a reflection on me. Everything you do is a reflection on me. You shame yourself, you shame me."

Throat closing and skin burning, I struggle to maintain eye contact. Not just because I'm even more embarrassed now than when I was hauled out of the game, but because I can feel my own tears coming.

"And you shame Windsor Prep." We whirl around to

a deep voice at the door we failed to shut, and Principal Meyer is standing there in all black like the grim reaper himself.

"Up until today, you've been a wonderful addition to Windsor Prep, young lady—a straight-A student and a natural leader. But tonight, you embarrassed not only yourself and your sister, but me and your school."

Again, the words are right there, ramming the barrier of my clenched teeth, begging to get out. What that bitch said. Why I hit her. That I was standing up for my sister and against hate.

But it all sounds so stupid right now. Letting something like that get to me. When I know better. When ignoring her ignorance would have been the best thing to do.

I sound like a loser with no control.

Which is exactly what I must have looked like out there with my fist cocked back the instant before it connected with Stacey's nose.

"Coach Rodinsky-Simpson, would you leave me alone with Miss Rodinsky?"

Miss Rodinsky. Just hours ago, at the assembly to see us off to this game, Principal Meyer shook my hand and called me Liv. As if what was going on here weren't already blaringly obvious, those two little words confirm it.

I really want Danielle to stay. As a family member, not my coach, but I know that's not going to happen. I'm in deep shit with her, too, and when she doesn't protest, I know it's more than her being a good employee to the man who runs the school where she's not just a coach but also an English teacher—she knows her presence will soften whatever is coming next. And if anyone subscribes to the tough-love approach, it's my older sister. Which, ironically, is why I love her so much.

"I'll be right outside," Danielle says as she steps out of the room, leaving the door ajar. I'm left alone under the sodium lights with the head of our school.

I've seen this movie before. I know what he's going to say. I know it, but I still don't believe it.

I'm the best in my grade.

I'm the star athlete.

I'm the anointed queen of next year's junior class.

But none of that matters right now.

All that matters is that I go to a private school, broke its private rules, and now I'm about to be privately kicked out on my ass.

"Miss Rodinsky, though I do believe what happened tonight to be out of line with the exemplary character you've demonstrated over the past two years at Windsor Prep," he says, pausing, and my heart drops fifty feet before he begins speaking again, "that does not change the zero tolerance policy for violence to which we adhere."

Zero tolerance. Words I haven't had directed toward me in my entire rule-abiding life.

Principal Meyer pauses again, and his weary eyes are

on my face, willing me to return in kind. He's not going to move on with my fate without looking me in the eye. I wish I were cowardly enough to look down forever so it won't happen, but instead, my eyes flash up to meet his.

"In accordance with our policy, I'm sorry to say that you are suspended for the rest of the school year."

I blink at him.

Suspended. Not expelled. Just out. For the rest of the school year—only three days, for the remainder of finals.

I'm not sure if that suspension will keep me from the state championship tomorrow night, but still, my hopeful heart rises back up to its rightful place and my gut reaction is to smile in relief. But he draws in a deep breath and I realize he's not done. I wait for it, nails digging hard into my clenched palms, even though I have no idea what else there could be to say. He's already said the worst thing.

Or so I think.

"Suspension aside, there is also the matter of your scholarship—"

My heart drops all the way through the bathroom tile to freaking China. I think I'm literally shriveling up to die as my mind races through what this means.

I am at Windsor Prep on scholarship—one deemed "academic," but *everyone* knows it should be described as "athletic," if only that weren't technically illegal.

There's no way in hell my parents could afford the $15,000 yearly tuition without it. My dad's a detective and my mom had to quit her job last year when her cancer came back. We even put our house on the market with plans to move in with Danielle and Heather because we can't pay for both our mortgage and Mom's mastectomy that's happening next week to save her from her own boobs, even with insurance.

I swallow.

I haven't so much as blinked at my scholarship documents since I signed them in eighth grade, continuing the very short tradition Danielle started of Rodinsky women leaving public school behind for Windsor Prep.

I have no idea what it says other than that my parents don't have to pay a dime for me to walk the expensively adorned halls I all but own.

"Under the terms of your scholarship, suspension voids the contract."

Stars float in front of my eyes. Principal Meyer's pruney face hovers, framed by their light, floating in the abyss. My educational abyss, apparently.

Owned. The halls I all but owned.

"This means if you would like to return to Windsor Prep next year, you will have to do so as a nonscholarship student."

3

SOMEHOW I FIGURED THAT IF I WERE TO HIT THE BOT-
tom of my own personal barrel at sixteen, it would've
been in the dead of a Kansas winter. Snow blowing,
skies as gray as my mood, maybe a patch of black ice
at the ready to land me on my ass physically as well as
metaphorically.

Instead, it's 98 degrees outside in August and approximately 410 degrees in my stomach as it stutters and flips
under the withering stare of Coach Kitt.

We're in her office at Northland—my new school.

Aka the place housing my now-ex-boyfriend (Jake,
who broke up with me a hot minute after I punched his
ex) and about fifteen hundred kids I don't know because
I grew up across town before we moved in with my sister.

My time in public school—elementary or middle—wasn't with a single person at Northland.

All this, plus the woman holding my softball dreams in the palm of her manicured hand, because of course my parents couldn't pay for me to stay at Windsor Prep.

In fact, even if they could have, they wouldn't have, because they were so pissed at me for getting in a fight. In front of everybody. Over something that they think had to have been stupid mean-girl stuff.

I still haven't told anyone what Stacey said, and I probably never will. The point is that I lost control. Even though I was in the right, how I handled it was so, so wrong.

And now, because I'm the luckiest girl in the world, my sister's house sits just inside the boundary for Northland. Two blocks over and I'd be enrolling as a junior at Central. They have a horrible softball team there, but at least I'd get to be a star. Here, I may not even get to play.

Not if Coach Kitt's face is any indication.

She actually hasn't said anything to me yet, and it's been five minutes since I walked into her office this afternoon—with less than a week to go before my first day of school. And so I glance at the personal photos over her toned shoulder—snapshots that include a husband and what looks to be a boy in a Northland letter jacket.

When I can't take the silence anymore, I start to talk again, even though I've already said varying versions of: *I'm sorry. I apologize. I want to be on your team this year. I can add value. I can be a good teammate. I promise I won't send another Tiger to see a plastic surgeon.*

What I don't say and won't say: *I need to be on your team to make sure I get a college scholarship.*

I clear my throat. "Coach, if you need a reference, I'd be happy to put you in touch with my club coach, or Chad with the Junior Olympic te—"

Coach Kitt holds up a hand. "Olive, I believe you're not only genuine in your remorse but that you're a genuinely talented player. My team would benefit from having you."

I take what feels like my first breath since I stepped into her office.

Junior year is *crucial* for a would-be college softball player. Senior year is a wash—all the scholarships have already been awarded and accepted before seniors even step on the field. Meaning that even with the attention I've already gotten, I can't fade away or my future will, too. And just like a Windsor Prep education, college isn't possible without a scholarship.

"Now, though you have impressive talents and are possibly the best third baseman I've personally seen play in Kansas City—"

"Thank you."

She doesn't even acknowledge the fact that I spoke. "—a successful team is made up of more than just talented players. A successful team is a careful balance of talent, drive, personality, and unity."

I nod because I know all of this. If a team doesn't mesh well, it can suffer, no matter how good the players are.

"And, honestly, at this juncture, my opinion is that you're not a good fit for my team."

"I—"

"That *opinion* may change by tryouts in February. But that's not a guarantee. I have to do what's best for my team. We were third place at state last season." This is a fact I know well, because *we* placed second, losing in the title game, with my suspended ass riding the bench.

"And I only lost one senior," she continues. One senior—Stacey. Gone to Arizona State. Good freaking riddance. "The group of girls we have this year is a terrific balance of talent and teamwork, and I want to nurture that, not upset it."

I swallow again. "And you think I might upset it."

"Yes."

"What can I do to—"

"To make me think otherwise?" She says it with a perfectly arched brow, red lips pursed at the question mark.

I nod.

"Show me you can be a teammate."

I'm not sure how I can demonstrate to her my stellar teammate chops without a team to be on.

To my surprise, Coach Kitt picks up on my confusion and helps me out. "Are you going out for any fall sports?"

I blink at her. In my world, there is no other sport to

play but softball. My little brother, Ryan, plays soccer, but I never did. For girls, it's a spring sport, anyway, so it doesn't matter. In fall, the options are slim—cross-country, volleyball, golf—and I'm not really cut out for any of them. Maybe cross-country. *Maybe.* I can run and I'm fast, but it's basically a group of individuals competing together. Not exactly the best showcase for teamwork.

Coach is waiting for me to answer, patience wearing so thin I think she regrets throwing me a bone at all.

"Cross-country?" I suggest weakly.

I know she sees the same holes I do. And I hope she realizes why that's my answer—that there is nothing more Olive Rodinsky would like to do than play softball. Even cross-country would be a means to an end, a way to stay in shape for the main event in the spring.

"Consider it," she says. "And maybe a winter sport, too. Basketball, not swimming, if you have a choice."

I nod. I better start shooting hoops with Ryan the second I get home. The kid's got a nice jumper and I hope to God my little brother has learned a thing or two about coaching from Danielle.

There's shuffling outside Coach Kitt's door, cleats on linoleum. Her eyes fly up, and I know it's time for me to leave. I'm dismissed. Students she actually believes in are waiting for her.

4

I WANT TO RUN AWAY FROM THIS PLACE, TO RUN BACK to Danielle's house, fall into bed, and fold into the fetal position with my sorrows. But I can't go anywhere. No, I have to be a good sister to Ryan.

Ry is trying to make the soccer team and, therefore, is participating in his third "optional" two-a-day workout before official tryouts on Friday. He walked to practice Monday with a buddy from down the street before delayed onset muscle soreness (aka DOMS) smacked them both so hard in the butt that they begged me for a ride today.

So I drove them, using it as an excuse to get to the batting cages early in the morning and to the track for laps in the afternoon. But when I saw Coach Kitt walk in the building as we were parking, I delayed my run for a chance to plead my case.

A lot of good that did me.

Still, I have my shoes, music, and water. And I have an hour. Plus, there's no chance of running into Jake here because his butt is all the way over on a practice field, separated from the track by a fence. If only juniors and seniors were separated by a magical fence once classes start. So, track time. Again, probably a good thing to do given the conversation I just had.

Cross-country stardom, here I come. Or maybe just Katy Perry's "Roar" on repeat for six miles. Or however far a cross-country race is.

I'd better look into that.

Turns out DOMS is the least of Ryan's problems.

"Coach is gonna cut me" is the first thing out of his mouth after his workout.

Jesse, Ry's bud from down the street, agrees with a "Dude. Parsons totally hates Ry. How many extra laps did you have to run today?"

"Ten. Or maybe twelve."

"Duuuude."

I nod in sympathy. "Duuuude. That sucks."

Ryan shrugs, and I notice he has a football wedged in the crook of one arm. At fourteen, he's all angles and sinew, even though he can down ten slices of Bruno's deep-dish pepperoni without swallowing. Two years older, I'm (barely) an inch taller at five foot ten, and probably ten to twenty pounds heavier—puberty, softball, and estrogen keeping me from the same geometric fate.

"I've got a backup plan. Get in the end zone, Liv." He hoists the football over his head and jogs onto the turf with way more energy than he should have after a second two-hour practice and the (supposed) inability to walk this morning. He turns around, jogging backward, smile wide and bright and exactly like Mom's, pre-chemo. "The football team is down a kicker. And I can kick."

Suddenly, I wish I'd taken up soccer. There are female kickers in both high school and college. If I'd spent the same amount of time on the soccer field that I had on the softball field, I might have a decent fall sport to play.

I also might not have punched a first baseman at state.

It might have been a midfielder instead.

Or maybe all the soccer players in Kansas City are smart enough to know that gay people aren't pedophiles. How is that stereotype even still a thing these days?

I scowl. Stupid-ass Stacey Sanderson.

Though, if I took up football, I most definitely wouldn't be able to avoid Jake, even on the C team.

"Heads up, Liv!"

My frown immediately opens into a soundless "Oh, shit!" as I throw my hands up in time to avoid a football to the eye that had *just* started to look truly normal a few weeks ago.

I catch the ball and immediately chuck it right at Ry's head. I've watched enough Chiefs games with Dad to know he's got some major technique issues. "That was a freaking line drive, dummy. To make a field goal, you've got to kick up. Not out."

"Hey, at least I got the distance."

He drops the ball to Jesse, who balances the point in the turf, finger holding the tip in place. Ryan takes a few steps backward and smacks another one low—it's slightly higher, but still dings into the goalpost and comes to a thud in the turf.

I throw it back to him. He kicks it low.

I throw it to him again. This one is waaaaay high and doesn't have the distance.

Again. The ensuing kick glances off the left post, bouncing out.

Once more, but Ryan's so frustrated he spikes the ball and whiffs at it. Kicking it down to the twenty-yard line all the way at the other end. When he retrieves it, his face is all scrunched up like he's a four-year-old about to have a fit.

"Ry, just kick the ball," I say. "Who cares if it isn't the same motion? Don't overthink it. You kick a ball *every* day."

Ryan gives me a choice finger and lines up a kick. Takes a step back. Lets it rip.

Straight through the uprights.

I catch it and hold it over my head. "FINALLY."

I spiral the ball back at him, laughing. The pointy end smacks him right in the chest. "Jeez, Liv," he shouts. "Take it easy on the man boobs."

I grab the dormant soccer ball and chuck it at Ry, too. Jesse is inherently lucky that I'm not violent with people I'm not related to. Well, except for the one time it hurt me the most.

And, just like that, I'm done.

I sigh. "Ry, time to go home."

We walk in the front door to the sweet-and-sour aroma of chicken pad Thai and the sizzle of Heather's wok. It's been a favorite this summer—cheap enough to feed six mouths, tasty enough to keep everyone satisfied. My sister's wife has plenty of ideas for feeding us, having been the oldest of seven, and she's mega-cheerful about it all. I wouldn't say cramming her in-laws into her starter home was a dream come true, but feeding us sure is.

Ryan takes a deep whiff of tamarind and lemon-grass, smiles conspiratorially at me, and whisper-shouts, "Caaaaaaaaarbs" before literally running to the kitchen.

"Whoa there! Shoes!" Mom snaps as he rushes past her spot on the couch. Mom may be on the downside of recovering from a mastectomy, but she's not about to let Ryan track turf dirt into our newly adopted house.

Ryan shuffles back, head hanging dramatically as I slip off Danielle's hand-me-down Nike Frees. "It's a compliment to Heather's cooking that I forgot the rules."

"No one believes that, Ry," Danielle yells from the kitchen where she's playing sous chef. "You'd eat those shoes of yours if we had enough barbecue sauce."

We all laugh, but I'm shocked when Dad's baritone joins us from the half flight of stairs that leads to our bedrooms. "Ryan, don't listen to them. I got the same crap from my sisters and I turned out just fine." Dad is *never* home from work this early. But now he jogs down the stairs, changed out of his detective gear and into ancient basketball shorts and a Royals T-shirt.

"Dad, you're here!" I say as he plops on the couch next to Mom and grabs the remote. "Uh, why?"

"Nice to see you too, Livvie. No case tonight, but there is a Royals game. Plus, you know, I like hanging out with you people when work doesn't get in the way." He suddenly, dramatically, shrinks back from my sweaty self. "Man alive, did you run six miles through an onion field?"

"Hey! I don't smell as bad as Ryan."

"Do too!" Ryan shouts from the kitchen, mouth full.

"You both stink," Danielle says, before adding, "Liv, come here."

I pad to the kitchen. Ryan's standing over the wok with a fork, testing noodles, while Heather's chopping peanuts for the final touch. Danielle finishes setting out silverware and yanks me out the sliding glass door and onto the deck.

The sun out here is unrelenting, even in the evening, cutting a laser-beam path through the trees. "Did you talk to Coach Kitt?"

I swallow. Putting on my lady pants and apologizing to Kitt was Danielle's idea, of course. She had some hare-brained notion that it would do me some good. "I did. But she's worried about my teammate compatibility."

Danielle frowns. "She's a coach. She'll take talent over teamwork any day."

"I'm not so sure."

"Make her sure."

"I'm trying," I say, biting my lip.

Her eyes narrow. The woman is all about the execution. "How?"

"She wants me to prove I can be a teammate, so I'm doing that." My sister's eyes narrow further. Vagueness is not a favorite of hers. "By running cross-country," I clarify.

"You are?"

I haven't officially looked into it or anything, but I kind of make it seem like I have. "It's not really a *team* sport, but it's what I can do. I mean, you know I suck at volleyball. And I wanted to show her I could do *something*."

Danielle's lips press into a thin line as she mulls the options. "It's not exactly going out on a limb, but at least you're showing that you're taking her request seriously."

"I'm trying."

She sighs. "You always do."

The door slides open and Heather's face pops out. "Dinner. Come and get it before Ryan eats it all."

That's enough of a warning. She doesn't have to tell us twice.

5

THE NEXT DAY, I'M ON THE TRACK AGAIN, EYES PINNED to the pitted white lines, earbuds struggling to drown out the thought that school is less than a week away.

I'd hoped running on this track during Ryan's practices would help acclimate me to the new environment, but I still don't feel any more at home. I'm my own little island in a sea of activity, surrounded by soccer players, cheerleaders, cross-country waifs, and the football team.

Even without setting foot in a Northland classroom, it's far too easy to imagine what it'll be like to be the new girl, drifting through a sea of fifteen hundred other students who've known each other for the past eleven years.

Sure, I'll recognize some faces (including the one I used to kiss, *ughhhhh*) but the chances of me eating my lunch in the bathroom still seem to be ridiculously high—the mythical 110 percent. I'm sure Mom's famed turkey and Swiss will taste extra delicious when consumed within spitting distance of a pink toilet cake.

Something solid bumps into my shoulder and my head pops up.

"Crap, I'm sorry, I—" I glance over and see a tall white guy in a red football jersey, basketball shorts, and sunglasses going stride for stride with me.

"Olive Rodinsky, star infielder and sometime pitcher, I presume?"

"Liv," I say slowly, tapping pause on my hand-me-down iPhone. "And you are?"

"Grey Worthington. Yes, it's a family name—we're not landed gentry but we sure sound like it." Even with the half smile, he's so deadpan that I stop moving for a second, stutter-stepping as he angles his giant body toward me, heels lapping at his hamstrings as he bounces in place. There, in his left hand, where I couldn't see it before, is a football. "Starting quarterback."

And so it begins. One of Jake's buddies, here to make my life hell.

"Say no more." I pointedly hit PLAY on my phone screen and take off.

Though I'm going at about 70 percent full speed—fast enough that it doesn't look like I'm obviously sprinting the hell away from him—the dude's right by me as if I didn't move at all. In fact, in two long strides, he's in front of me and stopping on a dime. Despite my supposed athletic prowess, I nearly smack into the white number sixteen on his chest.

"You have horrible manners, Grey Worthington."

Instead of recoiling, he pushes his sunglasses into his hair and honest-to-God *winks*. Who the hell winks in real life, other than serial killers and George Clooney? Yet, somehow it appears to be a natural movement for Grey Worthington. "Yes, I know who you are," he says. "But I'm not here for Stacey. Or Jake. I'm here for your arm."

"My...?"

"Arm. You have an arm, and I need one."

Still not buying it. "Both your arms look just fine." And they do. Tan enough that the hair on his forearms has been rendered blond, almost completely mismatched with the light brown shag on his helmetless head. I glance over at the football team, still deep in practice, running suicides in a whir of orange and white. Only one other kid is wearing red, and everyone has a helmet. My mind searches for any tidbit Jake ever mentioned about football practice, but I can't for the life of me reconcile the way this guy looks— no helmet, no pads, *sunglasses*—and the words "starting quarterback."

"My arms *are* fine. But I still need yours."

Sweat drips into my right eye with a sting. "Why?"

"I'll tell you in a second." He stuffs the ball to my chest

and backpedals down the track, dodging a power-walker in a Royals cap, his long shorts whooshing. The sunglasses slide back to his nose. "Just throw the ball, Liv."

"It's not even the same motion as in softball," I shout over to him.

A smile tugs at his lips. There is no denying Grey spied on Ryan and me yesterday when he says, "You throw a ball *every* day."

God, I'm blushing—my own words to Ryan tossed back at me with a softball-appropriate edit. I'm so flabbergasted I can't even say anything.

Grey pushes on. "Yesterday, you spiraled this ball twenty-five yards like you'd been playing for years. I'm over here at thirty. Just throw the ball."

"Fine." Before the word is out, my arm is back and the ball is gone, a wobbly spiral headed straight toward his big, fat overconfident mouth.

"Sh—" Both hands come up, shielding his pretty-boy face at the very last instant. The ball smacks into his palms with a huge *whoof* and falls flatly end over end to the track.

When Grey's hands drop to his sides, I expect at least a full "shit"—maybe something worse. But instead, I get nothing but another cool smile. "Try to hit me on a route."

Tossing the ball back at me, he backpedals another ten yards and cuts toward the infield. Cleats churning on the turf, he hauls butt toward the opposite sideline as I aim again for his stupid, half-smiling head. Grey has to leap about three feet in the air, but the ball lands safely in his big, outstretched hands.

He holds it triumphantly over his head. "Perfect."

I swallow a smile of my own—God, I miss being told I'm awesome—and give him the full-on game-day glare when he finishes jogging back to me. "Now spill. Why the hell am I throwing a football to some dude who totally trashed my daily cardio?"

He palms the football and points one end straight at my nose. "How does 'Liv Rodinsky, backup quarterback' sound?"

I laugh. "Sounds like you've been hit in the head one too many times."

The perpetual lazy curve of his lips dies. "Actually, that's not too far off from the truth."

I roll my eyes. Whatever. "Look, I have two more miles to run before my brother needs a ride home, so..."

He pops the ball up and I catch it out of complete habit.

"See? You look like a natural."

I shove the ball between the one and six on his chest. "And you're starting to look like a creeper." I really am so good at making friends these days. "Cut the crap. What do you want, Grey Worthington, nonlanded gentry?"

He shoves the sunglasses back again and smiles for real. There's a glint in his eyes, which I've suddenly realized are a shade of steel worthy of his ridiculous name. While I'm distracted, he lines up his pitch, straight and fast and right over the plate.

"I want you to be my backup. Yes, I know you're a soft-ball player. Yes, I know you've never played football. And yes, I do realize you've got two X chromosomes. But here's the deal: I broke my collarbone in June. Nonthrowing arm, but it's still a problem. I'm not cleared for contact until the second game of the season. We've got a freshman who can start, but there's nobody after him who can hit shit." Those steely eyes shoot away for a second, sneaking a peek of the football field over my shoulder. "That's where you come in. Just suit up, do your awful scrunchy-scowl thing from the sidelines, and buy me some time. Once I'm cleared, you can still ride the bench if you want, or you can leave the team."

He's just mocked my glare, therefore I can't turn it on him, so instead I start poking holes in his pitch. "First of all: You're a player, not the coach. You don't call shots like this. Second: Why the hell should I help you?"

At this, he smirks and tosses the ball at me. "Go long, Liv!"

This is so stupid. He's stupid. Nobody short of a mall mannequin with mashed potatoes for brains would want to make me into a football player. Grey sails into the end zone, arms extended, begging for the ball. So dumb. Oh, so dumb.

But I still bomb it in his direction. And the ball drops right into the cradle of his outstretched hands.

Now I'm smiling for real.

From behind me, a slow clap begins. My heart sinks. It was a setup. Of course. And I know, *just know*, that when I turn around, Jake will be there with the rest of his stupid buddies, and for the next month I'll be the girl dumb enough to think for two seconds she could play with the boys. Not that I want to.

"Nice work, Grey." The voice isn't Jake's. In fact, it doesn't even sound like someone our age.

I turn around and see a Dad-age guy standing there in a Northland Football T-shirt. A black knee brace pokes out from below his shorts, and a visor shades the beginnings of crow's-feet on his warm brown skin as a distinctively coach-like whistle rests around his neck.

"Liv Rodinsky, softball star, I presume."

He knows my name—the way I prefer it—and who I am. Or who I used to be, at least. When I don't answer, he smiles at me.

"You think half my squad sees the pinnacle of all girl fights and I don't get a play-by-play?" My cheeks begin to burn. Getting my GED seems like a really smart move right about now. He sticks out his hand. "Manny Shanks, offensive coordinator and quarterbacks coach."

I shake it hesitantly "Uh, nice to meet you, Coach."

Shanks is wearing the same pre–pep talk stare of appraisal I've seen on nearly every coach I've ever had.

"Liv Rodinsky, we need you."

My eyes flit over to the practice field where the other

red-clad player and the rest of his teammates are on bended knee, listening to some final instruction from a grandpa-age dude who I assume is the head coach. Helmets off and backs to us, they almost appear to be in prayer, rather than man-boys gaining instruction on how to plow other human beings into the ground. Before I realize it, my eyes settle on Jake's number thirty-two.

Of course.

I glance away. "I think you're mistaken, Coach."

"Oh, but I'm not. We need a *capable* backup quarter-back behind our freshman, and you've got one hell of an arm. We're a running team, but in the event he's injured while Worthington's out, we still need someone calling the plays and chucking the ball to our running back."

I frown. *Our* running back. Aka Jake Rogers.

Nope. Nope. Hella nope.

"Not interested."

I'm surprised when it's Grey who speaks next, not Coach Shanks. "I think you are. Because if you play with me, I'll make sure you have a fair shot with Coach Kitt."

I blink.

Coach Kitt. I think back to the figure standing outside her office, to the cleats on linoleum. And I swallow when I realize those were big-ass cleats. Much bigger than any girl would need.

The same cleats that are on his feet.

But, also, the same cleats that every Northland football

player wears. A horribly annoying shade of orange. And as much as I'd like to believe that Grey Worthington, starting quarterback, has the magical ability to make my craptastic life disappear with a single word to Coach Kitt, something here just doesn't add up. No kid would be able to make a coach do anything she didn't want to do. "Why would Coach Kitt—"

"Or, as I like to call her, 'Mom.'"

I swallow.

Grey is half-smiling his heart out, football cradled in his hands. I can see it now—the square jaw, wavy hair, long eyelashes—Trudi Kitterage's features chiseled in masculine relief. Even without Coach Shanks's nod of confirmation, it's suddenly completely obvious that Grey Worthington is most definitely Coach Kitt's son.

Over on the field, the players are done and walking away—helmets off, patting butts and all that machismo crap signaling another practice down. Jake is right there in the middle of it all, sweat glinting off his brand-new buzz cut. My heart drops at the loss of his dreads, perfect as they are in my memory against his dark brown skin—as he laughs. Probably at the farce going on over here on the track.

"There are fifty kids dressed out in jerseys over there," I say. "I'm sure at least one of them played quarterback at some point before getting booted to another position."

Grey hangs his head in a nod. "Sure did."

Coach nods, too. Wow. Maybe the other possibilities really are awful.

"What about the baseball team?" I ask. "Surely there's a pitcher you could harangue."

Grey serves up another half smile. "My mom's the softball coach. You think I don't play baseball?"

Duh, Liv. Duh. "Starting quarterback and ace in the rotation, eh?"

He shrugs, face still deadpan. "Outfielder."

I stare at him as Coach Shanks cuts in. "Look, I hate to say it in front of Worthington, but our baseball team is crap."

Grey shrugs. "He's not wrong."

"Our football team, however, was tops in the league last year, and we stand a great chance to do it again. But only if I bring in winners. And you, softball princess, are a winner. Plus, I saw that spiral just now and it was magnificent." Okay, now I'm sort of blushing. "And before you ask, yes, there have been female quarterbacks in high school. It's legal, and there's no rule against it."

Suddenly, I want to believe them. Both the kid who scouted me as a solution to his problem and the coach desperate enough to add a girl to his roster, ready to embrace the huge can of worms that'll come along with it.

"You guys must be in deep if you're willing to coerce a sixteen-year-old girl into joining your football team," I say.

A new half smile curls on Grey's lips, and he pops the

ball to me, my fingers snagging the point. Though he could wink, he keeps that move in the holster. "Ding, ding, ding," he says.

It's got to be at least a hundred degrees, and I'm still sweating in the blistering air, but a chill shoots the length of my spine when it hits me that I might actually want this.

I want a fresh start. I want a chance at playing for Coach Kitt, at a softball future and all the things that come with it. And I want actual friends at this stupid school.

Plus, Jake will hate it.

I grin. "What time's practice?"

6

THE SECOND I GET HOME, I HEAD STRAIGHT TO THE
room I share with Ryan, my cell phone in hand. I thump
onto my twin bed, which is shoved into a corner in my
half of the room, and dial the one person I know who
won't think what I've agreed to is batshit: Addie.

She'll pick up because I'm *calling*. An actual phone call
beats a 911 text any day. If I have to verbalize it to her, it
must be completely serious.

She answers the phone in two seconds flat. "Oh shit,
who's dead?"

"What? No, Addie, everyone in my family is perfectly
fine." At this, I hear shuffling and the metallic clang of a
locker—Addie's still at Windsor Prep for marathon practices with the volleyball team. "Well, Mom is as fine as she

can be," I add. Because it's hard to use definitive language when the subject has lethal boobs.

I hear Addie let out a breath. "Christ, O-Rod, don't scare me like that." In the background, there's some chatter from the volleyball girls—most I haven't seen since that night, too embarrassed to show my face to anyone from our circle. I have to swallow a hard lump that's formed in my throat at the thought of Addie walking through the halls of Windsor Prep without me, even though she's probably been doing it all week. And will be doing it at least for the next year. "What's up?"

"I'm calling with news."

"A reclusive, softball-loving benefactor paid for your Windsor Prep tuition?"

I snort. "Not even close." God, I miss Addie, and I saw her Monday. But hitting the mall together is totally different from sharing four classes and endless pop-up drills. "I just walked on to the Northland football team."

I can almost hear her eyes narrow. "Like, what the *boys* do?"

"Have you been going to an all-girls school so long you forgot what football is? Yes. Duh."

"Wait." There's some commotion as some of the girls drift past. When it's silent again, she says, "Like the same team Jake is on?"

I bite my lip. "Yes."

There is a beat of silence, then her voice goes up an

octave—zero-to-sixty *WTF, Liv.* "Does *he* know about this? And what the hell are you even going to do, anyway? Get them water?"

"Screw you," I say, voice light. "I was recruited as a quarterback. And Jake probably knew the second I said yes, but if they spared him he'll find out tomorrow at practice."

I give her the same abridged version that I'm planning to use on my parents in the near, yet still as far away as I can make it, future. "The starting quarterback recruited me. He needs a backup, saw me throwing a football around with Ryan, and figured I might be interested."

Addie hesitates. "I dunno, sounds like a setup, Liv."

"It's not; the quarterbacks coach was there, too. But get this—the injured starter, his mom is Coach Kitt. So he might be willing to put in a good word for me. A favor for a favor."

"Liv, please tell me he's hot, because that sounded kinda dirty."

"Um, yeah, he's hot in that Peter Kavinsky way. Like a surfer with a side career as a newscaster. Serious face, great hair." God, I sound all weird. "But I'm not joining the football team because Grey is *hot*, it's because—"

"Wait, his name is Grey?"

"Grey Worthington. He's a senior."

"You definitely need to check out the validity of this guy. That name alone makes him sound like he's a secret duke, or a type of tea or something. You've googled him, right?"

I probably should have, just to make sure he was who he said he was. But Coach Shanks backed him up. And he'd have no reason to lie to me, or to be twisted into helping Jake pull one over on me. So, I fib to Addie. But it's only a small lie, because I'm going to google Grey the second we hang up. "Yes. He's legit."

Addie can probably see right through me, just like she can read a pick-and-roll. I hear the whoosh of nighttime air as she exits Windsor Prep and enters the parking lot. "So, I'm guessing you have practice tomorrow?"

"Two-a-days. First one's at 7:00 AM. Guess it's a trial by fire to see what it's all about."

"And Jake will be there." There's a smile in her delivery. She's totally thinking of the revenge possibilities. "But you're on the team no matter what, right?"

"As far as I know. The quarterbacks coach already signed off on it."

"That's insane."

"Possibly. But I really think it'll work. Coach Kitt wants to see teamwork. What better way to show that than by being the only girl on a boys' team that includes her ex?"

"I can't think of one," Addie admits.

"*Right?* I've still got to get Dad to sign a waiver, but I can do a pretty mean Eddy Rodinsky John Hancock."

She snorts. "You said 'cock.'"

I roll my eyes. "Public school is already ruining me. I'm a social misfit."

"Admit it, you miss me."

"I do." I sigh. I really, really do. I wish Addie were going to be with me at practice tomorrow. "You sure you can't just show up to Northland to jog laps tomorrow at precisely seven to see this all go down? I need a wingwoman, even if you're a hundred yards away."

"I'll have to clear my schedule, but maybe."

"I'd love you forever."

"You already do."

"True."

I can hear her car dinging and know she's about to drive away. I know we need to hang up.

"Okay, lady," I say. "Drive home. Eat dinner. I'll talk to you tomorrow."

I'm about to hang up when she catches me. "Hey, Rodinsky?"

"Yeah?"

"Be careful. Please. With Jake. With getting hit. With all of it. You know what I mean."

"Don't worry, McAndry. You know I can take care of myself."

"I know. That's what I'm afraid of. I don't need to bail you out for assault."

I smile back. "Don't worry, Cop Dad will do the deed if necessary."

"Or leave you in there to rot."

"Or that. Love you." I hang up the phone, more optimistic than I've been since May.

1

"WAIT. YOU WANT ME TO LIE FOR YOU?"

I scrunch my nose as Ryan belts himself into the back seat of my ancient Honda, Helena, like I'm his freaking chauffeur. Which I am, taking the young mister to morning practice. I'm going to pick up Jesse from down the street, too, and it'll just be ten straight minutes of them giggle-snorting freshman boy secrets like I can't hear them. "I don't want you to lie," I tell him. "I just don't want you to rat me out."

"Until when? Until Dad finds your helmet and decapitates you?"

My hands tighten on the steering wheel—all I want to do is survive practice before telling Dad and Mom what I've done. "I'm going to tell him. Just not now."

In the rearview mirror, Ry smirks over the bottle of blue Gatorade he's got balanced precariously on his knee. "Uh-huh."

I really will tell Dad and Mom about football. Danielle and Heather, too—I don't keep stuff from my family. But there's no point in telling any of them if I can't hang past the first day.

"Just let me deal with it, please?" I say, frustration creeping into my tone.

I watch his eyes narrow in the rearview mirror. "Fine. But you owe me."

"I'm already carting your butt around like Jeeves. I think that's enough."

Drunk on power and Blue No. 1, my little brother coughs out a laugh. "You were doing that anyway, sis."

"Don't push it."

"*You* don't push it," he shoots back. "You're the one wanting me to lie for you."

Ughhhh. "Just don't say anything, okay?"

He goes quiet. Which is annoying, because I didn't mean to not say anything *now*, I just mean to Mom and Dad in general. And he knows that.

"Okay? Ryan, *okay?*"

"Fine." He takes another swig of Gatorade so loud I can hear it as I back out of the driveway. I know he's not done. "I still don't see how Dad would let you play. He won't even let *me* play."

I do a double take. "Wait, you totally sucked at field goals—but you asked him anyway?"

"I did." I coast to a stop in front of Jesse's house. "When you were in the shower last night. It—it did not go well. Even Mom freaked out. So now there's no backup plan for me once Coach posts the roster Monday."

Great. If Ellen and Eddy Rodinsky won't even let their son play the safest position, they most certainly won't be thrilled about their daughter playing quarterback, even third-string. Softball and soccer aren't without their chances at a horrific injury, but football is another beast altogether. Anyone who has spent a minute watching a game knows that. Dudes knocked unconscious, spinal cord injuries, knees bent the wrong way—all life-changing injuries. And given the fact that both Ryan and I need to keep our bodies healthy to play other sports well enough to go to college, my parents' reservations aren't a surprise.

My eyes go straight to the parental consent form that's still sticking out, unsigned, in my bag. I'd been half joking when I'd boasted about my signature reproduction skills to Addie, but now I'm not so sure I won't have to use them.

Jesse gets in the back, bringing with him the smell of dryer sheets and, oddly, strawberry shampoo. "Duuuude, what's up?"

Ry raises a brow and I catch a wolf's smile in the rearview mirror. "Liv says she'll take us to Burger Fu after practice. On her."

"I would *kill* for a burger, man." Jesse's eyes light up as I pull away from the curb, my brother's silence apparently purchased with Kobe beef and waffle fries.

"What's the deal with the red jerseys?" It's the first thing out of my mouth as Grey comes out of the boys' locker room and zeros in on where I'm standing off to the side, helmet in hand. I figured I'd pounce on either him or Coach Shanks, whoever I saw first. Coach left my uniform in the girls' locker room with a note. Ryan's two fields over, warming up. A quick glance at the track tells me Addie isn't here yet—all I see are some power-walkers and a mommy boot camp group. No six-foot-two black girls with legs for days.

"Good morning to you, too," Grey says. It's 6:59 AM on a nonschool Thursday and yet Grey is still all half smiles, gooey and infectious.

We fall in step and head toward the practice field, just on the outside of a huge throng of giant bodies. One of which probably belongs to Jake, though I haven't seen him yet. Heck, other than glimpses through the fence, I haven't seen him since he was in the stands at state, cheering me on. Haven't talked to him either—the guy broke up with me over text like a real man.

I've taken only about five steps, but I can feel dozens of eyes on me with each one. And not in the way I like, when

I'm the star on the field and people can't look away. Nope. This is the kind of attention an outsider gets.

I turn back to Grey. "No, seriously. Is red code for quarterback?"

"Sort of. It means 'don't hit.'"

"Oh." Addie will be pleased. So would Dad and Mom, if they knew.

Grey's excited to educate. "We don't want anyone purposefully laying out our quarterbacks in practice. That's what games are for."

This makes me wonder exactly how Grey managed to get injured so early in the season. But I don't get a chance to ask, because Jake Rogers has decided to wander over and block my sliver of sun.

"Olive," he says, all formal.

"Jacob," I reply stiffly, knowing he hates being addressed by his full name as much as I do.

He looks different, even though his jersey is exactly the same as the last night I saw him. On close inspection, his hair isn't just buzzed, it's razored to within an inch of its life, giving him a five o'clock shadow from forehead to the nape of his neck. Jake's face is different, too—not open and excited to see me, the girl whose curves and dark hair used to make him weak. Rather, he's stoic as shit.

Jake's eyes—dark brown and delicious—stay on me. The stares I felt earlier are still weighing in from the shadows, which makes the seconds tick by at a snail's pace as we stare each other down.

Finally, Jake's lips kick up. He looks cocky as hell—he's here to perform. He's the showman running back, bullying through anything in his way. Most currently his ex-girlfriend. "Missed me, huh?"

"Not for a second," I reply, way too fast.

Grey throws up his hands and steps between us. "Liv is here because she's got one hell of an arm for us to use while mine's out of commission. You can't hold up our offense with your legs alone, Rogers."

Steely, Jake eyes Grey and says, "Yes, I can." Something passes between them. Then he turns his attention to me, his voice amused yet annoyed. "So you thought it'd be a cute idea to enroll in your ex-boyfriend's school and join his football team for shits and giggles? Stalker much?"

Jake turns away and says loudly to his buddies, "Such a joke." He starts to laugh and a few of the dudes snicker along. I think of Jake's friends in the stands that night at state. They're just blurry orange blobs in my memory, but now they're *real* orange blobs. Blobs that probably know way more about me than I know about them. Especially considering Jake never really introduced me to any of his friends. And considering even Stacey knew I was dating him, he most definitely didn't keep his mouth shut about his Windsor Prep conquest.

With the laughter, something inside me snaps—the same something that made me take a swing at Stacey's schnoz. My helmet donks him right between the three and two on his back before anyone blinks.

When Jake turns, mouth agape, I point to my jersey. "No joke."

Grey picks up my helmet, which has rolled into his cleats. "See? Great arm."

A choice finger springs up on Jake's right hand and I grin at him. Just so he knows I don't give a crap.

"Hey now, this ain't rugby—what the hell's with the scrum?" a voice calls through the mass of bodies.

Coach Charlie Lee, in the flesh.

I'd googled him along with everything else I could about Northland football last night—right after I made sure Grey was who he said he was. A small-but-mighty black man in his sixties, Coach Lee wears his Northland hat lightly on his head, not bothering to push it down all the way. There's a whistle around his neck and a general air of authority that surrounds him like a cushion. He makes eye contact with me for the briefest second before eviscerating Jake.

"Put down that hand, Rogers, or I'm taking that finger as a sacrifice to the god of high school football. Might take that senior captain title, too, for good measure."

Jake complies, a mixture of anger and sheepishness

crossing his face. It's an incredibly handsome look for him, and that fact steamrolls me even though he's been a total dick for the past few minutes.

Coach moves on. "All right, Tigers, five laps around the complex and then meet me at the fifty."

I half expect him to call me back. To say hello or warn me not to cause trouble. Or maybe to tell me I can't do anything until he has my signed parental consent form in hand. But maybe he's not much for paperwork, because he lets me go and I fall into line with Grey, jogging lightly as the pads skip across my shoulders. It's a strange sensation, one that's going to take some getting used to.

"You sure know how to make an entrance, Rodinsky."

I'd elbow Grey if I knew him better. But I don't. Still, he's the closest thing to a friend I have at this school, and I'd better take what I can get.

"Just sticking up for myself," I say.

He winks so hard I can see it out of the corner of my eye. "And sticking it to Rogers."

We do a loop, and the crowd starts thinning out. Jake is about three yards in front of us, his offensive line buddies falling back so far that I'm sure we'll lap them by the time we're done.

It's then that I realize Grey is dressed differently from yesterday—in full pads. Not the jersey-and-basketball-shorts look I saw on the track. "Are you supposed to practice?"

"We're going to see how today goes. I'll probably just do drills alongside you. Nothing big. Just think of me as a helpful shadow."

"That works, with your name being Grey and all."

He grins. "I totally set that up, didn't I?"

"Well, you're an easy target."

"I'm a quarterback—I make the targets."

I drop my eyes to the big, fat white thirteen on my red jersey. "So am I."

Again, Grey winks. "And you're slow."

As soon as the words are out of his mouth, his eyebrows shoot up and he takes off for the last lap, legs churning in full sprint. I chase after him, dodging past Jake and up toward where the spindly, fast wide receivers and cornerbacks are leading the way.

We finish the lap and, breathing hard, I take a knee next to Grey as orange jerseys fill in, forming a rough circle around Coach Lee, who's standing in the mouth of the growling tiger at midfield. At his side are two assistant coaches—Coach Shanks and a reedy man who I assume is Coach Napolitano, the coach in charge of defense—and a couple of managers, including a girl with a long auburn ponytail. It's not until she looks up from her clipboard that I realize I know that girl and her cat eyes.

Kelly Cleary.

Because of course the girl who drilled me with a sixty-mile-per-hour fastball on the worst night of my softball career would be present for my first practice as a football player.

Awesome.

Now I don't just have to do damage control on Jake's bad attitude, I have to deal with her and her eyeliner addiction, too.

Kelly's busy counting us all, a single finger bopping to its own beat in the air as she ticks off each player.

When the linemen rumble in and join us, out of breath and red-faced, Coach Lee finally looks up from his clipboard. His assistants stare out at us in tandem, arms crossed.

"Hello, Tigers."

"Hello, Coach," the boys echo. I rush in a second too late, but manage to say "coach" with the group.

"Tigers, our first game is coming up fast." He grins at our impending doom. "Good thing we have three more chances for two-a-days after today. That's right, folks, you're mine through the weekend."

As at least one dummy grunts out a sigh, I realize it's not just today and tomorrow I need Ryan to cover for me, it's this weekend, too. As far as I know, he won't be having two-a-days this weekend because tryouts are over and the team is announced Monday, and Dad and Mom are totally going to notice if I'm gone for huge chunks of the morning and afternoon without explanation. Which means the kid has to lie hard-core for me. It's gonna cost me way more than a trip to Burger Fu, that's for sure.

"That better be the only lily-pants whine I hear for the rest of today or every single one of you is going to run twenty laps in pads to end practice, instead of five." Coach Lee might be small, but his voice is tough as nails. "Don't care who whines—you're a team, and you'll take the punishment together."

I could be imagining it, but I feel eyes on me again. I grit my teeth.

Sorry, boys, but you won't be able to blame this girl.

Coach pauses for a second to confirm everyone will stay silent. Then, "Tigers, I've got a compliment for you, and you know I'm not big on those. No point in blowing hot air up your backsides if you're just gonna get the wind knocked out of you on the next play."

Danielle would love Coach Lee.

"You kids have worked your tails off so far this preseason. Drive, focus, and determination have been high. Maybe the highest I've seen this side of the year 2000."

A crack of energy shoots through the manly glob of bodies surrounding me, though no one is dumb enough to beg a high five or even so much as whisper excitedly. But the thrill is there, the hairs on everyone's arms standing at attention.

"Will that translate to a winning record?" Coach shrugs his narrow shoulders, hands raised toward the sky. "That's up to you."

And it is. In softball and in football, the only control

you have is how prepared you are. Everything else is in the hands of chance. And chance only sides with you if you worked for it more than the other guy.

Danielle might have been the first one to teach me that, but it's a lesson I've had reinforced over and over.

"Would you like one more piece of motivation, Tigers?"

As a fifty-headed beast, we nod.

Coach checks his hands on his hips. His eyes drop to the ground for a moment before he looks up.

"Last season, we were 10–2. League champs." We nod again. "That's pretty good. Hell, any other year, I'd take any of those things and call it golden. But this year, I want all of that and more."

He pauses. There's weight to it—a heaviness. A cool finger sweeps down my spine, and I'm right back in that family restroom at state, waiting for bad news to tumble out of Principal Meyer's mouth.

"Tigers, this is my last year as head coach at Northland High."

No one breathes. No one moves. Even the sun seems to pause in its ascent, everything frozen except for the words rushing from Coach Lee's lips. Next to me, Grey has turned granite-stiff.

"I didn't expect to tell you kids this until the end of the season. But that seemed like a coward's move, and I'm no coward. And you kids aren't kittens."

He cracks a smile, and a few people exhale. I don't, though, completely stunned by the fact that I'm not just a novice on this team, I'm a player whose coach wants to ride off into the sunset a champion.

"Sharpen those claws, Tigers. We've got winning to do."

8

GREY'S TRUE BACKUP IS A SO-BLOND-IT-HURTS FRESH-
man named Brady Mason. He's number seventeen, and a
legacy in Northland football because his older brother,
Cooper, was starting quarterback before Grey arrived.

Like my brother, he's spindly—puberty slow to smack
him across his hairless cheeks. Like Grey, he's far too smiley. His parents must've paid a small fortune in middle
school orthodontia because his teeth are almost beauty-
queen pretty.

I'm not sure if he's smiling so much because he doesn't
know what else to do with his facial muscles or if he's just
awkward around girls, but he looks like a toothpaste com-
mercial as we warm up, passing balls in tandem, him to
Grey and me to Coach Shanks.

He's also totally checking me out. Not in a romantic way. The kid's watching my arm, catching my form for a split second before passing his own ball. He's left-handed, so we're turned toward each other as we draw back and aim.

I can't tell if I should be embarrassed or flattered. Because either he thinks I'm a hot mess or competition for the number two spot.

Which is kind of hilarious either way.

"Nice warm-up, folks." Coach Shanks blows his whistle. "Routes."

Shanks pulls over a pair of wide receivers, Chow and Gonzalez, and lines them up. As Grey fires off five different numbered routes, I study a multipage play chart binder with Brady. It's got more Xs and Os than a Valentine's card, but I think I get it.

As I line up, I get a clear view of the fence separating the practice fields from the stadium. And there, not even remotely pretending to be exercising, is Addie, long limbs pressed against the crosshatch of chain link.

She is truly *the* best friend.

Feeling Addie's eyes at my back, I line up the balls and dig into the turf, my softball cleats doing a fine job despite being designed for a completely different sport, just like the rest of me.

Chow and Gonzalez—who turn out to be Timmy and Jaden, both seniors—are swallowing huge gulps of air while waiting for Coach to call the same five plays.

Orange Five. White Two. White Ten. Orange Nine. Orange Three.

I only miss once, overthrowing Gonzalez. But to be fair, he was gassed and it was the last play.

They walk off, replaced by two tight ends—Smith and Tate, aka Trevor and Zach—who take turns running short routes.

By the time we've run through that, my arm is starting to gripe at the restriction of the shoulder pads. Not that I'm about to complain. Because that is something Olive Rodinsky never does.

"Nice work, folks." Shanks smiles, but there's something evil in it that I recognize from when Danielle has cooked up something especially... epic. "Now go rest up, because this afternoon is going to be fun."

After postpractice laps, I change back into my outfit from this morning, running shorts and a tank top, in a quiet locker room free of Kelly and any cheerleaders or volleyball players who've been banging in and out of the door since seven, heading to and from various practices. Besides the pad marks across my shoulders, I'm pretty sure I don't look like I just came from football practice. Hopefully Mom will agree when she sees me after I get home from taking the boys for burgers.

I push into the parking lot, expecting to spot Ryan

and Jesse right away, burger lust glowing stronger than the noontime sun. Instead, there's just a single figure. The unrelenting brightness blinds me, and at first I think it might be Addie or Grey waiting for me, but the proportions are all off.

Jake.

He's in a T-shirt and cutoff sweats, pads and jersey probably airing out in the locker room like mine.

"I want to apologize." He looks me in the eye as he says this. No one is forcing him to do this—he actually seems to want to say the words. "I was a complete asshole earlier, and that was stupid and immature."

"Yeah, it was, and you were."

He rubs a hand over his short-as-stubble hair. "I reacted without thinking, and I reacted poorly. I shouldn't have called you a stalker or said you were a joke. That was shitty."

I pitch a brow. "Thank you."

He coughs out a laugh, his eyes shining bright in the blinding sun. "I thought I could scare you away. Should've known better."

"Damn straight."

"Yeah." Now he glances at the ground for a second. "Anyway, can we start over?"

"Sure." The corners of my lips perk up, and I know there's no way I'm scowling anymore.

He smiles for real, and for the first time since May, I don't immediately hate the thought of looking at him.

"Liv."

"Jake."

"How've you been? How's your mom—the surgery go okay?"

Oh, my heart. He didn't forget that Mom's mastectomy was scheduled for the week after the state championships, even after we broke up. "It went well. She's getting better every day." Which is what she tells me, even if it's not totally true.

"Good. Your mom's a tough one." There's genuine relief in his eyes.

"How's Max?" I ask—Jake's little brother has always been a favorite of mine. There's a ten-year age gap between the boys, yet they're as close as Ryan and me. Like Jake, the kid's hella smart, and probably going to rule the world someday. "Ready to crush second grade?"

"Don't you know it. Already reading at a fifth-grade level like the badass he is."

"Little genius. Teacher won't know what hit her."

"That's a family specialty," Jake says, laughing. He slings his hands in the pockets of his cutoffs. "So, uh, what brings you to the team?"

"Grey scouted me."

Something passes across Jake's face. "I don't really like him using you like that."

I scoff. "That's a little possessive for a guy who called me a stalker four hours ago," I say. It comes out a little harsher than I meant, so I rush out the next bit. "He's not using me. I *want* to be here. I was scouted and I said yes."

Jake crosses his arms over his chest. "But why are you *actually* doing it?"

At this, I'm the one going sheepish. Might as well be honest. "Because I want to make the softball team," I say simply. "Coach Kitt wants me to prove I can be a team player, and Grey gave me the opportunity. I couldn't say no."

"Even though you knew I was on the team?"

I smile. "Especially because you were on the team."

I expect him to say "Because you knew I'd hate it," but he doesn't. Instead, he's slightly more flattering to the both of us. "Because if you can be teammates with me, you can be teammates with anybody."

At this, there's a half smile—different from Grey's, but nice all the same. We dated long enough that I know there's something hidden in it, but I'd rather keep this newfound civility than call him out. Instead, I ask, "So, we're cool?"

Jake nods with a real smile. "We're cool. See you at four."

"See ya."

He walks off and I head to my car. The boys are sitting on Helena's sunbaked blue hood, and Addie's off to the side, staring down Jake as he jogs toward his truck.

"What the hell did he want?"

"To apologize."

She raises a perfectly threaded brow. "For not having the below-deck bits to break up with you in person?"

"For flipping out on me this morning."

"What'd he do?" Ryan asks, brotherly discord clouding the dark angles of his suddenly mannish face.

"Nothing," I say quickly. "Just wasn't happy to see me. But he's over it now."

Addie isn't buying it. "Uh-huh."

Honestly, I don't really buy it either. But I'm willing to make an effort because he did.

The boys get in the car but Addie stops me at the driver's side door. "You're seriously okay with Jake?"

"You know I'd tell you if I wasn't."

Addie silently reads my face, like she reads the field before trying to blast through the gap. Then she cocks a brow. "Grey's number sixteen, isn't he?"

My face grows hot. "How'd you know?"

Under that raised brow, her eyes go mischievous. "He couldn't stop looking at you."

9

THE AFTERNOON SCENE AS I EXIT THE LOCKER ROOM alone is much different from earlier today. Most of the boys are already out on the field, running laps. No one's interested in trying me after what happened to Jake this morning.

The sun is heavy, the heat wet and strong and hovering around a hundred yet again. Already sore from the morning, I start toward the field, sweat immediately beading on my forehead.

The locker room door slams behind me a second time. More out of curiosity than anything else, because I thought I'd been alone, I turn and see a flash of red ponytail.

"Cleary."

"Rodinsky."

I actually smile at her, because I truly don't want to start off on the wrong foot with anyone else. Even the girl who left a massive, softball-size bruise on my back. "How's it going?"

Kelly balks, surprised at such a soft opening pitch. Not that I blame her. Still, she goes on the offensive, like I slapped her instead of smiled. "Save your breath, Liv. I have zero interest in being your friend."

I blink. "Um—"

"And before you ask—if you're dumb enough to think I'd give up my nights and weekends to spy for Coach Kitt, I'm not. I've been a manager here for two years."

"I didn't think that you were spying on me," I tell her. "Why would I think that?" I take in her stance—the crossed arms, squared shoulders, jaw set—and realize that whatever's there has been building all day. And suddenly, everything clicks. "You're wondering why they didn't scout you."

"Of course I am. I'm a pitcher, not a *third baseman*." She says it like my position is inferior, even though we save the heroes on the mound from themselves all the time. "I should be a more natural choice than *you*. Heck, half of our shitty baseball team would be a more natural choice than you."

Which is true—but I'm not looking this gift horse in the mouth.

"Cleary, look—" She resumes stomping toward the practice field. "Kelly." Her chin dips in my direction. "I don't know why I got scouted over you. But if you want to go out for quarterback, no one is stopping you."

"Someone is most definitely stopping me." She halts and I pull up short to avoid smacking my chest pad straight into her shoulder. "Coach Kitt would never let someone as valuable as her star pitcher play football. I get hurt, there go the team's chances." She raises a finger and stabs me in the chest, right astride the padding. "If *you* get hurt, it doesn't affect the team one bit. You're not a part of our team, and you never will be."

Coach Kitt said it *might* change, and I've got hope in that might. "I've already talked with Coach Kitt, and she understands my potential value."

She laughs. "We all understand your *value*, believe me." Cat eyes narrowed, Kelly swipes her claws. "Paid to play in high school? Yeah, everyone understands your *value*."

My hands curl into fists. "That's not how it worked."

"Right. You can spin it however you want, but here, you haven't earned a thing. We don't owe you squat—not the softball team, not the football team, not Northland." Again, she starts to stalk away but whirls back around at the last moment. Like I'm the one who dinged her, not the other way around. And maybe I did—maybe she's as close to Stacey as I am to Addie. "And I'm going to love watching you get hit."

I start my warm-up thirty seconds late, so Coach Lee is making his opening remarks to the team by the time I finish my laps, sweat pouring down my face and pooling between my skin and the shirt I'm wearing beneath my jersey and pads. I squeeze in next to Grey, trying to wipe the sour look from my face, and whisper, "What's up?"

"Scrimmage."

Oh. Shit. My heart bottoms out when I realize that those routes I worked on this morning are plays I might actually have to pull off in a game simulation.

On my first day. After everyone else has been practicing for two weeks, plus, you know, most of their lives.

Meanwhile, I'm a quarterback who knows ten of the plays and has never taken a snap.

I suddenly realize Grey's not dressed out in his full uniform. Gone are this morning's pads, tights, and helmet. Replaced with an undershirt, red jersey, and the same basketball shorts from yesterday. Plus, the sunglasses are back.

"You're not going to practice?"

Grey shakes his head, watching Coach Lee, who is rattling off numbers. "Nope. Can't get hit."

"But you're wearing red—doesn't that keep you from getting tackled?"

The Clark Gable angles to his face go all nightly news-man serious. "I want to be out there more than anything, Liv, but this is football. You get hit. The red's not a force field, it's a suggestion."

A suggestion.

As I'm processing that, Coach Lee calls my number. Thirteen. And I realize he's been separating us all into teams the whole time. One of which I'm the quarterback for—A team for Brady, B team for me. Nothing but side-lines for Grey.

Great.

~

My parents are going to kill me. Kill me dead. If not for playing football, then for the position I'm in right now with a guy nicknamed "Topps."

I don't know Topps's actual first name. I don't know his last name. But for the eighth time in so many minutes, my hands are hovering near the rear-end seam of his pants.

Like, right underneath his junk.

Big, bulgy, manly junk.

I have a feeling this is making him uncomfortable, too, because every time he's been upright in between plays, his cheeks have turned rosy red above his meandering dark beard.

But embarrassment won't save him, just like it won't save me when my parents see where my hands have been.

But first: Orange Nine.

I scream the play twice and huddle in as close to Topps as possible, waiting for the ball to hit my fingertips. The second it makes contact, I've got my eyes up and my feet are going back. The feeling isn't a whole lot different from making a catch and slinging it back to first for the out. Except that now I've got a wall of boys in front of me, and the "base" is a moving target. In this case, number eighty, streaking in a right-to-left pattern about five yards from the line.

It doesn't take much to spot him—thank God I'm not two inches shorter—and as my arm goes back, I see a huge body rumbling in from the left. I release the ball right before he gets to me, slowing just enough not to totally tackle me. But it's still hard to stop two hundred pounds on a dime, and this guy, number forty-eight, is easily that. My magical red jersey makes him veer away, yet he can't do that fast enough either, and his chest smacks into my nonthrowing shoulder, setting me on spin cycle on my way to the turf.

Again.

Clearly our offensive line needs to do a better job, because they're getting beat. Every. Single. Time. If not by number forty-eight, then by the dude on the other side, number fifty. If my reflexes were any worse, I'd be in traction already—much to Kelly's amusement.

I roll onto my back and pop up to my feet, realizing

only too late that there's a hand extended my way, ready to help. It's attached to number forty-eight, whose name I don't know. High school jerseys don't have names like they do in the pros.

"Sorry," he says. Beyond his face mask, there isn't a smile, just a wary look of trepidation.

I dust my hands off. "No problem." As he starts to stalk off, I shout, "Hey, wait! What's your name?"

He turns around and extends his hand again. It's calloused and heavy. "Nick Cleary."

I can't help it—I start reading his face. Baby-blue eyes. Rusty stubble. Very much a steak-and-potatoes Prince Harry.

Crap.

His identity registers in my eyes before I can stop it, and he smiles at what he sees there. "Don't worry, Rodinsky, I'm not going to drill you into the dirt. I have much more restraint than my sister."

"Lucky me."

He doesn't answer, just jogs back into formation.

Which means I need to do that, too.

Next: White Ten.

It's a ten-yard shot straight downfield to either tight end.

I yell the play twice, pause for a second next to Topps's back end, and then shoot back into the pocket. My target tight ends are tangled up by defenders and are slow to extract themselves and make it to their spots. Out of the corner of my eye, Nick is rounding in an arc toward me. On the other side, my throwing side, number fifty is already free of his defender and hotfooting it my way.

I have to get rid of the ball. I know it. But I don't want to throw it away. I want to prove I can stay calm and make the play.

My feet start moving toward the right-hand line, eyes high over the complete chaos in the middle. I plant my back foot and bring my arm back to throw, but something both hard and soft hooks me across the bare patch of neck below where my helmet ends and my jersey begins.

Down I go, face-first into the turf. If the landing knocks the wind straight out of my lungs, what comes next ensures I won't be getting any of that wind sucked back in for at least thirty straight seconds. Number fifty falls flat on top of me.

I'm immobile, my field of vision nothing but sun-dried turf and fresh dirt. Earlier, Shanks explained that if I get hit, the safest thing to do is to stay as still as possible while waiting for the pile to break up. So I stay still. But number fifty hasn't moved yet. He's taking his freaking time, and his girth is approximately equal to a Mack Truck lined with bricks.

"Hey, Sanchez. Get off her, man—she's not a mattress."

The voice is Coach Shanks's, and I'm suddenly embarrassed that he's noticed I've been squashed. Ten plays and this is the first time I've truly taken something resembling a real hit. And, God, it *hurts*. My ribs shudder like they're going to shatter. Efffffff.

"Just giving her a taste of what it's like, Coach."

"Red shirt. No tasting menu for her. OFF."

Number fifty—Sanchez—rolls off my back and onto my legs, his butt pressing into my hamstrings before the weight is finally lifted. I get to my knees, and there's a hand at the edge of my slightly blurred vision. Topps.

I snag it and stand.

"You're doing good, girlie. Real good."

I nod, words still impossible.

Topps shakes his head. "Sorry, you probably don't like being called that." He lowers his giant head like a freaking wild pony. "Do you have a nickname?"

I nod again. Swallow. Find my breath in three heaving gulps. "O-Rod."

Topps smiles. It's far too gentle for the mass of him. "Like A-Rod. I get it."

"Yep."

"You're doing real good, O-Rod."

I want to believe that.

10

FRIDAY IS MORE OF THE SAME. MORNING DRILLS WITH Grey—who totally got razzed by Shanks for trying to wear his sunglasses again—Brady, and select receivers, followed by an afternoon of scrimmage, aka Liv's red shirt doing *abso-freaking-lutely* nothing to keep her safe. I trust my feet more than a stupid jersey, even though my footwork sucks. I've been training my whole life to run from point A to point B, not elude four dudes who each have a hundred pounds and years of experience on little old me.

By Saturday morning, all I want is to sleep in and then raid the noontime doughnut selection at Dillons.

Instead, I roll out of bed, pull on my customary batting cage outfit of running shorts, a tank top, and cleats, and bribe Ryan with two of his own doughnuts if he leaves the house with me in his soccer gear.

"Four. I'll do it for four."

At this rate, he'll be asking for three courses at The Cheesecake Factory by the time the season's over. Teenage boys can *eat*.

I drop him off at Jesse's house with promises of carbs and head to Northland. I change, grab my helmet, and I'm at the field—cloaked in red and ready—at 6:59 AM.

By myself.

I do a loop in warm-up and scope out my surroundings. There are a few of Ryan's soccer teammates a field over, taking turns on corner kicks. Two cross-country girls are running the bleachers in bright orange singlets. The cheer squad works formations on the stadium turf, a flash and whirl of ombré-patterned tights and pineapple buns.

But nowhere in sight is a herd of fifty or so man-boys.

My phone is in the locker room. But I don't know who I'd call. I don't have Grey's cell, mostly because I've been too chicken to ask. Don't know how to reach any of the coaches. And even though Jake apologized, I'm not totally comfortable texting him all idiot-like with a "I thought we had practice?"

I do a loop back around by the locker rooms. No sound is coming from the boys' side. And the coaches' offices are dark.

But there are cars in the parking lot.

Lots of cars.

Jake's car.

My Timex warns me that it's now 7:14 AM.

A chill runs up my spine as a burst of heat climbs my cheekbones. Parallel swells of feeling—stupidity and frustration—arm-wrestle in the pit of my stomach.

I can't be late. I *am* late.

Not knowing what else to do or where to go, I end up back in the locker room. Check my phone. Nothing.

Screw it.

I scroll through and find Jake's number. I hold my breath as the ghosts of messages past pop up on-screen. And even though I know it'll be there, I still nearly drop my phone on the locker room floor when I see the last message in the chain.

Can't deal with the crazy. I'm out.

And by "crazy" he meant me.

I squeeze my eyes shut and start typing.

I can't find you guys.

To my surprise, a new message pops up instantly.

Weights. Meet me in the hall. I'll show you.

Oh, thank God.

I toss my phone in my bag, slam my locker, and light out of there like my butt is on fire... only to turn right around because my clothes are all freaking wrong for weights.

Off come the jersey and pads, tights, more pads. On go

my shorts. I don't have tennis shoes, but cleats won't be too weird. I hope.

"Took you long enough," he says as I finally exit the locker room.

"Wrong clothes. I'm new, remember?"

"How could I forget?" There's a little smile there as he takes a step toward the intersection of two halls, and I fall in beside him. The air is fat between us, a thick layer of blubber between normal and whatever we are as we learn to coexist.

"So, um, that was super lucky you answered right away."

Jake shrugs, shoulders straining against a neon Northland T-shirt. "Kelly brought me my jersey and I had to put it away. My phone lit up the second I opened my locker."

"Ah." I'm not sure what else to say to that. That I wish Kelly would do my laundry? Though, based on yesterday, it'd probably come back in shreds. "Anyway, thank you."

He snickers. "You might not feel like thanking me when you see how pissed Coach Lee is that you're twenty minutes late."

Having Danielle as a sister has paid off in a myriad of ways, but in this instance, the most valuable of those is that I don't look down when facing a pissed-off Coach Lee. I know how to take a look like that.

Eyes up. Chin up. Respect written across my forehead.

The rest of the team is going through what looks like a series of stations—back squats, bench press, TRX, clean and jerk, plyo, abs. And, though arms and legs are moving in my periphery, I know everyone is waiting for the yelling to start. Heck, *I'm* waiting for the yelling to start. But Coach Lee isn't yelling. His lips are drawn up tight. The silence is deafening, even with the clank and swish of ambient weight room noise.

I've already apologized. He didn't answer to that in any volume. No acknowledgment except the glare.

Finally, he says one word: "Squats."

I take off toward the back of the room as quickly as I can without looking like I'm running away, toward a series of squat racks lined up against a wall of mirrors. There's an open one on the end, the quarterbacks and secondary assigned to the same rotation.

The weight already on the bar is completely ridiculous. Quick math tells me it's 260 pounds. With the bar added in, it's 305.

There's no way in hell I can squat that.

I start reracking the forty-five-pound plates on either end. I have no idea what the rep situation is or how many sets we're doing. All I know is I can't do 305.

Grey silently swings over from two racks down and pulls a forty-five off the other side. Which is sweet and also completely embarrassing that he realized my problem right away.

Coach Napolitano meets me when I'm hauling the second forty-five off the bar. "Eight reps. Start with fifty pounds on the bar."

These are the first words I've ever heard Coach Napolitano say, but I'm going to have to refute them. "I can do more than ninety-five."

While Coach seems nice enough, it's obvious the guy doesn't like anything going against the tide, including me. But I can't sit here and squat two-hundred-plus pounds less than the rest of the team.

I can't. Not when I'm already wearing the "otherness" like a glove.

And without the benefit of pads and helmets, my differences are even more pronounced.

More glaring.

Every eye in here is judging me in my black tank top and the purple sports bra peeking out the back. The elastic is gone on my old shorts, meaning they're rolled at the waist a few times just so they won't fall down. And I'm damn certain they realize I'm still wearing softball cleats.

Grey huddles in closer to me, angling his broad back so that it's harder for the others to watch. Napolitano chews at his lower lip. "What's your one-rep max?"

"Two hundred," I lie. Because I have no freaking clue. In the weight room, I just do what my sister says—the weight's not mine to set.

"Start with a hundred on the bar," Coach says. "If that feels good, up it on the next round."

I nod, relieved if not still embarrassed.

One hundred forty-five pounds. Eight reps. No big deal.

But when I glance at my reflection in the mirror at the top of my first rep, that feeling of otherness crushes hard on top of that hundred pounds.

And then another weight: I miss my softball girls. I miss people I know. I miss being a true part of something. I know it's early, but just this scene alone is enough that I worry I won't ever fit in here. On this team, at this school, anywhere.

But I won't know for sure unless I try.

I close my eyes and squat.

Twenty minutes late to the start of practice means it's twenty minutes I have to stay *after* practice to make amends.

Luckily, it's just twenty minutes of running.

Unluckily, the person making sure I complete the laps is Kelly Cleary.

For the most part, she's sitting on her duff, ignoring me. Playing on her phone. Scratching out notes on her clipboard. Checking her silver-painted nails.

Basically, doing anything other than interacting with me.

Eight laps in and fresh perspiration crowds my hairline and rests under my eyes when the door to the boys' locker room clangs open. Out comes Jake with a few of the A team guys. Keys stuffed in their hands, pristine sneakers on their feet, and tank tops clinging to hungry muscles. They're laughing at something that feels a lot like they're two seconds away from high fives. Still, Jake notices us and waves an arm through the air.

My hand automatically shoots up in response as I scream around a turn. But as it's returning to my side, I see that Kelly's hand is up, too. I stop on a dime.

Her eyes catch mine. "That wasn't for you."

Ugh. I take three steps, but the second I find my stride again, it hits me.

Kelly brought me my jersey and I had to put it away.

Oh. God.

I stop and turn around. Kelly's messing with her phone. "Are you and Jake a thing?"

She doesn't look up. "Keep running, Rodinsky."

A subtle hint of satisfaction hangs in her answer, her cheeks pinking atop her freckled skin.

Goddammit. Kelly definitely did something with Jake last night that required the removal of his jersey. Wonder how Stacey feels about that.

I step away from her, glance at my Timex, and get back at it.

Two more laps and Kelly stands up and walks away

without saying a word. Fine. Whatever. I don't care. I decide to do a cooldown lap before grabbing my gear and running off to spend my allowance on brother bribery. When I finish and head toward where chain link separates the stadium track from the locker rooms, there's someone standing there.

Grey.

The sunglasses are back, his hair is wet, and the smell of soap hits me almost as hard as the fact that I must totally stink. He holds a hand up, an iPhone generations newer than mine in his big palm. "Your number?"

I put my hands on my hips. "So you can give me shit for being late between now and this afternoon's practice?"

"No, so I can make sure you're not late again."

He unlocks the phone and hands it to me. I see he's already filled in the contact information—"Olive Call her Liv or Else Rodinsky." I'm blushing, like *instantly blushing*, and I furiously hope he can't tell postrun flush from heart-flutter flush.

With shakier fingers than I'd like to admit, I type in my number as we meander toward the girls' locker room.

When I hand the phone back, my fingers brush his. And goddammit, I'm blushing again. But I look back up at him like there's nothing wrong and my face is always beet red.

"My mom's waiting," he says, gesturing toward the parking lot. They must have carpooled; Coach Kitt seems like the type to be in her office at any available moment. "See ya."

He leaves and my heartbeat slows as I push into the empty locker room. I grab my stuff from my usual locker and fish out my phone, ready to add him the second his text buzzes through. But, to my surprise, I've already got a text from a new number.

I click it open and it's a copy of the team's day-to-day schedule. And a winky smiley face.

Of course.

11

"HE *SAT* ON YOU?" ADDIE CACKLES, SHOULDERS quaking. "Like he just thought you'd be a good place to rest?"

"Yeah. Two hundred pounds of Goldilocks and I'm still not sure if I was just right or not."

Now she's laughing so hard she chokes midsip on her Dr Pepper. Instant coughing fit. More pop. She wipes her eyes, wetness catching the meager overhead lighting in the oregano-scented dim of Bruno's Pizza, our favorite carb-delivery supplier. Finally, when she's not going to cough or laugh anymore, she shoves two garlic knots in her mouth.

Starving, but ironically too exhausted to keep up with Addie in the food department, I spear myself a garlic knot and try to straighten my slouch from an *S* to an *L*. But somewhere in the middle, my back muscles seize up and I pitch to the side against the wall of our booth. It's Saturday night and I'm *zonked* from my third two-a-day in a row. Honestly, it's all I can do to stay upright across from Addie. My life's been a blur of laps, drills, and scrimmages since Thursday.

And I still have a final round of two-a-days tomorrow, right before dinner with my family—a dinner in which I can't look like I've been mentally and physically destroyed for four straight days. And the day after that, I get to trudge my way through my first official day as a Northland student. Yippee.

"So, other than being sat on, how's it going?"

"Fine."

Addie's eyebrows rise so high on her forehead that they graze the baby hairs that have managed to escape her head of tiny black braids. *"Liv."* When I don't say anything else, she blinks slowly, exaggerating her disbelief to the point of animation. "You're running around, getting tackled by a bunch of boys in tights, and all you have to say when I ask how it's going is *fine*?"

"Technically, they aren't supposed to be tackling me."

"But they're sitting on you."

"Yes, in lieu of tackles."

"Okay, whatever. Just give me the scoop."

I wave a hand. "Eh, enough about me. Tell me what's up with you—how's the volleyball team looking?"

Addie sputter-sighs into her drink. "We'd be looking a whole lot better if Barbie and I weren't the only ones to hit the court this summer."

"I mean, to be fair, you get bonus points because you hit the court with *me*, and I can't even keep the ball in play seventy percent of the time."

"God did not make you a volleyball player, that's for sure, but you were excellent target practice."

We both laugh, because that's totally true.

"And what about the rest of Windsor Prep? How's your schedule?"

"Well, I got into Danielle's Honors English section, so that won't be weird or—wait." She narrows her eyes. "You're avoiding talking about it."

I poke at my plate. "I am not."

"Oh, yes you are, Olive Marie." She pauses, eyes narrowing further as if she's trying to read my mind. Then her whole face lights up. "It's *him*, isn't it? Grey?"

I feel the sudden urge to stuff my piehole with ten garlic knots—I barely have the energy to eat, let alone manage Addie's expectations on what isn't happening with my teammates and myself. "Um, it's him *what*?"

Addie doesn't skip a beat. "*You know what.* You're being antidescriptive because you're afraid of describing something. And that something is Mr. Surfer Newscaster."

And suddenly I'm blushing because . . . yeah.

Just then our server materializes with an eighteen-inch monstrosity fashioned from mozzarella, cured beef, and stinky miniature fish. Oh, and carbs. Glorious carbs. The nectar of the gods. Or at least the nectar of athletes ambling through two-a-days.

Addie and I each yank a slice onto our plates and dig in. She takes a giant-ass bite and launches back into her assault—she clearly has it in for me.

"Seriously. You've been at practice. With boys. For *hours*." She presses both hands into the Formica tabletop on either side of her plate. "In case you've forgotten, there are no boys at Windsor Prep. None. Zero. *Zilch*. Feed my hormones, Liv. A girl's gotta eat."

I'm not exactly sure what to say. Yes, I've spent hours with boys. One of whom happens to be Jake. He's been fine since apologizing to me in the parking lot. I'm neither a stalker nor the girl who has somehow won back his heart. I'm just there. Even though I really do wish he weren't so stinking pretty. As for Grey—oh, God, he's pretty, too. And kind. And smart. And so damn good at what he does.

Addie chucks a burnt hunk of crust down on her plate and picks up another slice, her eyes never leaving my face. "You seriously have to think about this? What is there to think about?" She sighs. "If you don't start talking in about two seconds, I'm going to get up from this table and go assault that boy over there in front of his family, just to hear about his day. Information: *I needs it, preciousssss*."

She waves an arm in a grand gesture toward the other row of booths and I glance over, wondering if this poor soul knows what exactly he's in for. My heart immediately hits the floor when I recognize the curls and lantern jaw in profile.

Then it stops beating completely when a pair of steel-gray eyes meets mine from across the pizza-scented dim. Addie realizes exactly who "that boy" is without the football gear about .002 seconds later. "Is that—"

I move my head in some semblance of a nod. "Number sixteen, in the flesh."

A few words to the blond woman across from him—Coach Kitt—and he's walking our way. Hands in his pockets—he's the perfect, terrifying mixture of nonchalant and confident.

"Liv." He says it with his customary half smile. Which looks nice when paired with jeans and a golf polo. I've never seen him in real, nonathletic clothes, and that thought is so distracting that I totally don't answer him.

So my best friend does it for me.

"Hi, I'm Addie." She sticks out her hand for a shake.

"Grey Worthington," he says, taking her hand. "I've seen you play."

Addie blinks at him. "Volleyball, basketball, softball, or all of the above?"

He laughs. "Just softball, sad to say. Base hit to beat Northland at state."

He was there. He hadn't just heard about my infamous

game, like Coach Shanks. He had been there in person. But of course he was.

I should've known. Of course he'd seen my arm in person before that day on the track. Of course he'd been there to see with his own eyes the kind of arm I have—not just the one that can sling a deadly accurate softball, but the one that can pull back for a mean right hook.

Again, Addie's confidence rescues me.

"Too bad," she says. "Softball's the weakest of the three."

"I'll have to see you play the other two sometime."

"Liv will update you on my schedule." Her eyes flip to mine, all wide. "Won't you?"

I nod, trying to get my head back in the game. "I'm the keeper of the official Adeline McAndry performance calendar."

Grey laughs again. "So, while we're talking games, I'm assuming you're coming Friday?"

"Friday?" Her eyes skid to mine for a hot second, but I'm not exactly sure what Grey's getting at.

"Liv's first game."

I shrug, immediately brushing off everything—his enthusiasm, Addie's surprise, the whole idea that I'm actually going to have playing time. "I'll just be riding the bench. It's no big deal."

I laugh but Grey doesn't. "Just because Brady's starting doesn't mean you won't play."

My stomach rolls a hard left, garlic knots and all. Embarrassing myself in the privacy of practice is one thing. Being sat on by a two-hundred-pound behemoth from another school in front of a couple thousand people is quite another. "Sure. I guess if he gets hurt, I'll be ready to go."

Grey half grins at Addie. "She's being modest. Brady's scared shitless that he could get benched in favor of her."

Usually my confidence in my athletic abilities rivals Addie's, but the second Grey finishes speaking, I start cracking up. "Yeah, right."

Sure, I look good when we're doing routes, but in an actual scrimmage? I suck. Hard-core. Granted, that's my own estimation, but given my elite status in one sport, it's pretty easy to see my general suckitude in another.

The giggles keep coming...until Grey shoulders his way into my side of the booth. I immediately shut the hell up, surprised by the sudden warmth of him next to me.

Grey's face sharpens to an edge as he looks at me. "Why is that so funny?"

"You've seen me play, right?" I glance across the booth for backup. But Addie's face is tabula rasa–level blank. I guess she's pretty freaking surprised, too. "I've spent more time facedown on the turf than right side up."

Grey's head is already shaking, corners of his lips tipped up. "You've also made about 90 percent of your plays since Thursday. You're deadly accurate. And, despite the fact that, yes, you've taken a few body blows, you're extremely mobile. Brady can't move his feet to save his life. And that means he throws the ball away at least a third of the time."

I had no idea how Brady played. I hadn't been watching him scrimmage because I'd been busy enough trying to remember my own plays and stay upright. "If you say so."

"I do. And I'm not the only one who's noticed." He slaps me on the back, winks at Addie, and slides out of the booth. "See you bright and early. Don't leave the awesome at home."

"She never does," Addie calls out, and we watch him saunter—yes, saunter—back to his parents' booth. His mother's blond head is rigid enough that I know she's been spying on us.

Before I can think about if this is a good or bad thing, Addie snags my wrist, long fingers gripping the bones with all their three-sport might.

"That boy can sack me anytime. I *love* him."

The giggles come back. "Quarterbacks don't sack people. They're the sackees."

"Okay, who sacks them?"

"Linebackers, mostly."

"Then I'll mostly be a linebacker. And he'll be mostly on the ground."

I cut off my laughter and give her a chin tip. "How are those hormones doing now, McAndry?"

"They're well fed, but still hungry for more."

I rip a corner off my slice of pizza, grease immediately coating my fingertips. "Too bad you weren't the one who punched out Stacey Sanderson."

"Damn right. You've got all the luck, O-Rod."

I grin. "Something like that."

12

IT'S SUNDAY MORNING AND GREY'S WORDS TO ADDIE last night won't quit running through my head, swirling around and around like a nervous goldfish.

Brady's scared shitless that he could get benched in favor of her.

Her.

As in *me*. The only "her" with a helmet.

I'm here as a backup. As a teammate. As a means to an end. Not as a starter.

I don't *want* to start. I'm not even sure I would want game time if offered it.

But even though I am a much better third baseman than quarterback, I still want to be the best I can be. Even if I'm third-string, I don't want to be a distant third.

Which means Brady Mason has a freaking bull's-eye on his back.

I steal a glance at my target as Brady, Grey, and I take turns trying to hit an orange traffic cone Coach Shanks has whipped out and is repeatedly setting up at various locations downfield each time one of us knocks it down. We go like that for a solid hour, Shanks changing it up by moving the cone left and right, stationing it anywhere from point-blank range to sixty yards downfield, just to see what we can do. It's not a perfect drill because usually we don't aim to hit something a foot off the ground, but it's definitely a challenge in accuracy.

It's also something we're pretty equal at as a trio.

But what comes next has my eyes shooting straight at the too-blond back of Brady's head.

"Okay, gang, great job." Coach is smiling, eyes crinkling at the corners. He's got sweat staining stripes down the back of his Northland polo as he turns to dump the orange cone next to his piles of gear. Still bent over, he picks up a bag of miniature cones, the kind Ry uses in our backyard for soccer drills. "Footwork time."

Brady's face hardens as much as it can with baby fat still clinging to his cheekbones. The dude feels called out. And based on Grey's description from last night, he should.

"Seven-step drop-back, five-step drop-back with a roll-out, and then we'll do some resistance work."

Grey's face doesn't melt into the same despair that Brady's has. I don't let mine change either. Maybe it's the fact that we're both a few years older. Or maybe it's having coaches in our families. But Grey and I are most definitely on the same page.

Just do the work.

No moping. No fear. No excuses.

Just do the freaking work.

Shanks uses the soccer cones to set up a pocket-size square at the ten-yard line and calls over Smith and Tate, the tight ends we worked with on Thursday and straight A teamers.

Coach demonstrates what he wants—a conscious seven slide-steps back and then a zigzag through the far end of the box before planting a foot and releasing to one of the guys in the end zone.

Grey lines up, ready to go, but Shanks waves him off.

"Let's go youngest to oldest today." He holds the ball out for Brady, who has a look on his face I would never, ever give a coach. It's dripping with disdain. The glare my sister would give me if she caught me with his expression would singe my eyebrows to ashes.

"Why don't we do ladies first?" Brady offers, gesturing to me, though that's obviously completely unnecessary.

Shanks frowns. "Excuse me?"

Amazingly, Brady thinks there's room for an actual

conversation here. "I think Rodinsky should have to do something first for once." It's suddenly very obvious that his shitty agility isn't the only reason Shanks bought into my recruitment.

Shanks purses his lips, anger deepening on his features. I'm not sure if Brady is smart enough to know he's about to get yelled at or dumb enough to think that his power play here is opaque. Or all of the above.

"Coach, it's fine, I'll go first," I say. Shanks glances at me, but I'm glaring at Brady. "I don't care when I go. I just want to get the job done."

After a pause, Coach hands me the ball. For an instant, a winsome look crosses Brady's face, but as he lines up next to Grey, it seems to dawn on him that he might not have tasted victory there.

I start at the top edge of the box, launching myself backward.

One. Two. Three. Four. Five. Six. Seven.

Slinging myself forward, I cross around the cones in measured steps, eyes up the whole time, watching the receivers shoot back. The second I'm back to the top of the box, I plant my foot and release, aiming to strike Smith straight in the heart.

When it makes contact, the ball thumps off his chest before bobbling into his hands.

Caught.

I have to bite my lip to keep down a smile as I stalk past Brady's bowed head.

~

The angels have smiled upon me, because our afternoon practice runs short. Which means I'm home and hopping into the shower by six o'clock.

Which is of supreme importance because it's Sunday night. Aka Rodinsky family dinner night. When we had a house of our own, my parents would host, Danielle and Heather making the trek across town to our place. Now that we're all together, we still do it—it's literally the only way to guarantee all of us are at one table at the same time. Mom still insists on cooking, but if that's more than warming up pizza, it's too much for her, even though she's crap at admitting it. So, for pretty much the entire summer, Heather's made up some excuse about having a new recipe she wants to try, or wanting to make something she's already bought the ingredients for. Mom plays along, "making salad," but not trying to do much more. It's a game and we all know it and it sucks.

But it works. So we go with it.

Tonight's meal is pot roast, something Heather culled from a compilation of recipes from the 1970s. Which means dessert is probably elaborately molded Jell-O, because she loves to go all out on a theme.

While setting the table, I catch Heather glancing at me

and then twisting to lean into my sister's ear, her moving lips barely disguised by Danielle's wavy bob.

Something's up.

And the only thing I'm keeping secret from everyone but Ryan is football.

Which makes me extremely nervous, even if it kills me to be keeping secrets from my sister. Because I don't think there's been a single thing about my life I haven't told her. Okay, maybe not my entire life. Maybe just my athletic life. But up until boys started getting interesting, there was nothing we didn't share.

Until now.

Part of me thinks Danielle might actually be proud of me if she knew I was playing football. But most of me doesn't even want to attempt that conversation.

So, though present at dinner, I'm slightly off my game, letting conversation swirl around me.

Dad's asking Mom about her doctor's appointments next week, so he can make sure to be there. Heather and Danielle have gone from whispering to making eyes at each other. Ryan is on his third helping of pot roast and has totally splattered meat juice on his white T-shirt—*that* I can't keep quiet about.

"Ry, what the hell? You look like pot roast Jackson Pollock." I laugh and toss my napkin at him.

Danielle joins in. "They're not going to let you into high school tomorrow looking like that."

"What," he whines at both of us, not even touching my napkin. "It's not like I'm going to wear the same shirt. Jeez."

"It's the principle of the thing," Danielle says. "You need to look nice in high school."

"Oh, what do you two know about what a high school *really* looks like? There aren't normal-people clothes at Windsor Prep."

Danielle tosses back her head. "Fancy uniforms show stains just as well as stuff from Target, right, Liv?"

I'm supposed to laugh and agree, so I do. Like a champ. But my mind is stuck on the fact that tomorrow I won't be in my Windsor Prep uniform. I won't be with my friends. And even though I'm feeling slightly better about Northland after joining the team, it's still everything I don't want.

After the laughter dies, I grow quiet again. Maybe it's the two-a-days, or the secrets, or going back to school. But I suddenly really need to be alone.

"May I be excused?" I ask, eyes directed at Mom. The second it's out of my mouth and I'm looking at her, guilt pings through my stomach—I really shouldn't pass up any time I can spend with Mom.

She smiles and says, "We've got dessert coming—"

"Oreo cheesecake," Heather finishes, blue eyes flashing as she cuts off Mom. OMG, that's so much better than Jell-O in any shape, and Heather is the queen bee of desserts.

Still. My stomach so can't take that right now.

"Thanks, but I'm good," I say with a forced smile and stand up, hauling my plate and glass. "I've got to get ready for school in the morning."

Heather cocks a brow. "Preparation is Oreo cheesecake. I read that on the internet, so it must be true."

"SHHHH, Heather, I want her piece," says Ryan, gripping his fork and knife like Wile E. Coyote.

"Like I wasn't going to give you half," I say, forcing out a laugh before disappearing to collapse onto my bed. My jersey, pads, and tights are there, stinking up things while mostly hidden under the covers, and I know I should sneak to the basement to wash them, but for now, it feels good to be stationary.

To just be Liv.

Not a brand-new junior. Not a backup quarterback. Not anything but Liv.

Okay, I can sit still for only about thirty seconds before I *have* to do something. So out comes my phone, and I cue up one of the bazillion YouTube clips I've found featuring quarterback heroics from games of yore, plus newer clips of Patrick Mahomes, Andrew Luck, Jared Goff, Marcus Mariota, and Sam Bradford. I even pull up a clip of Drew Brees decapitating a piñata, just because.

"Liv?" A knock comes on the door, my sister's voice behind it.

I shove the phone under the comforter and make sure my stupid red jersey isn't poking out, either.

"Yeah?"

"Can I come in?" she asks. And she never asks. Usually she just barges right on in.

"Uh, sure."

Danielle bursts in alone, Heather nowhere in sight. Probably distracting the rest of the crew with cheesecake. She shuts the door and turns slowly, a false smile plastered across her suntanned face.

It doesn't work. It's weird. I stare at her for a moment longer than I can stand, then blurt out, "Oh my God, what is it?"

Her smile falls and her face lands into its regular lines. I can breathe again. "You didn't do anything, Liv. I just want to make sure you're okay."

Danielle's eyes lift and meet mine—dark meeting dark.

"I'm fine. I just didn't want cheesecake."

"That's not what I meant—you look like hell." She sits on the bed and I half expect her to pull out my dirty jersey. It takes all the strength I have left after two-a-day hell not to glance down at the rumpled covers. Why couldn't she just sit on Ryan's bed? Well, because it's a rat's nest of jock-straps and shin guards—but still.

She sighs hard enough that I can smell the Trader Joe's merlot on her breath.

"You don't need to play tough, baby girl." My lips drop open and I'm about to call for Ryan, just so I can give him hell for being a stupid snitch after all the crap I bought him. But then Danielle grabs my hand. "Anybody would be having a rough time starting a new school as a junior."

I blink.

She thinks I'm *only* stressed about starting at Northland. Not because she knows about football and thinks I'm being reckless.

"Look, I know this year isn't shaping up to be what you want—heck, it's not exactly starting off to be what I want either." I swallow, knowing that she means she'd much rather have me in the Windsor Prep weight room than across town. Maybe even in her Honors English section like Addie if Principal Meyer were cool with that. "You know me—I hate things I can't control."

Her fingers try to flatten the bumps on my comforter. Part of me would be fine with her discovering the jersey underneath. It would sort of be a relief to be found out. I think.

She stands but lingers by the bed, fingertips still grazing the edge of my comforter. "But really—are you okay? This new school thing is a big deal."

"No—no, I'm not okay." I take a shaky breath and press the heels of my hands to my eyes, trying hard not to cry. When I pull my hands away, Danielle grabs one and squeezes. I manage to take a deep breath. "I'm not okay, but if this is what I have to do to survive and advance, then it's what I'll do."

Danielle smiles and brushes a piece of hair out of my

face, her fingers cool on my hot skin. "Just like you'll survive cross-country, right?"

Oh. Shit. I nod, internally kicking myself. I should've known that she wouldn't just forget about that little detail.

"When's your first meet? I'd like to go."

Double shit. "I don't know yet. I'll find out."

"Good. And if your Saturday morning race times conflict with Heather's torture yoga, so be it," she says with a little laugh and a shrug. She squeezes my hand one last time. "And tomorrow, remember to be yourself and you'll be fine."

13

THE SECOND I PARK HELENA THE HONDA ON MONDAY morning, Ryan and Jesse barrel out and weave through the rows of cars, hot in pursuit of a couple of colt-legged freshmen cheerleaders.

No goodbye. No thank-you. No "That'll do, Jeeves."

Boys.

So I follow the gaudy orange paw prints through the junior-senior parking lot and up to the school's main entrance. I've never actually entered Northland this way, preferring to sneak in the back like a criminal or a celebrity. Based on whose side you were on at the Northland–Windsor Prep game, I'm either or both.

The weather is beautiful, and at least half the school is still outside on the front lawn, soaking up the clear morning sun, the atmosphere charged by the electric current that lights up the first day of school as much as the last. That little shock of promise and hope that's threaded through a fresh start.

And that makes me want to cry.

I had *all* of that exactly where I wanted it at Windsor Prep.

Now I can't even dress myself properly, because everything that fits me is either old athletic clothes or part of my private school uniform. And I'm not about to beg for new clothes for the school year; we can't afford that. So I settled on a pair of skinny jeans that I've got to roll up at the cuff because they used to be Heather's, and a tank top that has seen far too many hours in the batting cage. Still, I curled my hair, swiped on some black liner with my daily mascara, dabbed on some cream blush, and smudged on a lip gloss four shades brighter than my summer cherry ChapStick.

My shoulders droop more than I'd like as I make my way through a crowd of strangers, a familiar voice cutting through my thoughts. "Posture like that makes me think someone punched your pony."

Grey is dressed all preppy again, just like he was on Saturday night in a Lacoste polo and khaki shorts. He's kicked up against a stone pillar, hands in his pockets, rocking his newscaster-surfer look in all its chiseled glory, his shades pulled low against the strong morning sun.

"Punched? Nice."

"Touchy, touchy."

I skate past him and catch the door handle. "No offense, but I'd rather be starting school at Windsor Prep."

"Why? So you can play fashion face-off with a bunch of girls in the same skirt?" He bumps gently into my shoulder, but there's no wink. The deadpan game is strong with him this morning.

"No. So I can play fashion face-off with a bunch of my *friends* in the same skirt," I say, even though it feels like a lie. I've barely seen anyone but Addie since state.

"And here I thought we were friends." Grey's hand goes flat against the little Lacoste alligator over his heart and he falls with a clang against somebody's locker. A few girls stop talking and look our way. "That was a dagger, Rodinsky. A *dagger*. Oh, my heart."

"If you're saying you want to trade the shorts-and-polo number for a Windsor Prep uniform, I do own a sewing machine and about eight skirts I no longer need."

The serious planes of his face break. "Okay, nah, I'm fine." He pushes off the locker and raises his chin. The girls are still staring at him, and that's when it dawns on me that even though I'm a nobody here, Grey is a *somebody*. A major somebody of the "hot starting quarterback/senior football co-captain" variety. "Speaking of school, how's your schedule looking?"

My schedule just has the names of classes and the room

numbers. Not that I know where anything is, other than the locker rooms and weight room. Northland is the oldest school in the county and has been added on to so many times that it's laid out like a half-full Scrabble board.

As Grey reads down the line of classes and places, I glance up, ending up eyeball to eyeball with about two dozen posters with faces and names I don't know, all in various arrangements, all begging "So-and-so for Homecoming Queen!"

They let them campaign for honorary titles at this dumb school? And homecoming is still, like, five weeks away—I know because Coach Lee has it highlighted outside his office, the most important game outside of the league championship and anything else we get at state.

"Spanish first, huh?" Hope rises in my chest that he might be in that class, too, even though he's a senior—it is an elective, after all. "My class is that way. I'll show you."

"You're not in Spanish?" I ask, traitorous cheeks pinking.

"Not that section. But we do have Honors Calc together right after lunch."

Lunch—that sounded like an invitation. Thank God. "Awesome."

"We can discuss integrals for, like, two straight hours if we want." At this, he winks, completely oblivious to the fact that the sea of students is parting neatly for him and his broad shoulders. I have people skirting past me, knocking into my backpack in a way I've never experienced in high school. Mostly because Windsor Prep doesn't have nearly this many students, but also because I was so high up the social ladder, my shoulder wasn't in anybody else's airspace.

I start to laugh because though I don't know him well, I doubt that's what Grey likes to do for fun, but then suddenly his hand is twined with mine. "Liv, this way," he says, and then he's tugging me down a side hallway.

We're touching. And not in a shoulder-knock cutesy way.

Too soon, he lets go. "Two down, on the left."

"Cool," I say, though I'm most definitely not. Between the nerves, the dread, and whatever the heck just happened when we made skin-to-skin contact, I'm pretty sure I should've gone without any blush this morning. "Thanks for walking me."

"No problem. I'll play Good Samaritan anytime."

I open my mouth to respond, but suddenly—

"Grey?"

There, filling only half of the doorway with her slender frame, is Coach Kitt. Or, apparently, my Spanish teacher.

All the annoying color drains from my face.

"Hey, Mom." Grey cocks a thumb at me. "Just helping out Liv."

Coach Kitt's red lips smooth into a line, but there's a hitch at the end, her version of her son's half smile. "A new favorite pastime of yours."

Unfazed, Grey grins wider. "Eh, gotta have a hobby." His shoulder knocks mine. "Later, Liv."

When he's gone, I follow the stilettoed heels of Coach Kitt into the classroom. A quick survey tells me I know exactly two people in the twenty or so seats. I hope that Coach Kitt's love of team culture stops at the softball diamond because if we pair up for group projects at all, I now have a one in ten chance of having either Kelly or Jake as a partner.

They're sitting next to each other—of course—which adds credence to the epiphany I had on the track, though they aren't talking to each other at all.

Kelly is closest to me, cat eyes in finely drawn form as she stares daggers at the notebook in front of her. It's the same look she gives the clipboard in practice. So, either her eyesight really is as crappy as I thought after she beaned me at state, or she just stares that hard at *everything*.

Jake stands out in a bright orange Northland track-and-field T-shirt. He runs hurdles—really well, apparently—because it's the reason he was in *The Kansas City Star* spring sports showcase with me way back when we met.

I don't glance away quickly enough and he catches me looking.

Coach Kitt begins to rattle off the names and bodies start to move, all in alphabetical order. Which means that, sadly, I don't need to wait until she hits Rodinsky to know exactly where I'll be sitting at 7:45 AM every school day for the next nine months.

Right in front of Jake Rogers.

Because, as Addie pointed out, I have *all* the luck, my seat in Spanish actually isn't right in front of Jake.

Nope, the Rodinsky–Rogers split happened at the end of a row. Which means, because of the snaking layout, Jake and I get to sit next to each other in the back of the class.

It's something I would've seriously dreamed about five months ago. I probably *did* dream about it. Possibly while sitting in Mr. Sweeten's Honors English class, "listening" to him drone on about the merits of *The Scarlet Letter.* Possibly.

And now that daydream is a reality.

Which, despite our history, actually isn't much of a problem.

It was just like at practice—not exactly comfortable, but not exactly uncomfortable. It's fine but awkward. Probably the best scenario, all things considered.

Though I'd appreciate it if he randomly forgot his cologne for the rest of the school year because—*hot damn*—that's distracting.

Now it's hours later and I can *still* smell it, after sitting through two other classes where I knew exactly no one. And now I'm standing at the entrance to junior-senior lunch, paper sack in hand, scanning the room. It's filled with hundreds of faces, but I'm only looking for one.

But of course I spy Mr. Cologne first. He's sitting with Kelly and some girls I recognize from softball games. In my previous life, that would've been my table to curate.

I don't linger long as a familiar tan arm shoots up, hand open as casually as if it had just thrown a perfect spiral. Grey, calling me to a table by the windows.

As I get closer, I recognize other faces at the table, mostly as people I'm used to seeing in football gear—Topps, Chico Sanchez, Zach Tate, Trevor Smith, and, interestingly, Nick Cleary. I suppose twins don't have to do everything together, but separate lunch tables wasn't something I was expecting. Also unexpected: The only girl at the table is a brunette in a cheerleading uniform. I haven't seen her before, but she smiles at me like we've been best friends since macaroni necklaces.

"O-Rod," Topps says by way of greeting, beard even more striking when paired with a T-shirt emblazoned with the phrase I LIKE TACOS.

"Good one, Topps," Grey says, aiming for a lazy fist bump across the table.

Topps raises a bushy brow. "What do you mean?"

"O-Rod. Like A-Rod. And she even plays third like him," he deadpans, the corners of his lips curled. "It's clever."

"I didn't make it up. It's her actual nickname."

Grey kicks out the chair next to him. It puts me between him and Nick, and directly across from the cheerleader, who is still smiling—and stealing Topps's fries while he attempts to explain his lack of cleverness. It also puts me within Grey's wingspan, as he's got both arms splayed out and curled around the chairs on either side of him. Chico is on his left side—and not looking weirded out by the manspreading—while I'd be on his right. "Your nickname is O-Rod? How did I not know this?"

I slide into the chair and pull it up, conscious of his forearm making contact with my upper back. To cover for the flush I feel creeping up my cheeks, I sock him on the shoulder. "You didn't ask. Topps did."

Grey lifts his chin in appreciation. "Nice work, Topps."

"Now, I've got a question for you, Topps," I say, popping open my water bottle. "What's your actual name? Clue a girl in."

"Tobias James Topperman," the brunette says with a giant grin crowded onto her elfin face. She's got huge brown eyes that make her look like Bambi—in a good way. "And I'm Lily Jane Mack."

"My Lily Jane," Topps says with a smile, squeezing her shoulder with a bear paw. Said by anybody else, the "my" there would come across as misogynistic bullcrap, but with Topps, it's somehow sweet and endearing.

"Nice to meet you, Lily Jane."

"Likewise, O-Rod." She leans in. "Don't let the uniform fool you. I'm not like she-who-must-not-be-named."

"Oh." Frost settles over my skin as it dawns on me that I'd forgotten Stacey was on the cheer squad.

The chill spreads with further realization that—yet again—these people at Northland know a heck of a lot more about me than I know about them. All of them know about Stacey. And all of them know about why I'm here.

No use in denying our shared understanding, as much as I hate it. I match Lily Jane's smile, or at least I try to. "I'm fine with giving her the Voldemort treatment."

"Me too." Grey raises his knuckles to me in an offer of a fist bump. I offer my fist back, but as I do, I catch Nick and Topps in a whisper, both their eyes glued to Grey.

And I wonder what else I don't know.

14

I'M HIGH AS A FREAKING KITE AS GREY AND I WALK TO
the only class we have together. Honors calculus—with
Coach Lee as our instructor, as it turns out. Lily Jane,
Topps, and Nick are in the class, too, which is awesome
because it wasn't pleasant feeling so alone in my earlier
classes.

We pile into the classroom, Grey in front of me, which
is much more enjoyable than sitting next to Jake, and pull
out notebooks in a shuffle. Grey immediately wrenches
around in his chair until he's facing sideways, the sling of
his body oh-so-comfortable, both myself and Coach Lee
now in his sight line.

And as I'm writing the date at the top of my notebook, the bell rings, bringing with it a flush of last-minute

classmates. I glance up as the last person files in: Jake. Again.

He grabs a seat next to Kelly—who is here, too, because of course—and a pleased little look crosses her face as she arranges the pens and notebook on her desk.

I don't care. I swear.

"Afternoon, ladies and gentlemen," Lee says, underlining his name with a careful swipe of marker. "I do hope that though this class is directly after lunch, you will make an effort to be on time." He pauses, making eye contact with Jake for what seems like forever. I bite back a smile. Jake is soooo screwed tonight at practice, at least if he survives whatever weights workout Napolitano has already devised. "I expect all my students, but most especially my honors students, to take mathematics seriously."

He stops his speech with an appraising glare—as if to see if we're up to the task. After one last sweep across our faces, Coach Lee is apparently pleased enough to continue. He turns back to the board and yells out a name. "Topperman."

"Yes, Coach?"

"You take mathematics seriously, do you not?"

"As serious as I take my strawberry pop."

Considering he and Lily Jane just shared three cans over lunch, I'd say he's actually very serious about math.

"What's the difference between algebra and calculus?"

Topps seriously freaking strokes his beard like a philosopher. Still, I'm literally holding my breath for the guy because that is most definitely not an easy first-day-of-school question, but Lily Jane is smiling at him like he's a freaking rock star. When he answers, I see why. "They're partners in crime. Calculus finds new equations, algebra solves them."

Coach Lee writes Topps's definition on the board and when he turns around, it's with a smile like I've never seen. "Our district mathletics champ, ladies and gentlemen." Topps takes a little bow from his desk, cheeks bright pink. "We've got forty-six minutes remaining today, so let's see what new equations we can find."

The rest of the day is a blur of faces and assignments and new, poorly planned classroom locations, and my mind is toast by the last bell. I head straight from my last class to the athletics wing, the team's prepractice trip to the weight room so heavy on my mind that I don't notice the mass of boys huddled near the line of coaches' offices.

That is, until one of them peels off the pack, takes off down the orange-and-white checkered tile, and wraps me in a bear hug so strong that we plow into a nearby set of lockers. A metallic noise pings through my skull as it bounces off the empty steel box. The rest of me is stationary, pressed between a locker and this person. Who I now see is Ryan. A screeching, shaking Ryan.

"VARRRRRSSSSSITTTTY," he whisper-screams into the crook of my neck, where his face has landed.

I realize the mass of boys is gathered around a bulletin board above the drinking fountain and that nearly every one of them is wearing adidas from head to toe.

Jesse was right. *"Duuuuuudddde. Your sister is kind of an asshole."*

I've been so wrapped up in my own student-athlete drama at Northland High that I completely—and I mean *completely*—forgot about the team announcements today.

Football is a sport that needs bodies and cuts no one, the pecking order decided in a much more fluid A team and B team scenario of varsity and JV, plus the catchall C team. Soccer, not so much—there are far more bodies than spots. Tryouts matter, and if you're cut, you're not playing. Considering Ry's placekicking doldrums last week, I should've been on pins and needles all day, and instead I'm half-clueless and pinned to a locker.

I am a total asshole.

"Varsity?!" I whisper-scream in response. "I thought the coach hated you."

Ryan pulls back, cheeks flushed. "Turns out Coach Parsons is of the Danielle Rodinsky-Simpson 'the more I hate you, the more I love you' school of coaching."

I mock-punch him in the gut. "Harsh, man, harsh."

"You're right, not fair to Coach Parsons."

I shake my head and run a hand through his hair. "I'm so proud of you, Ry."

He raises a brow. "Any chance you might want to

express that pride in a double-dip waffle cone from Happy Cow postpractice?"

"It's a deal."

"Good, because I'm going to need all the calories I'm gonna get. Tonight's going to be killer."

I give him a knowing nod—I, too, was a freshman on varsity once. And, even worse, the coach was my sister in her first year. "Tough being a frosh on a squad of upperclassmen. Gotta work twice as hard to prove yourself."

Ry finally releases me, tucking his thumbs into the straps of his backpack in one cool motion as those cheerleaders he chased after this morning exit the girls' locker room in a fit of giggles and a swirl of plumeria body spray. He chin-checks them and then returns to me, right back to being dialed in to our conversation.

"Is this the part in the after-school special where I say, 'But not as hard as being the only girl on a high school football team, huh, big sis?' And you give me a wise smile with a flippant 'Not even close'?"

"We could go that route if you want," I deadpan.

He grins. "Nah. I won't patronize you. I'll just take your money and spin it into ice cream like Rumpelstiltskin."

Considering ice cream is basically gold to my little brother... Touché, Ryan. Touché.

15

FRIDAY NIGHT, OUR DEBUT IS AN ABSOLUTE BLOWOUT.

As in, we're winning by a lot, even though the Friday night lights did nothing to improve Brady's shitty footwork and entitled attitude.

No, it's a total blowout with a three-touchdown lead and counting (we're only in the third quarter) because of a single factor: number thirty-two.

Aka Jake Rogers, senior captain and all-area running back.

Aka the legs propping up the entire Northland Tigers football team.

I'd known that was the case ever since I was first approached by Grey and Coach Shanks. *We're a running* team, but . . . *we still need someone calling the plays and chucking the ball to our running back.*

But, still, *seeing* it in an actual game—as opposed to practice—is way crazier than being told about it by Grey, by Coach, or even by Jake himself. Though Jake only did his telling in dribs and drabs when we were first dating. A little show-off line here or there like, "Well, it *is* possible to score eight touchdowns in a game, because I totally did that against Central last year." I'll let you figure out how he totally worked that into a normal conversation with his softball-playing girlfriend.

And though he probably was exaggerating, he wasn't lying about his talent. Not in the slightest.

And sitting here on the bench with Grey, watching the team from Wyandotte Rural get steamrolled, I'm sort of dumbfounded. I mean, why did they even need a third-string quarterback? Brady's thrown the ball three times. Literally. And every time it was because Lee and Shanks intentionally called a passing play to fake out the defense for, like, five seconds. I almost feel as if I should ask Grey if he wants to go squeeze in between Addie and Ryan in the stands and eat the remainder of their popcorn, because there's literally no reason for either of us to be down on the field.

A slip of darkness falls over the bench, blocking out the scorching late-summer sun—Coach Shanks. He leans in and the shadows fade out and there's a big old crinkly smile on his face.

"Rodinsky, you're up."

I gape at him. "I'm *what*?"

"After this play, I'm putting you in. Orange Nine to Tate. Worthington, get her ready."

He disappears and Grey stands, but like my first day of scrimmage, my legs won't seem to move. My mouth, though, is sputtering my thoughts out loud, completely without a filter.

"But that's a passing play—" Tate shoots left, crossing before a catch and turn. Orange Nine. "Why would we do that?"

"He wants you to score."

Jake just ran seven yards for a first down. The ball is at the fifteen. Meaning, unless Jake doesn't score here or makes a rare mistake and actually loses ground, it'll be the perfect time to try a passing play. If it's unsuccessful, we still have another try before a field goal or going for it on fourth down.

Grey places himself right in my line of sight and squats down. The half smile he wears so well seems bigger at this angle.

"He wants you to score because he knows you can. Pass rush is extra tough just outside the red zone. Coach knows you're mobile and won't do something stupid with the ball, like give up an interception or stand still for a sack."

I blink at him. I haven't scored a thing since a two-run homer in the seventh inning of my final club game this summer. An entire month without scoring, because, let's be honest, scoring in scrimmage doesn't count. And somehow I get a chance to do it here and now in a sport I've played for just over a week.

How is this real life?

Grey pulls me over to the track for a quick game of catch, my body still warm from tossing with Brady at the half. Meanwhile, on the field, Brady covers the ball in a pretty shoddy attempt at concealment before dumping it into Jake's hands yet again. Jake is tripped up by the defensive line for once, only gaining two yards.

Which means we need eight yards to reset the downs. Putting on my helmet, I glance to Shanks—something he's completely expecting because his finger is already pointing to the field as he makes eye contact. "Orange Nine."

We're still doing the passing play.

No pressure or anything.

I get into the huddle, and it's the weirdest sensation ever because everyone is staring at me for word of what we're doing like I'm not the greenest of them.

"Orange Nine."

"What?" That comes from Topps, who got promoted to first-string this week, along with Nick Cleary.

"I know."

"Why?" This comes from Jake, whose face is curdling before my eyes.

"I have no idea, but that's what Shanks said."

"But—"

"That's what Shanks said," I repeat, staring down Jake and my own nerves. "So we do it." Jake, the rest of the huddle, and my nerves go silent. "Break!"

We jog out to our places. I bend my knees, stuff my hands way too close to Topps's junk, and call out again, all too aware of Jake's annoyed eyes pinned to my helmet from his spot deep in the backfield.

"ORANGE NINE. ORANGE NINE. HUT-HUT."

The snap comes and I've got the ball in my hands. I race back and look out for Tate, number eighty-two.

On the play chart, he's supposed to zoom in a right-to-left cross about five yards from the pocket. I hold my breath and look for a body in orange moving in that general direction. Instead, I see all too clearly a body on each side of me, rushing toward the pocket—linebackers on the move. And, unlike in practice, if they get to me, these two dudes are going to drill me into the turf.

No running wide at the last second. No stopping short. No mercy.

Automatically, my feet start moving and I shoot wide left, dodging the linebacker there, while trying to lose the guy on the right side. But the dude keeps coming. Faster than Tate is getting to his spot. And because I'm running the same direction he is, the whole play is falling apart.

And I'm being tailed by a rhino.

Christ.

In another step, I get my arm back and aim the ball straight at Tate. We make eye contact as I release the ball. Which is about two-tenths of a second before I'm steamrolled to the ground by the aforementioned rhino.

As I'm falling, I glimpse the ball sailing right through Tate's hands and into the mitts of some guy in Wyandotte Rural powder blue.

Shit.

The guy bobbles the ball up, and my helmet hits the turf before I can see if he catches it.

Double shit.

I stay still, hoping to God I didn't just notch an interception. I mean, that's what it looked like. And if that's what it was, I'm never playing again. Ever. It's a good thing Grey's supposed to be cleared for the next game because Coach Lee is gonna can the experiment that was Liv Rodinsky, backup quarterback.

Finally, the rhino rolls off me and I stand up.

The defense hasn't come on the field yet and the whole Northland offensive line still lingers in generally the same position as before, thirteen yards out from the end zone.

Okay. I take a deep breath.

So I wasn't intercepted. I was lucky as hell. The dude must have dropped it.

I breathe a sigh of relief as the down marker flips from second to third. Still alive. And somehow, this is all I need to know, the embarrassment and pain of the hit rolling off with the realization that we have a second chance. Football may be brutal, but the downs structure is actually forgiving in a way that softball really isn't.

Shanks mouths my marching orders—ORANGE NINE. I blink at him. And then run to the huddle.

I have to work to find my voice after that hit, but the words still come out firm and clear. "Orange Nine."

"Not White Nine?" That's from my freaking target, Tate, asking if it should be a running play.

"Coach said orange. We're doing it again."

"That's stupid." Tate again.

"That's the order." My eyes meet his. "Catch it this time."

Tate's mouth falls open.

Jake stays silent, which is half-amazing, considering I know he's itching to take a running leap over both lines.

But I don't care what either of them thinks, goddammit. I want to score.

"Break!"

One more chance to make the play. One more chance before giving it up to special teams for a field goal. One more chance to keep going.

I cozy up to Topps and yell out the play, loud and clear, daring Wyandotte Rural to wrap their heads around the fact that, yes, we're doing the very same play. Again.

Bring it.

"HUT-HUT!"

I shoot back in the pocket and scan the line for Tate. He's gotten free of his defender and is running the play at a perfect clip.

I line up for my shot as the linebacker to my left—the rhino's companion—comes charging my way. I dodge the other way, toward the blank space where the rhino would be if our line hadn't tripped him up. Line up my shot again. Throw.

Tate jumps up and to his right, hands out. The throw's slightly off, the ball grazing his fingertips and popping up for a split second. I hold my breath, but then both his hands wrap around the ball—right as I'm flattened by the Wyandotte Rural linebacker.

We go down in a rush, my helmet hitting the turf in such a way that it blinds me from the action. I lie still—breath gone but otherwise fine—waiting for the guy to get up, unable to see what's happening. But I hear something happening.

Cheering.

Lots of it.

When I get to my feet, my breath stops just as surely as it did when Kelly clocked me with her fastball at state.

There's Zach Tate's number eighty-two.

Far, far away from me.

In the end zone.

He's got the ball over his head, lets out a holler, and then spikes the crap out of some turf.

A touchdown.

My head whips around to the scoreboard to see that, yes, they've already added six points. I scored. Tate scored. *We* scored.

I know what scoring feels like—I've been sliding into home base for as long as I can remember—but this is just... I don't have *words* for what this is.

"O-ROD! TOUCHDOOOOOOOOOOOWN!" Topps screams—whirling around as quickly as 250 pounds of awesome can whirl—and picks me up.

Like, literally.

I'm in the air, nearly to his shoulders, smiling from ear to ear, when I glimpse Grey, over on the sideline, applauding with a huge grin on his face. *Huge.*

There's nothing "half" about it at all.

And it comes with a wink.

16

HE'S WAITING FOR ME OUTSIDE THE GIRLS' LOCKER room after the game.

I shouldn't be surprised. But I am.

I open the door and see him nearly in profile, most of his back to me. I stand there, my breath hitching. Gone are his pads and helmet, replaced with street clothes and the crisp scent of boy soap.

"Hey."

Grey turns, half smile in place, wet surfer-meets-newscaster hair glinting under the sodium lights.

"There she is: Liv Rodinsky, ringer."

A smile perks up on my lips. "A ringer would imply expertise."

He takes a step my way, a shadow casting over me.

There's not a soul near us—the locker room was completely empty of cheerleaders and Kelly by the time I finished getting ready. And I'll admit I took my time—mascara, blush, even a thin sweep of Addie-style eyeliner—hoping to look decent for the planned team trip to Pat's Diner for postgame pancakes.

"I'd say you gave Wyandotte Rural quite the seminar on how to score points—three passing touchdowns in one and a half quarters?" Grey's eyes meet mine and my heart flutters. "Master class."

"Or complete and utter luck."

"Or that." He takes another step, and suddenly we're just inches apart. "But it takes a lot of natural talent and hard work to make luck look that easy."

I punch him in the arm. Mostly because I'm not sure what to do with him so close. I'm used to feeling him against my skin, when our shoulders bump against each other or our hands brush as we walk down the halls, but he never stands there like this, with weight behind what he's doing. "Aw, shucks," I say, trying to will the heat away from my cheeks.

Grey's eyes narrow and the half smile freezes in surprise. "It can't be. Is mighty Liv Rodinsky, an immeasurably fearless quarterback on the field, actually afraid of a puny little compliment?"

Soap and giddiness surround him as the toes of his Nikes nuzzle up against mine. Suddenly more nervous than I've ever been in my entire life, I shove my hands in the front pockets of my jeans. Days ago, I didn't even know Grey Worthington existed. But now? Now I can barely breathe around him. Somehow, I maintain eye contact. "I'm not afraid of anything."

"Of course not."

The flutter in my heart quickens as Grey lets his hand close the distance between us, his fingertips grazing my cheek, moving down until they gently tip up my chin. My pulse stutters. He's inspecting me, searching for hesitation but actually seeing so much more—and that's something I'm afraid of.

He shakes his head. "No fear there right now. None."

I should play tough. Hang in my comfort zone. But instead, as so often over the past week, I feel a smile creeping up, and I have to hold myself back from snagging his fingers and kissing them. "Never."

Grey's mouth softens and he leans in, so close that his polo kisses my forearm. He raises a brow, smile falling from his lips in a way that's a good thing. All desire to hold back has evaporated. My breath vanishes and I tip my chin up toward his, the swoop of his lips my whole field of vision.

"O-Rod!" Addie's voice cuts through the slip of air between us and we jolt apart.

Addie flings herself at me in a jumble of long arms and legs, and I'm fairly certain Grey is grazed by friendly fire. "You. Were. AMAZING." She squeezes all the air out of my lungs. "Totally unbelievable. Outstanding. Genius. Every adjective in my arsenal."

"Thanks," I say, feeling a little guilty. She had two matches this week, and my practices went late enough that I didn't even try to make either one. But here she is, cheering me on like always.

"So, you *can* take a compliment," Grey whispers, but rather than getting a rise out of me, it has the effect of whipping Addie's attention from me to Grey.

"She's gonna take more than a compliment. She's gonna take your job, dude. Watch out."

I start laughing, but they both spin on me, faces hard.

"I'm serious," Addie says.

"She has a point," Grey says, nodding. "I was dying to get in there tonight, but if you keep playing like that, I'm going to have to bribe Coach for minutes."

I could brush them off. I could play coy.

But it's true. I did much better than I ever, *ever* thought I'd do as a quarterback in an honest-to-God football game.

Can I add another "ever" in there?

Because EVER.

The rush of what happened tonight is still zinging through my pulse points, even more than an hour after my last touchdown.

Forty-five minutes after shaking hands with the other team, my helmet off, hair down—the looks I got from Wyandotte Rural were fabulous.

Thirty minutes since I shot a confident smile across the locker room at Kelly, her annoyance level stuck at eleven.

Fifteen minutes since I hopped out of the shower.

And about a minute since Grey touched my face *like that*.

So I don't brush off their praise. But because I can't reconcile the thrill zipping through my veins with the burn of butterflies in my gut as I meet Grey's eyes, I go with a trick play to buy myself some time.

"Who wants pancakes? I'll drive."

Grey's got his arm around my shoulders. More technically, he's got it around my chair, Mr. Manspreader Supreme at work at ten thirty on a Friday night.

No one seems to notice or care. Jake and Kelly are working very hard to ignore us at the opposite end of five tables strung together. The boys between us don't seem to give a shit. And directly across from me is Addie, who would normally be cataloging every inch of Grey's body language in embarrassing detail to tease me about later, but who isn't paying a lick of attention because she's found something infinitely more fascinating: Nick Cleary.

The attraction was instant, like freaking lightning. He immediately recognized Addie as "the hot girl who trashed my twin sister at state."

Note to all boys: There is no better way to pick up

Adeline McAndry than to call her hot and talented in the same sentence. The steak-and-potatoes Prince Harry thing probably didn't hurt his chances.

Kelly was either not amused or a strawberry jam tub *just happened* to bean Nick in the jugular 2.3 seconds later. Addie immediately swept the jam off the banquet and squeezed in beside him, smile a bazillion watts.

"Earth to O-Rod," Grey whispers into my ear as a note of boy soap, crisply sitting atop his skin, drifts my way.

Rather than whipping around—which would put our mouths way too close together—I side-eye him with a little smile.

"Yes?"

"Seen a Martian yet?"

"Very funny, Captain Kirk."

His lips tip up at the corners. "Don't worry. It happens to everyone. It used to happen to me even."

"What did?"

"That posttouchdown buzz."

My smile widens. I can't help it. "How do you know I'm not always like this when I win? How do you know touchdowns make it different?"

"Because I know enough about your softball career to know that if you were like this every time you won or scored, you'd probably be permanently high."

"Is that a compliment?"

"Yes. You going to actually accept it?"

"I do believe I will."

"Oh shit," Addie screeches. "Liv, *curfew*."

My head whips around to where she's sitting across the table, stack of pancakes vanished in a sad swirl of used syrup and melted butter. Her eyes are wide, and Nick looks as surprised as she does that everything has come grinding to a halt.

I glance at my watch. Crap. It's now a quarter to eleven, which is pumpkin time in both our houses. Cop Dad is one thing, but Mrs. McAndry, Johnson County district attorney, is also not a person you want to defy. Neither set of parents is going to be happy if we're late, even if they think Addie and I've just been bumming it at the mall or movie theater tonight. Which is totally what they think—Ryan even asked Danielle to drop him and Jesse at the football stadium because I was "with Addie."

"I can take you up to Northland," Nick offers. He pulls out his wallet to pay. "Rogers, you drive Kell home?"

Jake nods, which doesn't help the fact that I'm still not thinking clearly, because I shut that shit down. "I've got to drop Grey off at Northland, so I can take Addie, too," I say.

Something passes between Nick and Grey. "I can take her," Nick reiterates and stands, dumping cash on the table. His blue eyes ghost to Grey's again.

Grey's hand drops from the edge of my chair to my shoulder. "I didn't drive to school. Would you mind taking me home? Nick's got this."

I share a glance with Addie, whose eyes are pleading with me to stop being an idiot. Pleading is the wrong word—they're screaming, "You go with your cute boy and I'll go with mine, dummy."

Because I'm a total genius right now, I manage a super-smart, super-sexy, "Okay, then."

GREY'S HOUSE ISN'T FAR FROM THE DINER. IT ISN'T FAR
from Northland either. I would say it isn't far from Danielle's house, but that would be an understatement.

It's practically in our backyard.

He lives next door to the house that butts up against
ours. If there weren't a wall of trees along his fence line,
I could see the back of his house from my bedroom
window.

Not that I would try to look later, for the record. Okay,
I might. But what I'd see then can't compete with what I'm
seeing right this second.

Grey is inches from me again, leaning in after taking
off his seat belt as I coast to a stop in front of his house.
Unlike my driveway, his isn't filled with cars. Instead of

a pile of parental and kid vehicles, his three-car swath of asphalt is completely pristine. Just like the house, which has the same manicured feel as his mother. If a brick colonial could wear lipstick, this one would. I mean, Danielle and Heather have a nice house, but it's on the smaller side for the neighborhood and needs some major renovation, so it isn't *this* by a long shot.

The house is quiet, too. Not a single light is on. Which makes the proximity of Grey's face to mine even more heart-stopping.

"Why are you giving me that death glare?" he asks.

Because we're so far apart, even though we're almost neighbors.

My brows shoot up immediately as I try to remedy my expression and shake from my head the fact that he's got triple the space for half the people, and I have to share a closet with my brother. "Oh, sorry."

Grey breaks into a wide smile. "Don't be sorry." Again, he catches my chin between his thumb and forefinger. "You're pretty even when you look like you want to burn me to the ground."

I snort. Real sexy, I know. "Is that what I look like? An arsonist?"

His smile collapses into its most comfortable half shape, but somehow he looks even more pleased. "Enough that I'd never hand you matches."

"Ouch."

His thumb grazes my lower lip. "Did you even hear the first part of that sentence?"

I blink at him, thoughts a jumbled mess on the cutting-room floor. Nothing seems adequate with his thumb on my lip.

"Pretty—I think you're pretty," he says. "Beautiful, actually."

My heart slows, just coasting on fumes until I'm staring at him with the whole of me—blood, breath, mind—still.

"Beautiful, smart, funny, and you've got one hell of an arm."

I sort of expect him to wink, but he doesn't. His thumb hasn't moved, and I struggle to give a straight answer. "You've made no secret of liking my arm."

"What if I said I liked more than just your arm?"

Something about the nature of his face softens, and my lungs collapse. "That would probably back up the beautiful comment."

Grey closes the space between us, his lips warm against mine. They're softer than I imagined, but the scrape of stubble pressing into my chin is 100 percent rough-and-tumble boy.

We stay like that for I don't know how long—one of his hands is cupping my cheek, but the other stays primly in his lap while my fingers grip the steering wheel—until a flash of light hits the backs of my eyelids. I open my eyes to see the light on his porch suddenly lit.

Grey's eyes spring open, too, but rather than freak, he rubs his thumb across my lower lip one last time and winks.

"See you in eight hours, Liv Rodinsky."

That smile doesn't leave my lips during my ride home. Thank God I only live around the corner and a boomerang block back up, because I seriously don't recall a single thing about that short ride. It's like the type of runner's high you get where you black out until you hit the front stoop and just then realize you're finished.

The past week has been an F5 tornado, with the last few hours the most dizzying part of the ride.

I kissed Grey.

I kissed Grey hours after scoring my first-ever touchdown. I kissed Grey and scored a touchdown without knowing either was a possibility just over a week ago.

I am in every way a different girl than the one who was running at the Northland track, earbuds canceling out everything other than my own pitiful thoughts.

I exit Helena with my eyes on the trees lining Grey's backyard. There's a light on in the back, spilling through a window on the second floor of the house and winking through the trees. It's got to be his room. A small voice tells me it probably smells of boy soap and just-washed basketball shorts.

A shadow catches my eye, interrupting my thoughts. I glance up the drive and my heart plummets.

Dad.

Eddy Rodinsky has a finger to his wristwatch, tapping at a ticked-off rhythm. The porch light backlights his dark hair, perfectly placed silver sparkling at the temples. I'm in deep shit. My dad prefers a tight ship, even if he's not around to steer it.

I've barely seen him since last Sunday's dinner, thanks to the case he's been working, so it'd be just my luck that he'd be home and awake the first time I've missed my curfew in six months. Awesome.

"I'm late, I'm sorry," I say—though a confession never works with Cop Dad. He's heard too many. "I was out with Addie—"

"And the team?"

My breath catches and the blood in my veins slows. The silvery patches at his temples blur.

"Dad—I—"

"You were going to tell me, I know." He crosses his arms over his starched button-up, dark eyes reading me. I don't know if it's learned or a parental instinct, but Dad always seems to know exactly what I'm thinking. And right this moment, I'm thinking about what he'd most hate about this situation—my deception.

"I didn't lie." It's the truth, and I hope he can hear it in my voice. I made Ryan lie, but I never lied.

"You did. You told Danielle you went out for cross-country."

Oh, shit.

"And before you ask, Ryan didn't snitch. The boy spilled his guts an hour ago, but I already knew. He didn't tell me."

I gape at him. If Ry didn't tell, then who? Addie?

Dad knows a stumped face when he sees one. "Sarge's grandkid plays for Rural. Better believe he was pissed that I hadn't told him about your new position. Called me up as he was filing out of the stadium to congratulate me—to congratulate you."

The way he makes it sound, the lilt of his voice, gives me hope that he thinks it's cool. That I did something smart and grown-up and he won't decapitate me for repeatedly sticking my hands an inch from Topps's junk all week.

But the taint of disapproval sits heavily in his body language. So I wait.

Dad rolls his shoulders and sighs, his eyes never leaving mine. "Would you like to explain why you lied to Danielle and neglected to tell your parents about your latest athletic endeavor?"

I know this is a kindness. Dad giving me a chance to share my story rather than weather his questions. My dad is strict, but that doesn't mean he's not fair.

"Ryan didn't tell you?"

"I want to hear it from you."

I keep my voice low, trying to prove I can be an adult and not throw a hissy fit just because he thinks I will. I can be calm. I can be better than the girl who lost her cool and punched Stacey. Or threw her helmet at Jake. I can be more.

"I went to talk to Coach Kitt about softball and she told me I needed to prove to her that I'm a good teammate and can add value to the Tigers beyond my talent. So, I told her I'd join a fall sport—probably cross-country."

I can't tell if he knows this already, but I figure it's as good as any place to start.

"And I really was planning to try out. But then the next day, the starting quarterback caught me on the track. He'd seen me with Ryan the day before, throwing around a football, and suggested I go out for backup quarterback. He's getting over a broken collarbone and the team needed an extra backup and he thought I'd be good at it. I laughed at him and told him it was a dumb idea, but he sold me on it."

"How?"

"Um, well, the quarterback, Grey, he's Coach Kitt's son."

Dad's jaw stiffens. "Did he tell you you'd have a spot on his mother's team if you went out for football?"

"No, not exactly. I mean, it was more of I help him out and he makes sure his mom knows—"

"That's coercion, Liv."

I shake my head. It's not like that...it's not *criminal* in the way Dad makes it sound. I can still feel the outline of Grey's lips on mine—and it's probably visible, too. "It's a favor for a favor."

Dad frowns. "You're doing a way bigger favor for him than you could ever possibly get in return."

"That's not true! The football coach signed off on it and—"

"That coach should've known better. And it's not his decision to sign off on. It's mine. It's your mother's. We know what's best for you."

Tears sting my eyes. "If you know what's best for me, then why am I not at Windsor Prep?"

"You know exactly why you aren't at Windsor Prep, young lady."

"I was stupid, yes. But you guys could've talked to Principal Meyer. Danielle could've—"

"Talking you out of trouble is not going to teach you to be responsible for your actions."

"But I'm being responsible here," I say, my voice breaking. "I went to Coach Kitt. I asked what she wanted to see from me. And then I took an opportunity to show her exactly that. *I* made those decisions. Me. I did." I could keep going, but my voice rises dangerously high and I have to stop or it's going to crack.

Dad shakes his head. "I'm glad you tried, but you're sixteen, Olive. Not an adult. You're a great kid and a smart girl, but your decisions since May haven't been the right ones. Football is dangerous. You need to trust your mother and me on this—"

"I need to trust you, but you can't trust me?" I feel like

a bitch cutting him off, but I can't let him go on. "You/ me to be responsible for my actions in one breath, but in the next you're telling me I can't make decisions without parental consent?"

Everything about Dad goes rigid. To me, it's so obvious and the truth, but to him I've gone too far.

"To make decisions, you have to have the ability to think things through." His voice is leaden with disappointment. "And punching that poor girl at state is the perfect example of you acting before you think."

"I *have* thought football through." The words are a whisper—much weaker than I mean them to be.

"Have you?" Dad takes a step toward me. "What happens if you get hit?"

"I've been hit."

He doesn't blink or pause or acknowledge in any way that I've said something. He keeps going—snowing me under in examples of my shortsightedness.

"What if you get a concussion? Tear your ACL? Smash your collarbone in two like this Grey kid?"

With each scenario, his eyes flash and it's almost like he's not seeing sixteen-year-old me anymore, but his youngest daughter, all dolled up in white for her christening. I've regressed to babyhood with one simple decision.

"If you get hurt, then where will you be?" He stares at me as if he expects me to answer. But I don't have one. And anything I throw out won't be good enough. The tears spill over as he answers for me. I grit my teeth and force myself to keep looking at his face. "Not on the junior national softball team or in college, that's for sure."

"I won't be on either if I don't do this! Coach Kitt is *never* going to let me on her team without extra brownie points—"

He cuts me off with a line so similar to Danielle's from the other night that I wonder if she told him everything we discussed. "Olive Marie, any coach worth her salt isn't going to look talent in the face and turn it away."

"This one will!"

I can see words forming on Dad's face about my club team, but we both know we don't have the money to pay for a premier travel team. "I *need* the kind of press that comes with a major run at state. The games I played this summer? They were fun. Were they enough to keep me on scouts' radar for an entire year? Probably not." My voice cracks and I draw in a big, shaky breath. "You know that."

I'm going to need both school and club seasons this year—junior year—to secure the only type of college ride I can afford: a free one. We both know it. And we both would do anything to make sure those scholarships and Olympic team accolades happen. Or I thought we would—apparently this method, my choice, isn't common ground.

Dad purses his full lips, hands on hips, the rest of his

body perfectly still. After a moment, his mouth drops open and the words come out at a precise pace.

"No more football, Olive. It's too dangerous. I know you're trying to prove a point, but if you get badly injured, you can kiss softball goodbye altogether. You have a much better chance of making the team healthy and repentant for your actions than injured and proud."

"Dad—"

"No more football."

"But—"

He holds up a hand and I go quiet, leaving my next words unsaid. *But I can't get a full ride without being on a team. And I can't be on a team without proving I'm teammate material. And the only way to do that is to play football.*

"No. More. Football. Do you understand?" I squeeze my eyes shut and nod. "And you're grounded this weekend. No cell, no computer, no car."

He presents a palm for my phone and keys. When I hand them over, he gives one last stoic Dad look before turning to go inside, no doubt to retrieve my laptop.

Conversation over. Concluded. Done.

But I'm not.

My lips quiver as I shoot words at his back.

"Dad, please."

He keeps walking. But I'm rooted to the spot. I force myself to be louder. Not to yell, but to make sure he hears me.

"Dad. *Please*. Please listen to me. I'm good at this. I'm part of the team. I won't get hurt." The tears are still spilling over my face. "I'll play. And Coach Kitt will see. And I'll play softball in the spring. I promise."

But he doesn't turn around.

18

I WAKE UP IN A STATE OF EMOTIONAL WHIPLASH—head pounding, eyes throbbing, the early morning sunlight too much. In basically five hours last night, I went from a stratospheric high full of touchdowns, applause, and kisses with Grey (not sure that's the right order, honestly) and then all the way to the lowest of freaking lows, with Dad effectively killing all those things with a single sentence.

I want to believe it didn't happen. That I'm going to be headed to practice in a few minutes where I'll see Grey, he'll kiss me (preferably in front of Jake), and we'll lift weights until Coach Lee calls a break to congratulate us all on a job well done.

But with a single open eye, I know that's all wrong.

The clock says 7:38 AM. An hour later than any time I've woken up in the past two weeks, and thirty-eight minutes past when I should've been in the weight room. Even Ryan is up and gone, his bed a still life: *Wrestling Match with the Sheets.*

My desk is bare—no computer there. And my phone charger is limp on my nightstand, phone-free.

Ughhhhh.

I step out of bed with a creak of the floorboards and give myself a once-over in my cheapo full-length mirror. My skin is mottled with bruises of varying sizes and colors. Dark purple on my thigh. Yellow in the middle of my upper arm on my nonthrowing side. Brownish-green on both shins.

A knock comes at the door.

"Liv?"

Ryan. I instantly wonder how long he's been standing out there, waiting for a sign of life. I squeeze my eyes shut and remind myself that I can't be mad at him. None of this is his fault. It's completely mine and mine alone.

"Yeah?" My voice is dry and I need water. Sweaty minutes on the field, late-night pancakes, and toothpaste leaving me parched.

"Can I come in?" The door opens a crack and he's shoved his arm through the space, a Krispy Kreme doughnut bag tight in his fist. "I got you breakfast."

Oh, how the tables have turned.

I sigh. "Ry, you didn't have to."

His head pops in as the door widens. "I didn't have to, but Heather wanted company for her cold brew, so these doughnut holes just happened to work their way into my life."

I smile weakly. This family's love language is most definitely food. Ryan scoots into our room, turns to shut the door, and when he's facing me again, I see he brought me a Pepsi, too.

His hazel eyes meet mine and he lights up in a smile. "Yes, I'm plying you with sugar."

I take the bag and pop open the can. The fizz burns at my throat, and it's exactly what I need. "Plying?"

A shrug. "It was in my English homework this week. Seemed appropriate."

"My little brother, using grown-up words."

He grins and dumps himself onto my bed. I sit down next to him and put the Krispy Kreme bag between us.

Just for him, I stuff an entire doughnut hole into my mouth and wash it down with more fizz. Even though all this sugar is totally going to make my headache worse. Still, I love him so hard for realizing I might need a treat.

"What did Dad do?" he asks.

"Told me to quit the team."

He blinks. "Did you tell him about Coach Kitt and being recruited by Grey? Did you tell him that you threw *three* freaking touchdowns?"

"He didn't want to hear it. He *informed* me that I didn't think things through."

"Sounds pretty similar to the speech he gave me about placekicking. 'What if you get hit, Ryan, what then?'"

I nod—my brother is definitely angling for a full ride to play soccer. Circumstance gave us identical plans. "Same speech. I told him I'd already been hit, but he kept going—didn't even acknowledge it. Had to stick to the script, I guess."

"What else?" Ryan stuffs three doughnut holes into his mouth before I can ask what he means, but I'm pretty sure I know.

"No phone, no computer, no car the rest of the weekend. Grounded."

He swallows. "Harsh."

Yes, but it's not the grounding that's cleaved a void in my chest. Who knew eight days could leave such a wound? I didn't know how much I'd enjoy football. I sigh.

Ryan crams two more doughnut holes into his mouth, slamming them down before speaking again. "So, what are you going to do?"

"Homework without a computer. Like a heathen."

"Total heathen."

"Good thing I don't have a paper due."

"You don't, but I do." He stands, and I realize he's in workout gear but not his soccer stuff—no weekend practices for him, even on varsity. "Jesse and I are going to shoot

— 152 —

some hoops. Paper later. Wanna watch a movie after? You aren't grounded from that, right?"

I haven't been grounded in forever, so I honestly don't know. "I don't think so."

"Furious 7?"

I grin. "It's a date."

He turns at the door. "You sure you're okay?"

A smile is at my lips, but I know it doesn't reach my eyes. That's just not going to happen today.

"No." My voice cracks.

Ryan ducks his head, takes three steps to cross the room, and crushes me in a hug. He doesn't say anything. Just squeezes me as tight as I need.

I haunt the edges of my room for the next few hours. I only pee and shower when everyone but Mom has left the house. Ryan to Jesse's, Dad to work, Danielle and Heather to brunch with friends.

At ten, I'm so hungry for something more than sugar that I have to venture to the kitchen. Mom's there, steeping some of her mega-antioxidant matcha tea. Yoga tights gone baggy hang off what's left of her butt; a Windsor Prep hoodie that used to fit gathers in a saggy pile at her waist. She's got a blanket around her shoulders, clutching it with one hand while minding the tea bag with the other.

This is when I should mention it's already ninety degrees

out, and my sister and her wife aren't big air-conditioning people. But Mom's shivering like she's just traversed the Rockies.

Cancer sucks.

SUCKS.

Worse, it's triple-negative breast cancer. Which means it doesn't respond to many of the treatments available. Even worse, it reoccurs more often than others. Which is where we're at now. Mom was first diagnosed four years ago. But last year it came back, more aggressive this time. Stage three, not stage four, but it's been bad enough all the same. This go-around it was a full mastectomy and chemo, paid for with money we don't have because we're still paying off the last round.

Mom looks up from her tea, blue eyes lighting up her thin face. Cancer has made her a husk of what she was even a year ago, but it hasn't taken her sparkle. It will never take that.

"If it isn't Peyton Manning," she says.

Jeez, Mom, *burn*. "Funny. Because he's retired."

She frowns. "I didn't know that. I thought he was still playing."

I laugh and lean into the counter, fiddling with the tea box. "Wait, so that's supposed to be a compliment?"

Mom places a hand on my wrist, and my fingers immediately freeze. I meet her eyes and there's a strength there that isn't in her grip. "Your father is upset because he's afraid you'll get hurt. And he's hurt that you lied to Danielle and to us by omission."

There's suddenly a lump in my throat, and never mind food because I'm going to throw up.

I'm usually so open with my family. It's what we're good at.

Mom catches my chin with a finger. "But that doesn't mean I'm not proud of you. You've always been fearless and loyal, and I have no doubt you led that team like . . . who's a good quarterback who isn't retired?"

I laugh again—clearly Mom has completely tuned out Dad on the Sunday afternoons he's parked in front of the TV yelling at the Chiefs. "Let's go with Marcus Mariota."

She brings her tea to her lips and cocks a brow. "That answer was quick enough that I assume he must be cute."

"*Mom.*"

Undeterred, she whips her phone out of her hoodie pocket and starts googling. "How do you spell Mari—oh, wait, there it is. He *is* cute! Who else is cute?"

"MOM."

"What? Indulge me. I know you didn't join that team without doing your research. You probably spent hours watching YouTube videos. Wait, does Marcus have a YouTube channel? Let's look. And don't you dare 'MOM' me again—this is bonding." She grabs her tea. "Let's go sit on the deck."

I follow her outside. She melts into an Adirondack chair

made of sun-bent plastic, her weight barely registering on its cracking facade. I know the other one will wobble on three legs, so I snag Heather's yoga mat from the corner and roll it out alongside Mom. Then I lie back and shut my eyes to the sun and to the corner of Grey's house I can see over the trees.

I think Mom is just messing around on her phone, but then I hear her swallow a sip of tea. "So, how cute is the boy?"

"You saw him—Mariota isn't bad."

"I meant the coach's son."

My eyes spring open and I sit up. "Mom, I did not join the team because Grey's cute."

"I know my youngest daughter well enough to know *that*." She finally takes a sip. "But, still, is he?"

My cheeks are giving me away. And besides, I'm not into lying to my mom about stupid shit like this. So, after a moment, I finally say, "Yes."

19

AROUND TWELVE THIRTY, I HEAR A KNOCK AT THE front door. Mom's taking her postlunch nap, so I tiptoe to the door before whoever it is starts with the doorbell and disturbs her. When I look through the peephole, steely gray eyes stare back.

My heart immediately begins a manic drumbeat. I don't want to tell him I have to quit the team. I don't want to tell him that Cop Dad thinks he coerced me. I don't want to do anything but go back to exactly the way things were when he kissed me.

Sucking in a deep breath, I pull open the door.

His freshly washed hair is curling at the edges, sunglasses atop his head. A polo, khaki shorts, and boat shoes round out the look.

"Hey." He kicks up a half smile when he says it, but immediately I see his eyes aren't in it.

"Hey." I force myself not to glance away. If I can look a fire-breathing coach in the eye, I can look this boy in the eye after kissing him and then vanishing behind a wall of absence and silence.

He unhooks a hand and pushes a lock of hair from my face. I am *so* glad I showered.

"When you didn't show up for weights, I texted you. And when you didn't text back and never showed, I bribed Rogers to find out where you lived. But it turns out he has the wrong address."

Oh shit. We hadn't moved into Danielle's yet when Jake and I were still a thing.

My mouth drops open, but Grey's not done. "But I'm buddies with the varsity soccer captain, so no worries."

A smile twitches at the corners of my mouth. "You're persistent."

"You weren't answering. And after last night, I just wanted to make sure nothing weird happened."

There's a lack of certainty in his eyes for the first time since we met, and before I know it, my arms loop his neck, lips to his. The sharp scent of boy soap hugs my body, and for a split second, I feel like maybe the last twelve hours didn't happen.

"So... not weird?" he says when I pull away.

"The new normal?" I suggest.

"I like that." Grey smiles, light reaching his eyes, the serious lines disappearing in a flash and bang.

But then we fall silent. The rest of the new normal needs to be discussed—but I don't want to start.

Grey touches my face. "I ran into Ryan on my walk over." He motions down the street to Jesse's house. "He told me why you weren't at practice."

"Everything?"

He sort of pulls away. It's subtle, but it's there.

"I don't know. What's everything?"

I frown out onto the street. I want to take him inside, but I know that won't go over well if someone comes home or Mom wakes up. Better they see us on the stoop, as if I'm turning him away.

"My parents didn't know about football. I was going to tell them, but I chickened out. And, well, the news got to them before I did."

"That happens when you're a badass who throws three touchdowns in twenty minutes." He knocks me on the shoulder and I almost smile again. But the truth keeps the frown steady.

"Yeah, well...I'm paying for that badassery. Grounded—no phone, no computer, no car—for the rest of the weekend." I raise my eyes to his. "And no more team."

Grey's mouth sets into a line. If Ryan told him this part, he probably didn't believe it. "That's bullshit."

"It's reality." I suck in a deep breath. "It doesn't

matter that I was good or that I enjoyed it or that the team needed me—"

"*Needs* you, Liv. Present tense."

I shake my head. "You'll be back next week. The team will be fine."

"No. We need you." He places both hands on my shoulders. "I'll admit I didn't think much about your effect on the team when I dropped your name to Coach Shanks. But now that I've seen how hard you work and witnessed how that work motivates the other players, I know we need you. You have to be there."

When I hesitate, his big hands gently squeeze my shoulders.

"*You* need this," he says. "We both know why you signed on to begin with—"

"Yeah, for softball. Which is exactly why Dad doesn't want me to play." Dad's line of questions runs straight through my heart as each echoes in my ears yet again.

What if you get a concussion? Tear your ACL? Smash your collarbone in two like this Grey kid?

I blink at him. "How'd you break your collarbone?"

"Not playing football, so your dad can chill on that if he's worried the same thing will happen to you." He brushes another lock of hair behind my ear. "Look, I know what it's like to have pressure on you to be the best. What do you think it's like to be the only child of a softball ace and a college football star?"

Probably not that much different from needing a college scholarship to do more than work for minimum wage after high school. Same pressure, completely different reasons to crave success.

But still.

"Look, my dad said no football. The Pope wouldn't be able to convince him I should play." Which is completely accurate. "He's worried about me getting hurt, because then where would I be? No softball, no college."

"Maybe I can talk to him. Or Shanks can. Or even Coach Lee—" When I shake my head, Grey throws his own head back and reads the sky, sunglasses bobbing. "What about my mom? What if she sat down with him? Told him her concerns?"

I figured he'd overheard some of my conversation with his mother that day in her office because of how he pitched joining the team. But now I'm staring at him, trying to figure out what else he's said. He startles when he sees the look on my face, so I just decide to go for it. "Did you talk about me to her?"

"What—no, I…Wait, the whole point of you joining the team was for me to talk about you. I mean, right?"

"Okay, yeah, but I…It's weird," I finish, not sure why it bothers me, even if it was him just living up to his end of the deal. But considering we've made out and I'd love to do it again *rightthehellnow*, the thought of our deal suddenly makes me feel sort of…cheap.

His lips pull up in the corners, and though the smile is subtle, it meets his eyes with a shine and a sigh. Which makes me feel cheaper. Or, I don't know, *something.* "Look, she knows I think you're a super addition to the team, and she saw the evidence for herself Friday night. She was there; she saw you enter the game. She knows you're kicking ass."

My head is already shaking. "She's not worried about my athletic talents, Grey. She's worried I'm a bitch whose mere presence will suddenly blow up the girls' batting averages and tank Kelly's ERA."

"Well, you're not a bitch. And if either of those things happen, it'll be their own damn fault."

I smirk, the ick from five seconds ago already dissolving with the fire of his clenched jaw. "Yeah, well, that's what she's worried about. That's the whole point. I need to prove I'm a great teammate. And even though I had a good game, I'm off the team now. So that's all the collateral I have. I'm not getting any more unless I join cross-country or something."

A little pang hits me in the chest when I think about how I really did lie to Danielle. God, I hate that.

"While I do love the idea of you in those little shorts," he says, and smiles wide enough that I want to kiss him again. Like, *now.* But I don't, because the thumping of a basketball on the sidewalk is too close to ignore, which means Ryan is probably making his way down the street, most likely with a full view of the stoop. "I really would rather see you in pads next to me under the lights."

My chin is caught in his fingers, rough from the day's practice. He tips my face up, and the light haloing down behind his head makes those eyes almost look blue.

"I didn't get to ask you this last night…" The memory of his mother watching from the window passes between us. "But at the risk of complicating things with the team… would you go out with me?"

My heart thuds to a melty stop. *God, yes.* I answer him with a kiss. Hard and full and undeniable from literally any vantage point on Danielle's street. And it's totally worth whatever the hell Ryan is going to say to me the second he rolls up.

But instead of Ryan's voice echoing toward me, I hear one come from behind me.

"Liv?"

I jerk apart from Grey so violently, the back of my head bonks off the doorframe.

"Mom! Grey was just leaving—he knows I'm grounded," I blurt, hoping to hell she didn't see that kiss.

"Wait, this is Grey? Coach Kitt's son?"

Mom may just have been napping, but damn if her eyes don't light up like the Fourth of July. The inflection in her voice hides exactly nothing, and if he hadn't just kissed me and had no idea how I felt about him, I'd be about ten thousand times more embarrassed right now. Though I'm already pretty good and embarrassed as it is, and it appears Grey might be a little bit, too, a light blush crawling across his cheeks as he realizes we've clearly discussed him before.

I'm about to formally introduce Grey, but he's already taken a step inside, charm going full force toward my very receptive mother. "Mrs. Rodinsky, my name is Grey Worthington, and it's completely my fault that Liv joined the team."

"Oh, it is, is it?" Mom cocks a downy brow, amused grin still plastered across her face.

"Yes. It is. And I can explain."

Mom waves him off. "I know my daughter takes an opportunity when she sees it." Mom reaches out and pats him on the shoulder, and...oh my God. I watch her hand flex, fingers squeezing. And *I'm* the one who seizes opportunity?

Grey flushes some more, my cheeks burn, and I'm now 100 percent sure my mom just saw us kissing. Our embarrassment is so palpable, we're about to register on the Richter scale. I seriously want to melt into the floor. But then Mom decides she hasn't claimed every opportunity this little conversation has given her. "But I do want you to tell me exactly how Liv's predicament is your fault. At dinner, tomorrow night?"

Oh. God. The last boy invited to Sunday dinner was Jake. He survived the Rodinsky family full-court press of scrutiny, but he didn't do anything wrong. Not that I think

Grey did, but Dad sure does. If Danielle and Heather side with Dad and not Mom, he's toast.

"Mom, I'm grounded. No friends over," I say, hoping to save Grey from Dad's likely interrogation.

"You didn't invite him, I did. And you'll come, won't you, Grey?"

"Of course, Mrs. Rodinsky."

Mom beams at him and takes the opportunity to press her palm to his chest, which I can tell you is nice and firm and *jeez*, she is seriously doing this to mess with me. "Call me Ellen. See you at six. Thanks for popping by."

"Sure thing, Ellen."

As Grey steps safely onto the stoop, I pull the door in close to my butt and lean out toward him, shielding us from view of Mom, who is totally eavesdropping.

"Your mother is lovely," he says, and I can tell he means it.

"She is. My whole family is." I clutch his forearm, hoping he can feel the warning in the press of my fingers. They *are* lovely, but they're also going to eat him alive if he's not prepared. My grip does the trick and Grey catches my eye. "Bring a helmet," I whisper.

"And obstruct your dad's view of my face while I explain what a fantastic football player you are? Nah." Grey winks. "See ya tomorrow, Rodinsky."

Hands in his pockets, Grey heads down the driveway and I haul myself back inside, feeling warm and fuzzy yet completely anxious all the same. I feel like I need to run it all off—maybe Mom'll be cool with that. Is it acceptable to jog while grounded?

When I shut the door, Mom is right there, waiting, as expected, wicked smirk lighting her papery skin.

"Well, he *is* cute."

Cute and totally toast.

20

I'M ON EDGE THE REST OF THE WEEKEND, RUNNING scenarios in my mind for everything that could go wrong at family dinner on Sunday night. Luckily, Mom seems to think letting me out for a jog is okay under the terms of my grounding—mostly because Dad has disappeared, the case he's on sucking him away from us every waking hour.

Without my phone, I'm musicless, and so I'm left with my thoughts and my nerves for a six-mile run Saturday afternoon and again on Sunday morning. On Sunday morning, I turn the corner back to our house to see Danielle and Heather, leaving for a run of their own, all sparkly and sweat-free. I wave, sweat sizzling into my eyes.

I've managed to avoid Danielle for most of the weekend,

and maybe she let that happen, so pissed at me for lying that she didn't even want to see my face. Might as well cut to the chase before the pair of them literally run away from me. I catch Danielle's arm before they pass.

"I'm so sorry for lying. I—I don't know why I did, but I'm sorry."

Danielle squints back at me, smile incredulous. "You lied because you knew I'd freak about football just as much as Mom and Dad."

"Okay," I admit. "That's true."

My sister flips her hand around so she's gripping me as much as I'm holding on to her. "But that doesn't mean I'm not totally impressed."

My eyes widen. "You're *what?*"

"I'm totally impressed. Coach Kitt wanted you to prove you could be a good teammate. And what did you do? You joined the most brutal, boy-centric sport possible and then you crushed it."

"We saw a video," Heather pipes in. "Ryan shot it from the stands Friday night." She's grinning—and so is Danielle. "My brother played football for a decade before starting in high school and he could never throw a spiral like that."

"Really?"

"Really," Danielle confirms. "You were great—Dad should let you play."

Tears prick at my eyes, mingling with the sweat crowding my lash line. Danielle squeezes my hand. "We have a plan to convince him."

"Dani's making enchiladas," Heather says proudly, beaming at my sister. Literally the only thing Danielle has ever learned to cook is enchiladas, and somehow they've become Dad's favorite food. If he had a choice of a last meal, that would be it.

A game-day glare slides across Danielle's face. "And I don't know this quarterback boy of yours, but if he can't convince Dad you should play football, you better believe I will."

"So…" I say, trying to add it all together. "We're going to lull him into complacency with cheese and enchilada sauce and then attack?"

Danielle's face breaks into a grin that is seven shades of wicked. "Exactly."

Sunday afternoon, Danielle's enchilada sauce is simmering and Dad's texted Mom to confirm he'll be home for dinner. He's missed family dinner night before for a case, but the combination of enchiladas and "Grey what's his name" is apparently worth pulling strings to get a night off.

Nerves flutter in my stomach, and I have nothing to do. I set the table, including an extra place for Grey, furnished with the rolling chair from Danielle's desk. I fixed my makeup. Cleaned my half of my and Ryan's room. Even washed my jersey and game-day tights, because there's no way in hell I'm returning something grass-stained and nasty.

Finally, around four, the doorbell rings. I jump, thinking it might be Grey, over early. But I know the car in the driveway—Addie.

Ryan answers the door and calls my name before scurrying away. When I see her, it's clear why he's so quick to duck for cover. My best friend's face is puckered into a sour-lemon expression, eyes ablaze, her long arms crossed tightly over her chest.

"Where the *hell* have you been?"

I pull the door closed and give her an apologetic smile, which only makes her launch into another assault rather than letting me answer.

"I have things to *tell* you, O-Rod, and you go all Casper on me and freaking *vanish*. You're my best friend—there should never be any vanishing. Ever. Especially when *boys* are involved. There's a code about that, I swear. *You broke the code.*"

Addie wants to be a DA like her mom. They're both hella good at making an argument and I totally gave her all the material in the world to eviscerate me. I automatically feel like an asshole, and I am, because my vanishing was a symptom of my lying and just…ughhhhh. "I'm sorry! I'm grounded. No phone, computer, or car until tomorrow."

This softens her face. I snag her wrist. "What did I miss?" I arch a brow. "Nick?"

At this, she squeezes her eyes shut, face lighting with a smile before they flash back open, all her anger gone. "*Yes, Nick*. I have so much to tell you—wait, can I tell you?" She glances at the house behind me.

I shrug. "You're probably the one person my parents don't care about when it comes to me breaking my grounding sentence. Yes, please, tell me everything!"

"Wait—first, what happened? I mean, why are you grounded?"

"Football," I say grimly.

Addie's eyes go wide. "The form?"

"Yep. Never got it signed. Never told them. Dad found out from his boss, who was at the game."

"Oh, shit."

"Exactly."

"So are you *just* grounded or…?" She trails off, but I know exactly what she's most worried about.

"Off the team. No more football."

"But…but you're good. But *softball*. But Grey—wait, what happened with Grey? Does he know? Does his mom know?"

"He knows, so I'm sure she knows, and, by tomorrow morning, the whole freaking school will know."

Tears sting Addie's eyes. God, I don't deserve her. "I'm

so sorry. If I'd known, I wouldn't have marched over here. I'm so—"

"It's fine," I say quickly. "Grey's coming to dinner tonight to help convince Dad. Danielle's even in support of me playing."

"He's coming to dinner? On a Sunday? To confront Cop Dad?" Addie's eyes grow wider with each building question. "He must really like you."

"Or he's got a super-bizarre sense of fun."

Addie's face melts into a smirk. "Oh, shut up."

I cock a brow. "And Nick?"

Addie's smile flashes, her eyes completely dry now. Her voice dips low, glee bursting at the edges. "That boy is hella good, Liv. HELLA. GOOD."

We plop on the stoop, Addie hugging her knees with a sigh. I've never in all my life seen Adeline McAndry swoon over anyone, but *this*, this is definitely swooning. It takes her several seconds to compose a sentence that won't come out like gibberish—which totally thrills me.

"He's not one for words, but the things he says are the right ones. That cannot be overstated. And in addition to not being shy at all about how much he appreciates my athletic awesomeness, he's also super thoughtful and a total gentleman."

"A gentleman?" I arch a brow at her. Seems like super-high praise for a boy who literally may earn a college scholarship for how hard he can nail people into the ground.

"I mean, he held my door! Who does that? And don't say Grey—let me have my moment. And then today we met at Happy Cow after his practice, and he didn't get all annoyed and machismo when I forced him to split the check. So after that, we went over to the pedal boats at Shawnee Mission Park—"

"Wait? Pedal boats? You *hate* the lake. Remember when you took those freshwater mussels home from our freshman field trip there, they killed Beluga the betta fish? You started calling it Shawnee Murder Park and wanted your mom to investigate the marina master."

"Well, yes, but admittedly my case sucked—Beluga's demise is on me because I put them in the tank. It wasn't that guy's fault I didn't do my research on deadly ammonia spikes caused by decomposing mussels."

I do a double take. "Who are you?"

She waves her hands overhead. "I'm a whole new woman, Olive Marie."

"I'd say so."

"Okay, so we did an hour on the lake and then we were hungry again, so we…"

I listen as she jabbers away, glad we have two hours until dinner.

Grey beats Dad to dinner, arriving smelling of a recent shower and dressed in yet another Nike polo and khaki shorts. He's got a half smile and wink for me when I answer the door after checking my makeup for the millionth time. "Hey, Liv."

"Hey," I reply, trying my hardest not to blush, the part of me that worked so hard to deny my initial attraction to him now on overdrive with it all out in the open.

"Is that Grey?" Danielle says, wiping her palms on her apron, dirty from her duty today as head chef. She offers him a hand. "Danielle, Liv's older sister."

"*The Kansas City Star*'s Softball Coach of the Year two years running—the youngest since my mom. It's a pleasure."

My sister beams. "Liv, I like him."

"Grey knows how to make a good first impression," I say, my cheeks burning.

"That's what I hear." All our heads swing around to the door off the garage where Dad is standing in full detective gear: button-up, slacks, and his Glock in a shoulder holster. Sweat has plastered all the wave out of his hair, and he looks totally exhausted from so many back-to-back days, but damn if he isn't dialed in, with his full cop glare aimed at Grey.

To his credit, Grey squares his shoulders, walks right over, and offers a hand to Dad without a millisecond of hesitation. "Mr. Rodinsky, I'm Grey Worthington. It's nice to meet you, sir."

Dad checks the grip on Grey's handshake, but his face

is closed up tight, not betraying whether he's impressed, annoyed, or anything else. All Dad says is, "I'm going to go change."

He disappears upstairs, and I introduce Grey to Heather. He and Ry have already talked a few times, so they just exchange chin nods. In the kitchen, we somehow squeeze ourselves around the table, Grey sitting between me and Danielle, and across from Mom and the spot we've left for Dad.

When Dad appears, he's wet down his hair and changed into the shirt he got for winning a department shooting competition last year.

Subtle, Dad.

If Grey's intimidated, he doesn't show it. He just spreads a napkin across his lap and tucks into the salad Mom pulled together. Across the table, my sister takes a sip of her wine and lobs a verbal grenade onto the table.

"Dad," she says, with no prelude, "let Liv play football."

All the breath leaks out of my lungs as I look from Danielle to Dad. Under the table, Grey finds my hand and cups it in his as the resulting silence spreads. Dad doesn't say a thing; instead, he pops open a beer. No one else has visibly moved except Ryan, who's fidgeting in the rolling chair, swiveling nervously between Heather and Mom.

Unfazed—though, in reality, she is never fazed—Danielle continues. "I shouldn't have to explain why she should be allowed to play, but because you seem blind to the obvious, I'm going to lay it out for you, Pops."

She pauses briefly and I hold my breath.

"First of all, the girl is allowed to make her own mistakes, which you know quite well from what happened in May and how you handled it afterward. Sure, you could've taken out a loan or deferred Liv's tuition or even let us set up a Kickstarter, for God's sake, but you didn't want her to return to Windsor Prep for a reason: to teach her accountability for her mistakes. Correct? You allowed her to have real-world consequences for her actions. Why is this any different?"

My gut twists—I don't want Grey to hear this, even if it's basically stuff he already knows. But he's listening like his life depends on it. When my dad stays silent, Danielle shifts to round two.

"Liv made a decision. A much smarter decision than last time, obviously"—I wince—"and had *success*. She scored three touchdowns in a football game, against boys twice her size. Boys who have been playing for years. Boys who were extra motivated to kick her ass the second she put on a helmet. She's a freaking Disney movie, Dad."

I can't help the grin that breaks across my face. Holy shit, I am a Disney movie.

By the time she finishes, Danielle is breathing hard. Ryan fidgets more in his seat and pulls out his phone, holding it aloft over the salad bowl. "Want to see a video?"

Rather than accept the phone or acknowledge Danielle's argument, Dad simply takes another long gulp of beer and looks to Grey.

"And what do you have to say?"

Grey doesn't clear his throat. Doesn't hesitate. Doesn't drop his grip on my hand. He just greets Dad's challenge with the same confidence he has when throwing routes.

"Liv Rodinsky is the most natural quarterback I've ever seen in my life. You can blame me all you want for recruiting her, but the truth is that our team is better with her on it. I'm proud to play by her side."

Dad's lips flatten into a line. He's still playing a hardass, but Mom's face is so bright and cheery that he softens when she aims all that energy at him and places a hand on the meat of his shoulder. "Oh, come on, Eddy, how can you say no to that?"

He doesn't respond. Still, hope rolls through my gut, my heart whispering *Hail Mary*.

We don't talk about it for the rest of the dinner. Instead, Grey manages to visibly charm literally everyone at the table. Even maybe Dad.

He raves about Danielle's enchiladas and asks for seconds.

He gamely answers Mom's nosy questions about what product makes his hair curl like that.

He says yes to literally every topping my family has to offer during postdinner ice-cream sundaes.

He elbows in on Heather and does the dishes for her like a freaking champ.

And while we're sitting down, watching the Sunday night Chiefs game, he gets Ryan going enough about Premier League soccer that they end up reenacting some botched play for Dad on the living room floor like complete oversugared goofballs.

Which leads Ryan to giving me shit for missing his first game of the season. But to be fair, it was literally all the way across town and started before football practice ended. I guess I won't have that excuse anymore. Maybe.

When it's grown dark and it's clearly time for him to leave, I step out to the stoop with Grey, planning to walk him to the turn of the block. The night is still warm, but there's a chill in the breeze, and without me even asking, he puts his arm around my shoulders as we hit the sidewalk.

I look up at him. "I have to say, that wasn't the complete disaster I was expecting."

"Complete disaster? There wasn't even a whiff of disaster." He winks. Because of course he does.

"Well, I don't know, I was pretty worried when Danielle went all in on Dad right away. Definitely a whiff there for me."

He waves a hand. "You worry too much, Rodinsky. From the second your sister opened her mouth, I knew it was going to be amazing."

"Well, yeah. She *is* amazing." I place a hand on his

stomach and we come to a stop, not yet to the corner. The trees wave in the breeze, and the moonlight flashes across his face as I palm his cheek. "But you were, too. Thanks for coming. Thanks for saying your piece. Thanks for fake side-tackling Ryan to the floorboards and making Dad laugh."

And then I kiss him.

21

MONDAY MORNING, I WAKE UP TO MY LAPTOP AND phone sitting on my desk. Not charged. No note. No suggestion that this means I can play football—just that my grounding is over.

I plug them in and they both light up like that one huge-ass Christmas light display in our old neighborhood.

Texts. Texts. Texts.

Missed calls.

All from the people who care about me enough to wonder where the hell I went Saturday. Addie, of course. And Grey.

A little flutter flips alive in my tummy when I think of Grey last night—of him grabbing my hand under the table and making a case to Dad, of him saying good night with yet another great kiss. The flutter swells for a faint second before I blink and see a slip of orange in my field of vision.

My game jersey.

Ready for return. The red practice one, too.

The flutter dies a quick death as I collect my stuff for a shower.

An hour later, Grey's there on the Northland steps as I walk up to school. Foot kicked up against the faded brick, wet hair curling against his temples, signature half smile in place.

I will myself to look thrilled that he's there. I mean, I am thrilled.

I am.

But all I keep thinking is that I won't get to see him tonight at practice. It'll just be our walk to Spanish, lunch, calc. That's it. He'll be at practice until seven, and I'll be at home, probably working on my jump shot for basketball tryouts in a couple of weeks.

"Hey," I say and he smiles in answer, his hand kissing mine as he holds open the door for me. I wish it were a real kiss, but I've never gone to the same school as my boy-friend, and I'm not sure of the etiquette.

"Liv!" I turn around and a freakishly tall guy I've never seen in my life is there, grinning like we're BFFs. "Awe-some game Friday."

He fist-bumps both me and Grey and stalks off. When

Shaq's body double is out of earshot, Grey leans down. "Micah Jellison. Starting big man."

"Oh." Okay. Basketball—so other athletes noticed. They also had no idea I didn't show up for practice on Saturday.

We keep moving and, like the first day, Grey grabs my fingers and tugs me around the corner, his lips to my ear. "Jellison wasn't the only one who noticed your kick-assery."

And it might be true—the collective masses are parting for both of us this time, eyes lingering on my face before skipping to our intertwined hands and then up to Grey's familiar features.

"Hope they savored their one and only chance to see Liv Rodinsky, backup quarterback, in action."

His shoulder taps mine. Which feels approximately 3 bazillion percent more sexy than it did a week ago. "They'll get an encore."

When I enter the classroom and take my seat, Jake Rogers wastes exactly zero-point-oh-nada seconds before pouncing on me. The moment my butt makes contact with molded plastic, he's snared my forearm, his eyes pinned to Coach Kitt's turned back.

"Where the hell were you, big shot?"

I almost remind him he could've texted me. But instead I decide to take the high road.

"Good morning to you too, Jacob." I wrench my arm free and turn away from him, digging through my backpack for my notebook. A ginger streak whips through my periphery, and I know Kelly is spying from her seat two rows over. "I'm off the team."

Jake's eyes widen, his confusion plain. "You're what?"

"Off the team."

"I knew Coach would be pissed about your absence, but that's super harsh, even for him."

He's trying to quantify it, but he doesn't know the half of it. "Lee didn't kick me off. My dad did. I didn't tell my parents I was playing."

Jake's eyes go fuzzy as I let that sink in. He met my dad approximately twice while we were dating—that family dinner and my spring formal—and the memory of those meetings clearly has his spine stiffening beneath yet another issue of Northland orange T-shirt.

"Oh, shit. So . . . that's it?"

I don't even have to nod and still, his face softens enough that my heart pings with recognition of the Jake I like most.

I don't get a single glimpse of Coach Lee until calc. I walk in with Grey and, without turning around from the whiteboard, he requests my presence in his office immediately after the last bell.

Perfect.

I can't wait to get this over with.

But, of course, because the universe has the absolute freaking best sense of humor, I make it all the way down to Coach Lee's office and the door's shut. The blinds are half-closed, but I can see the outline of a person in the chair that faces Coach's desk.

I don't knock, just start running through all the things I'm going to say.

Thank you for the opportunity.

I really enjoyed my time on the team.

It was a great experience, but—

But. But. But.

But I can't. But I knew this would happen. But I'm a liar.

Without preamble, the door opens and Coach Lee peers into the hallway, his guest still inside. "Come on in, Miss Rodinsky."

I raise my chin, square my shoulders, plaster a smile on my face, and walk inside.

And there, sitting in his office, is someone I definitely wasn't expecting.

Dad.

22

COACH FOLDS HIS FINGERS AND LEANS FORWARD, elbows set on paper piled into disheveled stacks across the dinged metal of his desk.

"Liv," Coach starts, and I'm stunned by the use of my first name. He has never used my first name. Not on the field or in class. "I've been a coach for forty years. There have been a lot of firsts in that time. First win, first loss, first championship. First drug scandal, first serious head injury, first hazing incident...the eighties were a mess.

"Honestly, I expected you to be a first *and* a last—that you'd fail the first practice and that would be my first and last day coaching a young lady. But what I forgot was that I don't make the decisions. The talent does."

A smile cracks his lips, and it has a level of mischief to it that surprises me.

"I forgot my own core belief until it was staring me in the face. I mean, you're greener than a fresh dollar bill, but at least 20 percent of the time, you look like an actual quarterback. Imagine what you could be if I had had the chance to properly coach you from freshman on up?"

I steal a glimpse at Dad. These words are meant for him more than me, but his stoic cop face is in place and I have no idea what's going on in his brain. Does he view "20 percent quarterback" as a compliment? Because I do.

Coach Lee straightens and pauses to unlock his fingers. "I had planned to *properly* coach you this afternoon with a hundred suicides for missing Saturday. Maybe a hundred more, because when I sent Coach Shanks to retrieve your file and call your parents, your consent form wasn't there. Hadn't been turned in—and you better believe me, Shanks's ears are ringing from what I had to say about that." My stomach twists—I know Shanks can handle it, but he didn't deserve that. I did. Coach Lee's eyes meet mine. "What I didn't know until thirty minutes ago was that you were never even on my team to begin with."

My heart stops beating.

"But your father was kind enough to stop by and discuss the situation with me."

Dad clears his throat. "Coach Lee is adamant that you

have a knack for making those around you more focused and more dedicated to the sport." This compliment actually feels good, even if it's also sort of a knife to the back. Because unless Coach Lee plans on sending a memo to Coach Kitt, his admiration means nothing since I'm no longer his athlete. "I'm not surprised, of course," Dad adds, and my heart floods with hope.

I tug out a breath and use this as an opening to run through the spiel I practiced in the hall. "Thank you for the opportunity to be on the team," I tell Coach Lee. "I really enjoyed my time here and I appreciate your belief in me and—"

"Slow down there, slugger," Coach Lee says. "Don't you want to know how our discussion ended?"

My eyes shoot between them. "Wait, what?"

At this, Dad raises a single brow, poker face still in place. After taking the longest freaking pause in the history of humankind, Dad shifts in his chair and plucks a sheet from Coach Lee's desk.

It's a brand-new waiver. Complete with an Eddy Rodinsky John Hancock scrawled in loops along the bottom.

I half tackle Dad in a hug, squeezing my eyes shut against the nape of his neck.

Holy shit. Holy shit. Holy shit.

"Save that hug for Danielle—we'll talk more at home." Dad extricates himself from my grip and stands, tight-lipped smile on his face. He tips his chin to Coach Lee and steps toward the door. "I have to get back to work."

"So do we." Coach Lee stands and they collide in one of the firmest handshakes known to man—the veteran coach and the veteran cop. I stand to follow but Coach waves me down with a glance and shuts the door with a rattle and swoosh of the blinds as Dad leaves.

He looks at me sternly. "Rodinsky, why do you want to be a Northland High football player?"

He doesn't want a Miss America answer. I straighten up in my seat. "Because I want to be a Northland High softball player."

I could've couched it—could've said that I already love being part of the team. That Friday night was amazing. That I'm having fun. But I don't, even though all of that is true.

Half of Coach Lee's mouth quirks up. "And you think playing a ruthless contact sport will make Kitterage think you're less of a hothead?"

His delivery is so direct and deadpan that I cough out a laugh, surprising even myself. "When you put it that way, I seem like even more of an idiot."

Coach stands. "I don't think you're an idiot, Rodinsky. I think you love a challenge."

"Guilty as charged," I say, my confident old softball smile perking up.

Lee turns to his coatrack and collects his cap and whistle. When he's facing me again, he's got a real smile spread across his face, though his eyes are dead serious. He pats me on the shoulder.

"Good, because you're starting Friday."

23

I'VE NEVER BEEN SO THRILLED OR TERRIFIED BY FIVE little words in all my life.

The feeling is so overwhelming that I do something I've never done in my athletic career: I pretend it isn't happening.

I don't call Danielle. I don't text Addie. I don't squee at my locker in glee.

I simply make the decision not to say a peep until Coach Lee does.

I'm trying to be logical. To protect what I have with Grey. He was supposed to start this Friday, and stealing his starting quarterback title was *not* part of the deal.

He's a senior who wants to play college ball.

He needs all the games under his belt he can get.

I know he's been dying to get out there.

And so logic tells me to keep my mouth shut until the coaches realize their mistake and start a fully healed Grey on Friday instead of me.

But the problem with logic is that ambition is deaf to it.

And my ambition is shooting through my belly, yelling at the top of its lungs, "Starterrrrrrrrr!"

That night, Grey and I scrimmage with the A team, switching off every five plays. By the end of it, I still have absolutely no understanding of why I'm starting at all. This should be his comeback game.

Grey's wearing his old form like a glove, rolling back smoothly on each play. Releasing the ball with unhurried confidence and connecting 90 percent of the time. And 90 percent of his misses are definitely the fault of the receiver. I think. He stops to sneak some Tylenol midpractice, but to my undertrained eye, he looks great.

I run through his form in my head as I change into street clothes, just-showered skin sticking to my jeans. I get them up over my butt and my back pocket vibrates with a text.

Road game tomorrow, volleyball ended early. In the North-land parking lot with Nick. Grey's here, too. I hear we have stuff to celebrate because you're back on the team. So, dinner? Burger Fu on the line.

I smirk. **And if I say no?**

Your choice to celebrate solo but just FYI, my burger-eating skillz are quite sexy. It's on you if the boys start fighting over me.

Then: **Protect Grey from himself and come. I don't want to break his face or my best friend's heart just because I'm trying to eat my dinner.**

Outside the locker room is the rapidly cooling night— my wet hair immediately plastered to my face by a breeze. **Who's saying Nick would win that fight?**

Addie doesn't waste half a second in coming up with a response—as quick in life as she is on the field or court.

Nick plows people into the ground every day, don't think he won't go all linebacker in the name of Adeline McAndry.

Are the boys standing there watching you type War and Peace?

Yeah, and they like it. But I'm hungry, so hurry the hell up.

Two seconds.

I fire off a text to Ryan to make sure he's already gotten a ride home, and one to Mom, letting her know I'm with Addie, before rounding the corner to the parking lot.

The boys and Addie are holding court in front of my car, all of them just showered and in street clothes. In Addie's case, she's doffed her Windsor Prep uniform for black leggings and a stretchy shirt that her mom would incinerate on sight if she knew it existed.

Addie groans. "Two seconds? That was *three minutes*. A hellacious eternity when we're talking carbs. Come on— less talking, more driving. You're chauffeur number two."

I give her a salute and unlock Helena the Honda. Grey drops into the passenger seat and I'm still putting on my seat belt when Addie burns rubber out of the parking lot.

"Hey." Grey's fingers graze my cheek as I put the keys in the ignition. There's a softness in the hard-edge planes of his face as he leans in without a response, lips pressing against mine, warm and wanting. I sink into him, the ignition dinging despite time standing still.

When he finally pulls away, it's a struggle to open my eyes, they're so heavy. I must look like a used candle—my features melty and warm.

"I wanted to do that all day." He winks. "But there's no kissing in football."

I swallow and compose an answer, lips numb with heat. "Ah, yes, just as iconic a phrase as 'there's no crying in baseball.'"

"I'm sure Tom Hanks said it at some point."

"That is the definition of iconic," I say, grinning. "But... I mean, really, is there any reason we can't kiss in football?"

Grey runs a hand through his just-washed hair. "Well, no. I just don't want the coaches to freak. Team chemistry and all that."

That's a thing or two I know about—heck, it's part of the reason I'm in this situation to begin with. And so I nod, though I'm not totally sure what I think about when and where we *can* kiss.

I press on the gas and Grey places his hand on my knee. It's all I can do to keep from gunning it into traffic.

"I'm glad your dad caved, by the way."

I smile at him. "Me too."

By the time we get to the restaurant, Addie and Nick are waiting for us outside, looking like a painting in the broad brushstrokes of sunset. They're so into each other, they don't realize we're coming their way until the last second, when Nick catches Grey's eye as he's nuzzling Addie's cheek.

"If it isn't the starter and the spare." Nick says it as a joke. As if we hadn't seen each other ten minutes ago.

"Dude, don't call my girl a 'spare.'"

My heart stumbles in my chest as Grey half laughs. *My girl. Starter.*

Nick laughs, and it's not half. "You're the spare, Worthington. Haven't you seen the clipboard?" When it's clear he hasn't, Nick's ears flush. His next words come more quietly. "Liv starts Friday."

I want to demur. To squeak out an "I do?"...but I can't. I know it's true. Nick knows it's true. I can justify ignoring it for the past few hours, but outright lying now would be a huge mistake.

And I'm done lying to people I care about.

Grey tenses as reality sinks in, his competitive side flashing, but in a blip, his features relax. "That's awesome, Liv."

As Grey bumps my shoulder, Nick tries to read between the lines. "Shanks didn't tell you?" he asks me. "You seriously didn't know?"

I'm trying to keep my face brave.

"Coach told me when I met with him about leaving the team—I just didn't believe him." All of which is true, but I suddenly feel like a total lying asshole.

"O-ROD!" Addie squeaks, obvious excitement over-riding any worry about me and Grey. Addie lunges and suddenly her arms are wrapped around me, so strong and warm, her bevy of newly done braids blinding my vision. She's absolutely vibrating with joy.

I wish I could see Grey's expression. Instead, I hear Nick laugh. "Jesus, what a tackle. You transfer to North-land, McAndry, and I'm B team again. Guaranteed."

Addie slides off me and straightens her shirt, the fab-ric riding up and flashing enough of a taut brown tummy to make Nick's cheeks flush yet again. "Don't tempt me, Cleary."

I check Grey's face—the surfer is winning out over the newsman, all relaxed and sunny. Like he's enjoying Nick and Addie's banter. But I know how badly he's wanted to start. And he's a senior. There are only so many games left.

I need to know he's truly fine. I don't want him lying to himself any more than I want to lie to him.

The sun is gone—the only illumination is Helena's ancient dashboard and the partial moon as we pull up in front of Grey's house. Because he's Grey, he still looks good, the light and shadow playing to the newscaster lines of his face, the wave of his hair softening the intensity.

"I really didn't think Coach meant it," I tell him. "About me starting on Friday. I figured he'd change his mind and it wouldn't be worth bringing up."

That half smile settles in. "My ego's that fragile, huh?"

I snag his hand and turn it over, forcing open his fingers and interlacing mine within his. My eyes pin to his face. "No, you're just that important to me."

The weight dissolves at the sigh in his eyes and I lean forward, lips to his before he can respond. His mouth is even warmer than his fingers, shampoo scenting his hair, chin rough with scruff.

When I pull away, his lashes flutter open and his jaw sets, lips slightly red from contact. "You're important to me, too."

I squeeze his fingers. The silence flies over. *Fragile*. "Are you ever going to tell me how you broke your collarbone?"

"Are you going to ask me why I don't drive?"

It seems like an odd question to ask in response. My vision blurs on his house—the three-car garage and the manicured lawn. He's never driven me anywhere. I don't even know if he has a car, which seems absurd, given that he's a senior and his parents aren't exactly pinching pennies.

"Wait. Am I in a movie?" I glance over his shoulder and whip around to look at the street. "Where's the director?

Casting got it all wrong. You're a horrible pick for the role of 'hot guy haunted by his mistakes' in *Cautionary Tale Number Twelve*."

His grin widens, though there's weight behind it. "Car accidents happen outside of the movies, Liv. In real life. With real people. Who really get hurt." He taps his collarbone.

"Yeah, but…you didn't…nothing…"

"I didn't kill anyone, Liv," he says, looking me in the eye. "I just totaled my car, busted my collarbone, and my hard-ass mom took away all my driving privileges and refused to buy me another car."

"Oh."

I don't know why, but I expected there to be more. Like some sort of moral to the story. But instead it's black and white, just an accident that happened. A mistake he made. One he's paid for in borrowed rides and sideline time.

One that led him to me.

"Why is the death glare back? You think I'm into you just for your wheels?"

I shake my face blank. "First my arm, then my wheels, right?" I plant one on his cheek. "No, sorry, I'm confused. Like, should I be happy that you got in an accident and that tossed us together, or sad that you got hurt? I mean—"

"That's easy. Happy." He touches my chin and I sink into his palm. "I'm happy about it. There's absolutely nothing to be sad about."

"But you were hurt—"

"*Was.* I'm fine now." His thumb rubs my cheek. "More than fine because you're in my life."

I should just melt into his words and take my liquefied self home for the night, content. But I can't let it go. It's stupid, but I have to make sure he's okay. "And you're *fine* with Coach's decision? Because if I were you, I'd be super pissed."

He barks out a laugh and unhooks his seat belt. "If it were Brady getting the start, I'd be pissed. But it's you. If anything, it's validation for my talent-scouting skills. You *are* really good."

A smile cracks my face and I see him visibly relax before I say a word. "So, you're only happy because I still make you look good."

"Basically." He opens the door and steals another kiss, our lips matching up horribly despite the fact that we're both grinning. "And because your butt looks really good in tights."

"I've been waiting for you to say something like that."

He steps out of the car, arms resting on Helena's roof and door, broad chest blocking his house enough that I almost don't notice the porch light pinging on—Coach Kitt is watching. Again.

"See you and those tights tomorrow, O-Rod."

24

GREY WORTHINGTON PUTS ON A GOOD SHOW, BUT the field hides nothing. So he can banter and kiss and laugh like everything's peachy—but when he's taking snap, it is crystal clear that, despite his assurances, my boyfriend is 100 percent, unequivocally *not fine*.

Since he learned about me getting the start, his scrimmage play has been off-kilter. He's a half step behind, his passes a foot too short, too long, too left, too right. Even his decision-making skills are suspect—he's throwing into traffic, holding on to the ball too long, refusing to go rogue on a collapsed play to make it work.

I've noticed. The receivers have noticed. Surely the coaches have noticed.

And it's all my fault. I know it.

On Tuesday, Nick pulled Grey aside at least five times for one-on-ones that always ended in helmet patting and nods. At one point on Wednesday, Jake got so frustrated, he straight stripped Grey of the ball on a passing play, just for the chance to move the A team forward.

But that's not the worst thing to happen. Getting called out in front of everyone is, and that comes as we're doing our final laps Thursday night.

Grey didn't practice any better than he did over the last two days, and he's uncharacteristically sullen as he, Brady, and I run next to each other, closing in on the finish line. I'm thinking of asking Grey if he wants to go with me to Ryan's soccer match after practice, to get his mind off things, but then Jake pulls in next to us.

"Worthington."

"Rogers?"

Jake speeds up, sliding in front of us, running backward. When he gets to the finish line, he stops on a dime. Grey hits the brakes and they're suddenly two inches apart, chin to chin, our two senior captains. Jake is smiling that annoyed smile of his, and the way his lips are curling, I know he's about to lay one out. And so does everyone else.

"You've been playing like shit ever since Liv got the start."

He doesn't look at me as he says it, and neither does Grey.

"I have not." Grey's voice is smooth. "I could play a

flute and it wouldn't matter anyway, because I'm not running the offense on Friday."

"No. No, you listen. Right now." Jake leans in, teeth
bared. I've never seen Jake like this—*ever*—and I wonder
how long his frustration has truly been building to this
moment. "I'm not losing to busted-ass Central because
your ego can't handle Liv's talent."

Grey doesn't blink. "It doesn't matter because *I'm. Not.
Playing.*"

But we all know this isn't the truth. Hell, I lived the
fact that it isn't the truth when I played last week. Back-
ups play all the time. I could play one snap and then Grey
could come in for the rest of the game, either because of an
injury or because Coach just feels like switching things up.

Rather than calling him on it, Jake dodges and goes in
a completely different direction—just like he does so often
on the field.

"Quarterbacks lead whether they're in the game or not.
Shape up."

I can barely admit it to myself, but I agree with Jake
there. Even still, my instinct is to stick up for Grey—
everyone has an off week now and then. But before I can
say something, Grey's eyes narrow in a way I've never seen
and suddenly I know exactly what opposing defenses see
when they cross him. "Or what?"

All Jake does is raise a single brow and shift his eyes my
way. It happens faster than I can process. Jake is looking at

me and then he's on the ground, Grey on top of him. Sanchez and Brady immediately dive for them, hauling Grey back by the shoulders.

There's a whistle and a flight of khaki-clad men swarm us, Coach Lee front and center. He blows on his whistle one more time, long and high, and places a hand on each boy's heaving chest.

"I don't think so. Save that crap for somewhere else. On this field, you're teammates, and I won't tolerate it. I *won't*." Coach Lee glares at each of them, spitting mad. "Both of you are on the bench tomorrow."

Jake's mouth falls open. "But—"

"Yeah, butt on the bench, Rogers. I don't care what your stats are"—Coach rounds on Grey—"or that you're already scheduled to be there. Neither of you sets foot on the field."

"I—"

"But—"

They're both cut off by Coach forcibly spinning them in the direction of the locker room. "One more peep out of either of you and we'll have to elect new senior captains."

As they're stalking away, my stomach bottoms out. There goes my safety net. Both my top backup and the team's leading scorer—gone.

Tomorrow, it's all on me.

And it feels like my fault. I want to grab Grey's hand. To remind him that he's an amazing player. That it's okay to have another off week. Second-string isn't who he is. I want to tell him that Jake knows that, too, which was why he was so hard on him.

But I don't. Because I'm not convinced it won't make things worse.

And so I watch them trudge away—Coach Lee, Grey, Jake, and the rest. Fifty-plus people who are all counting on me tomorrow night.

I'll need to run the plays. I'll need to *make* the plays. And I can't get hurt. I can't leave the team with Brady in the pocket and no Jake behind him.

Or we'll lose.

It's only for a game. But it might as well be an eternity.

25

"OH MAN, WHAT A FACE," GREY SAYS. "CENTRAL'S D IS going to shit bricks."

Grey peels off a huddle of giant bodies and does a drive-by knock of my shoulder as I stalk toward the bus, game-day glare on. Outside, I know I look hard as nails, but inside I'm a puddle of nerves. Not something I'm used to being, that's for sure.

Grey places a hand on my shoulder, right on the pad, as we find a seat. He's been like this all day—not a hint of frustration in my presence or a word about what happened last night. Jake's got apparent amnesia, too, though a deep purple shiner the shape of Grey's fist is imprinted on his right cheek.

I cock a brow and whisper, his presence immediately

dulling some of my nerves. "I thought you liked my face, Worthington."

Too close, he stares at my lips. "Don't tempt me, Rodinsky."

"No kissing in football. Yeah, yeah."

"Let's continue this discussion after a Tiger victory, shall we?"

I smirk at him. "Oh, I don't need a discussion to win this argument."

"No, you don't."

An hour later, we've been through warm-ups, the national anthem, and Central's pep song. Our junior captain—Nick—took the coin toss and happened to win it, telling the refs we'd receive. Which means I'm out on the field in less than a minute.

I'm more ready than I was before boarding the bus. But I'm still nervous as shit.

Alone with five thousand high school football fans, Grey and I stand side by side in the Central stadium, his energy seeping into mine at a much faster rate than the Gatorade I just chugged. Watching Jaden Gonzalez do the offense a solid and run Central's kickoff back past midfield and down to the thirty.

My eyes shoot up to the crowd, and within a few seconds, I find my family and Addie, up in the topmost corner of the visitor's section. They're easy to spot—Addie and Danielle, straight from school in Windsor Prep purple,

Heather in a criminally cute sundress, Mom and Ryan in Northland orange, and Dad looking ever the detective in a button-up, straight from work. He might not like me playing football, but he'll support me anytime.

Ball down, chains moving, the turf glittering under the lights, the weight of Grey's hand appears on my shoulder. "Good luck," he says.

I run out onto the field.

~

Turns out Central isn't as terrible as Jake insisted they were a day ago.

Their defense isn't the greatest, but their offense is right in line with ours. Our defense is okay, and our linebackers are excellent—praise Nick Cleary—but the Central quarterback is a senior who's seen it all on some really bad teams. He knows how to move, get rid of the ball, and fight.

Me, well...every inch of my being is exhausted from nearly four full quarters of football and at least twenty full-speed hits. And *that* is compounded by the fact that despite it's completely clear I've done my duty—282 yards and five touchdowns—we're tied.

Tied.

With a minute left. And Central has the freaking ball in the red zone.

They're killing time—the team's kicker warming up

with a Rockettes special on the sideline. One field goal and it'll be on us with seconds remaining to tie or win on a touchdown.

I'm on the bench, muscles tightening, waiting for my turn, because even with my exhaustion, my heart bursts to be out on that field, to go haul that win in. Next to me, Grey's so dialed in he can't crawl out, all the usual comfort sloughed from his skin. Where I am so tense I'm frozen in place, his legs bounce like Ryan's after one of Heather's colossal Sunday evening desserts. His mouth won't stop moving either—the coaching genes in his DNA whirring his brain up to eighty-eight miles per hour.

"Better go short and safe and hope Tate breaks free for a run than go long and miss an opportunity." His shoulder pad clicks against mine. "Not that you can't go long. It's the Central secondary I don't trust—scrappy and experienced. They've been holding up our receivers all game."

"Mmm-hmmm" is all I have energy to say.

The ball is up, up, up and then...not.

Batted down by a fingertip and rolling downfield.

The clock is still running and the second it's called as a Tiger ball—*Thank you, Sanchez*—Coach Lee is screaming for the offense to get out there. Shanks's call: Orange Sixteen.

I sprint to where the ball was downed—the twenty-two—make eye contact with Tate, and scream out the details. We haven't missed this one all game.

"ORANGE SIXTEEN. ORANGE SIXTEEN. HUT-HUT!"

Ball ready, I shoot back, eyes hunting for Tate's number eighty-two.

After a second, I spy it, but not anywhere close to on route—sandwiched between two red jerseys just beyond the line.

Shit. We haven't missed it all game, but that doesn't mean Central hasn't figured out a solution.

I dodge right, searching for any open receiver—pesky defense indeed. The closest thing to open is number eighty-four—Timmy Chow—out wide right, beating two defenders in his route downfield.

Holding my breath, I aim, hoping Chow actually thinks about looking for an incoming ball, even though he knows the play isn't designed for him.

The ball rockets out and over the fray. Chow's helmet pops up and back, his arms reach, and he leaps.

But so do the defenders—earning extra time in the half step Chow slowed to turn.

The ball crashes into Chow's chest, right between the eight and four. But the ball squirts out, skipping up end over end.

Catch it, catch it, catch it.

The ball hangs for an eternity as three pairs of gloved hands scrape fingertips against the leather. One leaping defender gets to it first, batting the point.

I release a breath as the ball makes contact with the turf, interception avoided.

Ten seconds left.

The coaches are all yelling at once for everyone to return to the line—the Northland players moving two times the speed of Central. In the mess, Shanks calls for White Twenty-Two.

Seven. Six. Five. Four.

Everyone settles into place.

"WHITE TWENTY-TWO. WHITE TWENTY-TWO. HUT-HUT!"

Three. Two. One.

I get the snap off with a second to spare and rocket back, eyes out for Trevor Smith's number eighty. He comes in on cue, trailed by a defender. Arm back, I fire, nailing him right in the hands. Smith takes the guy behind him on a spin move and points his body downfield, end zone in his sights... until two bodies come flying in. He dodges one but is stonewalled so hard by the other that the ball slips out.

This time, the defender catches the fumble and boomerangs in our direction—head down, plowing past the line before anyone can react.

Whatthewhatnow.

Every Northland jersey is immediately chasing him—including me. But the element of surprise is good enough for a five-yard advantage.

The whistle blows. The kid in Central red raises the ball high above his head. The end zone at his feet.

Nononononono.

The scoreboard says it all.

Home, 48. Visitor, 42.

Time remaining: 0:00

There's no need for an extra point. They've already won.

26

WE MEET IN THE VISITING TEAM LOCKER ROOM, AWAY
from the prying eyes and celebratory chants of the Central faithful. Heads down, hearts on the tile. When
Coach Lee enters the room, none of us can make eye
contact. Not even me.

Our coach. Retiring at the end of this year. And we just
laid an egg on his final football dream.

To get to state, we can't lose more than two games.
It's almost mathematically impossible to make state with
three losses.

And now we're 1–1.

Even worse, both games were against the cupcakes of
Kansas City.

In the coming weeks, we have to play Tetherman and

Eastern at home, plus South County on the road. Not to mention we get Jewell Academy, brother school to Windsor Prep and state champs, as a treat for homecoming.

One loss in that onslaught and chances are we won't play for the league title or make the regional finals, aka substate. No substate, no actual state.

Shame and exhaustion squat in a cloud over the room. Coach's voice comes through it all, sharp enough to hack through the gloom.

"Hello, Tigers."

"Hello, Coach."

At our answer, there's a pause. Coach taking his time to find the right words. I barely know him and his hesitation hurts as much as the loss.

"Tonight we got beat. That's the simple truth of it."

There's a tangible sinking to the room, even though everyone is standing. We can't sit for this man. Not after letting him down.

"Oh, I know the scoreboard doesn't tell the whole tale. It doesn't give Sanchez credit for blocking the field goal attempt and landing on the damn ball. It doesn't account for the fact that Rodinsky should've gotten her sixth TD for the night the second that ball hit Smith's fingertips. It doesn't account for those who didn't play tonight."

Coach Lee nails each of us with eye contact as he goes down the line. It stings. Jake can't even look at Coach, his eyes scrunched shut.

"The final score doesn't give credit or an explanation. All we get is a loss. That's it. That's football."

It is. And every other sport. There's no gray area. There's winning and losing. Pass/fail—no B-minus.

"This team was 10–2 last year. That number doesn't account for all the close calls that could've made that number more like 7–5 or 6–6. It doesn't take into account that we were five yards away from taking Jewell Academy out in substate."

I purse my lips. I was at that game, before I started dating Jake, shivering in sneakers and a Windsor Prep letter jacket with Addie and the softball girls. Five yards and Jewell's season would've been over. And all those boys wouldn't have been nearly as big of assholes at the winter formal.

"I know this isn't a 1–1 team. I know we're better than 50 percent. I know you're capable of so much more. But how much more is up to you." Coach straightens his visor. "Let's hit the buses, Tigers. Weights in the morning."

The coaches file out and the remaining air sags into the locker room's corners. Last week, we convened after the game around the benches. But this time—away from home, after a loss—this room feels the safest. We should follow to the buses and head home. But alone, we all hesitate, maybe waiting for one of us to say something.

Maybe me. I'm not a captain, but I was the quarterback. The leader.

I steel myself and hop onto a bench so that I'm a head above everyone—even Topps. "Tigers, we're going to make this right. This team is going to win every single game through the end of the season."

Through the forest of man-boys, I get some nods and turn up my inner Danielle. I'm not nervous or anything, but I'm sure not used to a bunch of boys staring back at me during a pep talk. Danielle, though? She could motivate a pack of polar bears to hula.

"We're going to take our 1-1 record and wear it like a badge of pride. When we make it to state, we're going to say, 'Hell, yeah, we're imperfect. And that makes us all the harder to beat, because we're not planning to lose another game this season." I pause. "This loss is our fuel. We use it or it burns us. Our choice, Tigers."

"Hell yes," Grey says, backing me up.

"That's right," Topps says before picking me up and setting me down on solid ground.

Others are nodding, too, a second behind. Even Brady. Even Kelly, way in the back.

But Jake takes a step forward, his jersey pristine for once. "Bullshit. It's not our choice. Our choice was to win tonight. We should have won. And we didn't."

He spits off "we," but the cut of his eyes says *I* didn't. *I* didn't win. The quarterback. The leader. I let him down.

I don't break eye contact. Just absorb his words and move on. "No, we didn't win. But that doesn't affect our choices from here on out. We learn, we move on. End of story."

But it isn't. Not with Jake. This Jake is the same bluster and fire I saw that first day at practice; that I saw last night picking a fight. The boy who offered apologies and admiration is stuffed down deep below the bruises and disappointment.

"A story is exactly what that sounds like," Jake insists, his beautiful dark eyes flashing. "This is reality. And the reality is that we got beat by shitty-ass Central because we weren't good enough tonight."

He's right. But that attitude's going to get us nowhere. I smile at him. "Oh, good, then you'll feel inspired when we lose to fantastic-ass Jewell Academy. That's when we'll make our upswing. First two-loss team to ever win league. Let's do it."

There's a tittering of laughter as I clap my hands together, faux-pumped. I swear I spy a hint of a smile from Jake before his competitor's armor slides back into place. "I'm not planning on losing any more games this year."

"Good, then we're on the same page."

Head held high, I turn and walk out to the bus.

27

I TRY BUT FAIL TO WASH THE LOSS OUT OF MY HAIR—
Garnier Fructis can only do so much. Still, I'm back at
Northland, clean after five minutes of furious scrubbing,
and it must say a lot about how I feel about Grey that
for once after a loss, I don't want to crawl into the fetal
position, rehashing what I could've done differently.

In my defense, it took Danielle twenty-five years to
truly believe the sort of stuff I said in the locker room.
Growing up, she was the queen of postloss moping. So: role
model. It didn't help that before he was promoted to detective and started working a million hours per week, Dad
had a tendency to drill us on how we could've improved
that mistimed throw or the whiffed tag.

So, yeah, breaking it down until we know exactly what

went wrong is a Rodinsky family specialty. Letting go? Not so much.

This feeling isn't going to go away, but somehow that's okay, because I know Grey is outside the locker room at this very moment, waiting for me.

And even though this time I'm expecting him, it's still a shock to see him there, clean and patient. His hands are in his pockets and that little half smile makes an easy spread across his face, despite the stench of defeat that followed us back to Northland.

"Hey, beautiful, wanna get out of here?"

I cock a brow. "You know that line doesn't really work when I'm the one with the keys, right?"

"No. I was literally asking," he deadpans.

"Of course you were." I roll my eyes and try to sock him in the shoulder, but he palms my fist before I can make contact and uses it to draw me into him, his lips catching mine midsmile. All my forward momentum stops, my free hand landing just above his hip, and the only thought in my brain is suddenly OBLIQUES.

We stand like that for I don't know how long, the starry night and yellow glow of the security lights flowing together into some sort of timeless vacuum. When we separate, I just grin at him and say, "I think you just made me miss curfew."

He fishes his phone out of his pocket and the screen flashes up at us—10:06 PM.

Nearly an hour. We have an hour alone. With the loss, everyone's bailed on pancakes at Pat's Diner.

What Grey says next is something I most definitely don't expect. "My parents are out of town."

Grey's house is pristine. I mean, I knew it would be, but seeing it is something else. Not rich, per se—two years of private school gave me plenty of access to people with houses like *that*. This is something classic.

Like Danielle's house, his was built in the fifties. Brick colonial, but not supersize. Hers is smaller—an in-need-of-an-update dinosaur she and Heather scooped up for a steal. Grey's house is magazine perfect, with glossy white trim, polished oak floors, and real wood furniture, heavy and refurbished.

As promised, it's empty. Which makes my heart race far more than it did at any point during tonight's game. Grey grabs a La Croix for each of us—no sugary soda in Coach Kitt's fridge—and I follow him up the stairs.

We turn the corner and all the doors are shut but one, the silver light of the moon combed over the rug, his blinds obviously open to the night.

When I step in, his room isn't far from what I imagined—a blend of sporty and serious in a preppy palette. The walls are a muted blue, but covered in orderly—and meticulously aligned—posters.

Classic Joe Montana taken during the blip of time he was with the Chiefs, and Patrick Mahomes in a more recent shot. Colin Kaepernick kneels over his dresser, Marcus Mariota and Drew Brees chill in smaller pictures around the room. Various Jayhawks are sprinkled around—"Mario's Miracle" frozen in time and Danny Manning bookend his closet. There are baseball players, too, of course, mostly Royals players like Salvy, Moose, and Duffy.

The furniture is dark wood and everything matches, nothing stitched together as money allows. Place ribbons of every color hang from the window frame, a shot of personality layered over white wood blinds. Trophies line two open shelves placed over the pristinely made bed.

Grey shuts his blinds and turns on some *Andrew McMahon in the Wilderness*. As the chorus of "All Our Lives" hums to life, I suddenly find an interest in small talk I never knew I had.

"So, um...where are your parents?"

Grey sits on the bed. It's not an invitation—it's like he needs to sit down for what he says next. There's a tick to his shoulders I'm sure I've never seen. "Touring the wineries of Hermann, Missouri." The way he says it, the way he's sitting, there's something more. "Last-minute trip. Preemptively celebrating Mom's fortieth birthday."

Wait. Hold the phone. I'm suddenly doing math in my head, trying to figure out how old she was when she had

Grey. He reads the mental gymnastics flipping across my face. "I wrecked her chances to make the 2004 Olympic team."

I wince.

But that's not the more in his voice—what comes next is. "Her birthday is actually next weekend, but I guess they figured they wouldn't miss much with my butt on the bench tonight."

Well, that's shitty. I claim a piece of the bed's corner and place my hand on his arm. "That's not the vibe I've ever gotten from your mom. I mean, pride practically shoots from her eyeballs when she sees you."

Through a wicked smirk, he sighs. "It's not that she's not proud of me—Dad either. It's just…things have been different since this summer."

The car wreck. A pang reverberates through my heart, and suddenly I have a lump nestled against my windpipe. We both made mistakes this summer. And the recovery keeps on going—relationships, trust, expectations—what we did bleeds over to all of it. "I know that feeling."

I meant it as an aside of solidarity. That I totally understand what it's like to disappoint those you love most. But then Grey reaches out and takes my hand, turning my palm over, his long eyelashes pointed down, examining the lines there—love, fate, life.

"Liv…" he starts, and then stops himself. There's something heavy hanging off my name. Something substantial enough to hurt. Grey glances up at me through those lashes. "There's more."

Not for the first time do I think that maybe he injured another person. But I googled the accident, and got nothing more than two sentences in the *Star*'s weekly off-season prep roundup about Grey's collarbone. And it would've been something much more if he'd wrecked someone else's life, along with his left arm. Grey hauls his legs onto the bed and crosses them, his bare knee grazing mine. Even through my jeggings, it's warm. He leans back against the wall, his thumb running slow circles against my skin.

His mouth drops open, but he still can't get the words out. I swear I can see fear churning in his eyes.

"What is it?" I ask. "You can tell me, whatever it is."

The words rush out of him in a single breath. "I think I might have gotten a concussion."

I blink. "In the car accident?"

His eyes shoot to mine, lips closing before immediately opening again. "Yes—well, I think so."

"You *think* so—you don't know?"

He pauses. "I don't—I mean I feel like I did after I got one freshman year."

As his words sink in, the signs solidify in my mind.

Sunglasses to practice when he knows better: light sensitivity.

Our exchange the first day on the track:

Sounds like you've been hit in the head one too many times.

— 221 —

Actually, that's not too far off from the truth.

The Tylenol I've seen him pop when he thinks I'm not looking.

Even his half-step slowness during scrimmage—just like Jake, I thought that was Grey's injured ego, but now it's suddenly startlingly obvious that something else is.

"How bad was the concussion you got your freshman year?"

He clearly doesn't want to say the words, but under my fiercest glare he finally does. "A grade three."

Oh. My. God. I'm no medical professional, but I have been hit in the head hard enough that I know Grey Worthington lost consciousness in that car accident.

"Grey..." I say, and get to my knees, one hand on the wall, and press my fingertips to his temple, as if doing so can magically tell me if his brain is no longer bruised.

He sort of laughs and takes my hand in his, kissing my fingers. "I'm okay. I'm really okay."

But I'm not fazed. "Are you really okay to play? I swear to God if you lie to me, I'll knee you in the nuts."

His eyes pointedly shoot to my knees, which are indeed pretty close to the crotch of his shorts. "I'm *not* cleared," he says, and then looks up from my knees and straight into my eyes. "But that's only because they don't know either."

"Who doesn't know?"

Grey swallows. "Everyone. The coaches. Mom. Dad."

Holy shit. HOLY SHIT. "Why don't they know about it?"

"Because I don't want college recruiters to find out."

I'm absolutely stunned.

And the thing is, I understand. I get not wanting to be judged forever for something stupid in your past—that's my summer on a plate.

Grey's talking again. "Dad's a lawyer, so we can swing college and all, but I don't want to just walk on somewhere. I want to play. And I don't want anyone passing me up my senior year because of it."

I understand that, too—it's part of why I need to make Coach Kitt's team. Not just to get in front of recruiters for a full ride, but also so anyone interested in offering me anything won't think twice about the reputation I dinged when I decked Stacey.

"How'd you keep it from them...? I mean, you had to be checked out after the car accident. I mean, your arm—it's not like you refused medical attention. How could they not...? How did you keep it from them?"

Again, Grey looks down. Embarrassed or regretful or both. "I came to before the ambulance and cops arrived. They didn't know I'd been out. And I don't know how, but I made it through every test. They were way more concerned with not jostling my arm—someone recognized me as Northland's starting quarterback."

Wow. Luck and way more deceit than I ever expected from Grey Worthington add up to one big-ass secret.

"So...no one knows but me?"

Grey doesn't break eye contact, the steel gray reaching into me. Pleading. "No one. Promise me you won't tell. Please? I can take care of myself."

The way he says it, I'm back on the stoop that night Dad found out about my secret football career, hearing my own voice as I beg him to listen. Trying to prove that I know what's best for me. That I can handle it. That I know what I have to do for the future I want.

I search Grey's face again, doing the math in my head. It's been more than eight weeks since his accident. I've had two concussions in my softball career—both grade twos at ages ten and fourteen—and I know that's long enough to heal. Still, I have to hear him say it.

"I promise I won't rat you out." He smiles briefly, but I put a finger to his lips, ruining the expression. "But I need you to promise me that if you're *not okay*, you'll tell me and we'll get you to a doctor immediately."

"I promise."

I sit back on my heels, appraising the whole Grey Worthington package. And it's a nice one. "Good. I don't want my boyfriend to have mashed potatoes for brains. I rather like your brains."

"Boyfriend," he says with a grin that makes me wonder if I've ever actually said that word to him. How could I not? Grey sits up off the wall and turns to me, and I swear I see the muscles shifting under his white polo in a way that I've never seen under his jersey—the pads most definitely get in the way. He runs a finger under my chin and then slips a lock of still-wet hair behind my ear. "I know I'm the one who nixed kissing in football, but I'm fairly certain Jake's real reason for being so pissed Thursday was because of how I look at you."

It shouldn't, but this gives me a little thrill. Right in the darkest corners of my heart, the part that still aches, that's stitched with that final text from Jake—**Can't deal with the crazy. I'm out**.

I close the distance between us, twisting to push up onto my knees, draping my arms over his shoulders. This is a position I've never had with him—the kind Helena the Honda doesn't allow. I'm looking down on him, my chest touching his, the ends of my hair pooling against his collarbone.

"Keep looking," I say. And then I kiss him.

28

DAD IS WAITING UP FOR ME WHEN I KILL THE IGNITION exactly two minutes until eleven, sitting on the cooling concrete of Danielle's front stoop, beer in hand.

I get out of the car with my head hanging, furiously trying to remember how I felt back in the locker room. Before Grey made me forget everything. My lips are pink enough to give me away—my head hangs further. I'm actually upset somewhere deep down, but still, I have to work to be the sore loser Dad expects me to be right now.

"Ah, hon, everyone loses." Dad sets down the bottle and hotfoots it my way. He takes me in for a hug, and despite the beer, he smells of sandalwood and the cinnamon disks he keeps in a bowl on his desk. I melt into him, arms limp at my sides, face buried in his shoulder. "So you lost. But no one can take that performance away from you. Running, leaping, throwing—you were outstanding."

I sigh into him as he rubs my back. My muscles ache from being drilled to the turf too many times, but it still feels good.

Hearing him say those things feels good, too, especially after months of feeling like nothing but a disappointment.

Dad kisses my hair. "Next week is your week, Livvie."

And I almost think he's right.

The next week is as close to my new normal as I allow myself to hope. A steady blur of school, practice, a few stolen moments alone with Grey, dinner with the fam. I miss Addie's match again, but I make it for a few minutes of Ryan's, so maybe I'm not totally a horrible person.

By Friday night, the weight of the loss is gone—the bulk of it eaten alive by good old hard work during the week. I'm tired but jazzed by the home crowd, the night air filled with the scent of popcorn as we take the field. There's a hint of crispness there, too, fall clearing its throat. It'll be here soon enough. Next week we have a bye, also known as an entire week off from competition. Which means I'm fairly certain by the time we're on the field again—homecoming, against last year's state champs—I'll be blowing into my frozen fingers before every snap.

Tonight, though, there's just enough humidity to make

the ball slick in my fingers. Despite the loss, I've gotten the start. Again. I don't know if Coach Lee is benching Grey because I'm actually better than him or because he's worried his collarbone still isn't healed. I don't force Grey to speculate. We just don't talk about it.

Whatever the reason, Coach Lee has decided to go for a mix of plays against Tetherman, trying to break through a defensive line that's been giving Jake a literal headache the whole game. Frustration sits heavy on his broad shoulders, and I know he's getting pissed when he starts mouthing off to guys who easily have fifty pounds on him.

"Dude, shut it. We'll get them," I say, cuffing his wrist. "Show, don't tell."

Jake meets my eyes and does a Grey-style deadpan I didn't know was in him. "You're one to talk."

I just smile. "Learn from my mistakes. Jawing gets you nowhere."

By halftime, we're tied 10–10, and Jake is still livid, stalking to the sideline for a word with Coach. So I'm not surprised when the first call out of the gate in the second half is yet another rushing play. Jake badly wants to break through this line like he's mowed over everything else.

We push into the huddle.

"Orange Five, Tigers."

We throw our hands in the middle and break.

At the snap, I turn and cover the ball just enough so that the defense thinks I'm running for it, but not so much that Jake can't sprint past and snag it. With the ease of a pickpocket, he tucks the ball under his arm and hurtles through the tiniest crack in a wall of bodies.

Jake breaks free on the other side and becomes a blur of orange, the white three and two on his jersey jumbling together under the lights as he speeds in the direction of the end zone, forty yards downfield.

With two white-and-silver bodies in worthless pursuit, he flies into the end zone in a sweeping arc and spikes the ball so high it sails up and over the goalpost.

All that frustration gone in a rush of satisfaction that comes with a breakthrough. And damn, if I don't feel better, too. Relieved we've figured out how to score on the ground.

The crowd feels it, too, becoming a stream of noise. There's a chant rising above the general screams of people too excited to realize they should join in.

"Tigers! Tigers! TIGERS!"

Jake swoops back downfield, helmet off, soaking it up. Arms raised to the star-speckled sky, he insists the crowd go louder.

It's magnetic.

The ground pulsates as I jog toward him—a rumble and roar rolling through Tiger Stadium. The rest of the offense is ahead of me, rushing in for fist bumps and high fives.

So when Jake goes down, I think it's under the weight of love.

Until a scrap of white-and-silver wedges in my eye, Jake's orange-clad body smothered into the ground, helmet rolling toward open field.

And then all hell breaks loose. Helmets and fists flying—an all-out brawl at the end zone. The benches dump onto the field, bodies all running full speed at each other, screaming like boy banshees.

FFS.

Jets on, I get there the same time as Kelly, tearing into the fray, determined to pound some skulls to get to Jake. But no matter what's happening between the two of them, she can't go in there. Kelly was right that day she yelled at me outside the locker room—she can't be on the football field. As much as I hate to admit it, she really is too important to the softball team to get hit. And she doesn't have a helmet. Or pads. Or any protection at all.

Shit.

Automatically, I pin her arms to her sides and hug her to my chest pad.

"The coaches have it, Kelly. The coaches have it," I tell her, hauling her back over to the sidelines. Deaf to anything but the fight on the field, she lunges forward anyway, trying to pull me along. But I stay upright, hands drilled to her shoulders in focus, grimace set.

"Think of the team," I shout at her. "You join that mess, you could be out for the year. The *team* needs you to pitch. You get hurt, there go your team's chances!"

Logic settles in and she quits struggling so much, softening enough that I finally risk searching for Grey. I twist around to look at the bench—empty as Chick-fil-A on a Sunday. He's in that freaking mosh pit.

And though I know he said he was all right, that he was healed, that he was only keeping quiet for the scouts, I still squint into the crowd, searching for number sixteen. I mumble a silent prayer that he grabbed his helmet before rushing into this mess of bodies.

It's all a blend and a blur—scraps of clothing, slips of skin, noise and fury.

Coach Lee's voice lifts above the din, but, like Grey, it's impossible to locate him in the fray. My legs itch to run in and find Grey, to grab his hand and pull him away. Keeping him safe seems like a much better use of my time than holding back my ex-boyfriend's girlfriend. But still, I stay with Kelly, who's thrashing less now, finally coming to her senses.

Somewhere behind me, an engine revs—Coach Napolitano is driving the cart over. The one used to collect bodies from the field, zipping them to the locker room or, worse, the ambulance.

No. No. No.

It's a precaution. It has to be. It can't be that someone—Jake, anyone—can't get up.

Napolitano noses the cart's bumper into the heart of the scuffle. The forced motion sends most of the Tetherman players packing to their bench. A few remain, white flecks in a sea of orange.

Unmoving orange.

Everyone has stopped. Eyes drawn forward and down. Napolitano disappears into the mass, hand up—signaling for help.

My fingers slip off Kelly's shoulders and I hop to the first metal bench, balancing on cleated tiptoes, reaching for something—anything. But the angle's bad. I can't see a single thing except helmets reflecting the glare of the stadium lights. My eyes shoot to the crowd—Dad and Danielle have identical emotions telegraphed across their faces: grim, grim, grim. Mom has her hand pressed to her mouth, eyes pinned to the field. A few rows down, I find Jake's parents—Jerome and Angela—and Max. Oh, Max. Max has his head buried in his mother's Northland hoodie, little seven-year-old shoulders quaking. Jerome and Angela are talking and then Jerome nods and starts to scoot out of the row. Headed down to the field.

My stomach drops and my blood pressure rises, breathing near impossible. For all the weirdness of our postbreakup-current-teammate relationship, I would still call Jake a friend. And even if we hated each other's guts, there's no way on earth I'd ever wish him hurt. Ever.

After a long moment, something stirs in the center and I recognize Jake's buzzed head.

There are hands on his shoulders. Three visors—Lee,

Shanks, and Napolitano—surround him. I exhale as I realize that though they're keeping him steady, not a single one is gripping him like he's not moving under his own power. I can see Jake's mouth moving. Blood streaming down from a cut over his left eye.

When he gets to the cart, Jake takes a seat next to the medic and lifts his head until he's looking me right in the eye. Even at this distance, I recognize the order.

Win the game, O-Rod.

Jake lifts both arms straight to the sky—touchdown!— and the crowd roars, knowing he's okay.

"Go get him," I whisper to Kelly. She immediately starts running after the cart, but then hesitates for a moment, and it's clear she's looking for her brother. "I'll check on Nick and let him know where you've gone," I add.

And then she's sprinting again without a reply.

I turn back to the fight, now broken up, the coaches and refs turning both sides back to the sidelines. I tell myself he has to be okay. They didn't bring another cart. Another medic. No one is circled around someone unable to get up because they've suffered yet another brain bruise.

And then, there is Grey—helmet on (thank God), gait strong, walking off next to Nick, who's helmetless but appears fine. When he sees the look on my face, Grey breaks into a run, taking off his helmet when he gets to me.

"Are you okay?" he asks, eyes searching.

"Are you?" I ask Grey, and my voice is all weird and

stilted. There's so much in it I don't say, and the fact that Nick doesn't know about the concussion looms large in the front of my thoughts.

He winks. "Rogers is gonna live and we're ahead by a touchdown—I'm most definitely okay."

29

GRADE ONE CONCUSSION, DELIVERED BY THE RIGHT
hook of a Tetherman lineman immediately after the
dude plowed Jake into the ground on a super-duper late
hit. Not even close to Grey's injury, but a prescription
all the same for butt-to-bench therapy.

Jake's out the rest of the game. Just like the delinquent
who took him down, and it doesn't seem fair that they have
the same punishment. That's not an eye for an eye, it's a
slap on the wrist for a brain bruise.

My mind is a jumbled mess once we're back and settled. Tetherman scored on the next drive, and so now we're
tied at 17–all. But with fewer than thirty seconds left, it's
our turn to end this and avoid overtime.

The kickoff return was a great one—Chow getting us

all the way down to the twenty. Coach Shanks signals for our first rushing play and Jake's backup—a runny-eyed sophomore named Levi Towson—looks like he's just been asked to scale the Taj Mahal.

"Orange One."

There's nothing different about my voice in the huddle. But there's everything different about the reaction.

All ten boys are silent.

Towson just stares at me, glinting eyes begging me to take it back.

So I repeat myself. "Orange One." And give a descriptor. "Straight through the middle."

Blink, blink—Towson stares at me. Tate isn't having it—that eye roll could probably be seen from Pluto. "Let's just Orange Nine it up in here and finish this on first down. Kid's not ready."

He isn't. But that's not the point. We respect our coach and our teammates.

"Orange One."

"But—" Towson begins. I don't let him finish.

"Orange One." Handclap. "Break."

That buzzing crowd comes in now, an entire wall of orange, on its feet, a wave of noise crashing over our movement toward the line. I settle in behind Topps. Towson is a yard behind me, shaking like the wimpiest leaf known to man.

Dude, grow a pair.

"ORANGE ONE. ORANGE ONE. HUT-HUT."

Topps shoots the ball into my hands and I rocket left, ready to pick up Towson before he jukes through a hole made by the offensive line and leading straight toward the end zone.

Only Towson isn't there.

He's gone the wrong way and gotten tangled up in the meaty palms of a defender on the right side.

Shit.

I tuck the ball against my body and jerk two steps until I'm lined up with the hole, narrowing by inches each second. I grit my teeth, twist my shoulders, and dive through, aiming for the white end zone paint just beyond a Tetherman lineman's back foot.

A body comes flying in crossways at my ankles, pushing my lower half into a spin and throwing off my balance. I brace for impact, the turf rushing up toward my face, my body now parallel to the white line of the end zone.

Wait. The ball can't just hit the ground. It's got to hit before my knees.

My knees—which are being driven straight toward the plastic grass by some hippo in Tetherman white and silver.

Shit.

I thrust the ball away from my chest and reach for the green beyond the white line. The ball's point touches and

I have a split second to smile before the freaking hippo crashes down, crushing my knees into the turf so hard I'm sure I tag China.

The crowd roars, and somewhere in the storm there's the shrill of a whistle. Through the corner of my eye I glimpse one of the refs, arms up.

Oh, thank God.

Touchdown.

The hippo peels away, but not before grinding his shoulder into the outside of my top knee one final time before the refs run over to break it up. When I can stand, a pair of arms immediately hooks me under the shoulders and flings me around in a rough circle.

"O-Rod!!!!" Topps's cheeks are rosy with glee as he winds up for another revolution. Gentle giant that he is, he sets me down as if I'm landing on a flower petal, my other teammates approaching for high fives. It's only as I'm walking away from them to the sidelines as special teams set up for a field goal that I feel it.

Mixed in with elation and realization that I should've spiked the ball—because when else am I going to get to do that?—is a twinge in my left knee.

It doesn't hurt, not with the white-hot certainty of a true injury, but it doesn't feel right either. There's a hitch on the outside of the joint, like a violin string that's skipped the bridge.

"Rodinsky," Coach Lee yells from down the line, "you're

a sorry excuse for a running back, but at least you managed not to get caught."

My heart rises. That almost feels like a compliment.

I stick my head under the hand dryer for just long enough that my hair won't paint wet streaks on my shirt before grabbing my bag and checking my phone.

Addie: **Have Nick. Meet you at Pat's. We might be late.**

I text back: **Don't miss curfew, Adeline.**

Addie immediately answers: **I don't miss anything and you know it.**

I laugh. Kill, block, shot, catch—she's right. She doesn't miss.

I step out of the locker room with a smile on my face.

Like the past couple of weeks, Grey is there. Again, he's pushed up against the building, smelling of boy soap, the curling pieces of his hair catching the dying stadium brights.

But this time, he's not alone.

A girl in a dress is there, too, blond hair shimmering in the same light. She's pressed into Grey, one palm flat against his chest, the other hand in his hair, sweeping the curls off his temples.

I'm so stunned, I stand there for a second, the locker room door open, wedged against my backside.

"Look—don't." Grey's voice is insistent. I could just be

imagining it, but it almost looks as if he's trying to jerk his head away from her hands but not getting anywhere. "Stacey, don't," I hear him say.

Stacey.

That Stacey?

I stiffen and my butt loses its leverage as a doorstop and the heavy metal door slams shut behind me. Grey stumbles off the wall and out of the girl's grasp.

"Liv," he says, eyes wide and hands out, defensive. "It's not what it looks like."

For a moment, I believe him—he didn't look like he was encouraging her or enjoying her touch. But Grey Worthington knows how to evade the grasp of a two-hundred-pound linebacker. Surely he could escape a scant one hundred pounds of teenage girl.

Then the girl turns and it *is* her. She's not at school in Arizona. Stacey's *here*.

Touching my boyfriend.

The light's not the best, but she's definitely recovered from my right hook. Stacey's face morphs into a little smirk. She's had her brows filled in and her blond hair is less softball-practice-and–Sun In and more super-expensive balayage.

Her palm is still on Grey's chest. Grey realizes it the same moment I do and hastily moves away.

Stacey laughs, her eyes shining as they loop from my

face to Grey's, reading the situation. "And is *this* what it looks like?"

"Yeah. It is," Grey says, and pointedly steps around Stacey and grabs for my hand, tugging me away toward the parking lot.

But Stacey's not done.

"What is it with you and my sloppy seconds?" she calls after me. "First Jake and now Grey?"

I stop dead in my tracks, pulling Grey to a halt.

"Oh, you didn't know?" she says. "Grey and I dated for the last two years. Who do you think held my hand on the ride to the hospital after you punched me?" I wince, and this hurts more than what Stacey did to my eye at that last softball game.

Grey tugs at my hand. "*Dated*. Past tense. Come on, Liv, I'll explain."

But my heels are planted on the concrete.

"Oh, yeah, explain," Stacey says. "Don't forget the part where I dumped you and you were so upset you wrapped your car around a tree."

I shut my eyes.

The wreck.

I just totaled my car, busted my collarbone, and my hard-ass mom took away all my driving privileges and refused to buy me another car.

"I wasn't upset," Grey snaps.

She cuts him off with a single laugh. "You were three beers in—which is worse. Too drunk to drive, too emotional to Uber."

When I open my eyes, Grey's face is pale and his hand has gone clammy around mine.

He didn't just want to hide his concussion from recruiters. He needed to hide the fact that he drove drunk, too— no college wants to touch a quarterback stupid enough to do that with a ten-foot pole.

The concussion. The drunk driving. *Two years* with Stacey.

What else is he hiding?

And then—I see it. As clear as the perfect pitch coming my way, begging to be smashed.

Recruiting me, befriending me, even the starry eyes and kisses no one saw.

I'm not just his girlfriend—I'm a means to an end.

Because what better way to push back against a broken heart than to date the girl who shattered Stacey's nose?

And the *lies*. The lies by omission over the course of our relationship are suddenly so dense, piling together and splitting apart until I'm blinded by the spread of them.

Again, Grey tries to tug me away, to the privacy of Helena the Honda and then to celebratory pancakes with friends. But I'm frozen in place.

I slip my hand free of Grey's.

Now Stacey's the one moving, sweeping past us. She

turns midstride, teeth flashing. They're whiter than they were all those months ago, too. It's like she got a makeover simply for this moment. "Rodinsky, I almost feel sorry for you. Not only is your whole relationship a revenge plot, but it's a shitty one. Because guess what? I don't actually care what Grey does with his time. Or *who* he does."

And that's when I walk away. Because I don't need to hear a single thing Grey has to say.

30

"LIV! HEY! LIV!" GREY IS ON MY TAIL AS I BURST OUT OF the shadow of the main building and into the parking lot.

Oh, hell no.

I pick up the pace until I'm literally sprinting toward where Helena's parked next to an island.

A crush of disappointment, shame, and anger constricts my lungs until I can't breathe. It's like I'm piled under a bunch of bodies yet again, nose to the turf. Still, I weave through the cars. Why the hell are there so many people still here?

"Liv! O-Rod, *please*."

The tears squeak through my eyes now. Goddammit, why can't they wait until I'm in the car?

I will not sob. I will not break down. I can't—

"Olive." There's a hand on my shoulder.

Fresh tears immediately fall as I wrench myself away. I don't want him touching me again. Not now. Not ever. I wheel on him, backing toward my car.

"Don't."

Grey's hands are raised in front of his body. I want to slap him. I want to leave angry red fingerprints on his cheek.

"Liv. Listen—"

"Don't you dare."

"If you'd let me explain—"

"Explain what?" Car doors are swinging open, people coming to see what the commotion is all about, and I suddenly don't care. Let them see and hear the whole damn thing. "That you didn't mean to use me as revenge? Against Stacey?" My eyes tighten. "To make yourself feel better about *your* colossal mistake?"

Grey draws himself up to his full height, hands down, features granite. Bastard. "Don't act like you weren't out for revenge, too." He leans in, suddenly mindful of our growing audience. Out of the corner of my eye, I recognize Jake taking a step toward us, only to be pulled back by Kelly. "You can say it was all about getting on the soft-ball team. But I know you. I know that deep down in your heart, being on this team was just as much about steam-rolling Jake as it was about impressing my mother."

He's right. I saw my opportunity for revenge before Grey and Shanks had even finished their pitch.

"Maybe that's true," I shoot back at him, not bothering to lower my own voice. There's definitely a crowd now. The bodies are a blur—teammates, classmates, teachers, parents. Hell if I know. A big fat tear rolls into my mouth as I draw in a breath. "But you *lied* to me. I believed you when you said you wanted to be my friend. I believed you when you said you liked me. I believed you when you kissed me. I'm *your girlfriend* and you still used me. I may have had my own motives for joining the team, but I *never* lied to you."

I place both hands squarely on his chest and shove him away.

But Grey's not done.

"I overheard you in Mom's office and I felt sorry for you—I know how much of a hard-ass she can be. And then I saw you play with your brother and I had to tell Shanks. So what if you punched my ex-girlfriend? Who cares what she would think?"

"Then why didn't you tell me about Stacey? She ruined my life. *You* knew that. A lie by omission is still a lie." Staring him down, I dare him to glance away. Dare him.

And suddenly, there's real anger in his face, not just frustration. "She didn't ruin it. *You* punched her. You broke her nose. You got yourself kicked out of that fancy-ass private school. You did that. Nobody else."

The words sound like something he's told himself over and over since his stupid car crash. Maybe something his mom drilled into his head.

But, even still, the words hit their mark and anger rips through my veins, shoving past the sadness. The embarrassment. The shame.

I finally get my fingers wrapped around my keys. I yank them out of my bag and stare him down. "I'd do it again in a heartbeat."

I turn and stuff my keys into the lock, but Grey dares to touch me again. "I did this for you. Ninety-nine percent of my motivation was to help you and the team. I swear."

I want to believe it. But I just can't.

"Bullshit, Worthington." Jake's wiggled out of Kelly's arms and moved next to Grey, his left eye swollen shut. Behind him, I see half the team there—not just Kelly, but Topps, the whole offensive line, Sanchez, Brady, Tate, Smith. I don't see my family, though, or Addie and Nick, and it's a major relief. "You were using her and we all knew it."

Jake's defending me. But somehow that makes it worse. I've been a part of this team for weeks—so many sweaty hours together, and no one, *no one*, warned me that Grey had a past with Stacey. Any one of them could've pulled me aside and filled me in on the backstory so that I wouldn't be so blindsided.

I wheel on Jake. "So you knew about all of this and you didn't tell me?"

Jake's lips fall open in surprise. A memory of us in the parking lot that first day flashes in front of my eyes, when he told me he didn't like the thought of Grey using me. But that could've been anything—if Jake had really wanted me to know, he could have said something else in any of the days since then.

I search the faces of my teammates. Topps. Brady. Tate. Smith. I even spare a second to read Kelly's face.

"You *all* fucking knew?"

Silence. I take the collective lack of an answer as a yes. They all knew about what happened with me and Stacey, and they all knew about Grey and me. And yet not a single one of them had the balls to come clean.

I swallow, willing my voice not to break, and turn to Grey. "I'm a human being, not some pawn. If you got burned by some stupid girl, how dare you bring me into it? How dare you bring the *team* into it?"

A few of the players' heads nod in my periphery, but I don't care. They should have said something earlier if they didn't agree with what Grey was doing.

"I was taught that a team is a family," I say, my voice like iron. "And families don't do this shit to each other. Human beings don't do this shit to each other. And this human is out."

Every eye is on me as I jam my keys back into the lock, wrench the car door open, and slide into the seat. As soon as the door latches, the tears fall free. I hope against hope they can't see.

31

BY THE TIME I DRIVE HOME, BAWLING MY EYES OUT THE whole way, Dad's out front again, Danielle drinking beer with him. When I reach the top of the drive, he's taking a swig of Boulevard Wheat, and so Danielle speaks first, a big stinkin' grin on her face. "There you are, superstar."

Though I should be all cried out by now, I burst into tears.

Confusion crosses Danielle's face and she pushes up to her feet, tucking me into her arms. Dad's standing now, too, hand on my back. "Liv," he says, "what's wrong?"

When I shake my head into Danielle's shoulder, she gently pushes me to arm's length, the two of them trying to read the words I can't say.

That Dad was right. That I couldn't trust Grey. That the people who play football are brutal.

It doesn't help that I can feel my left knee swelling, my jeans too tight around it.

Two car doors slam.

"Look," Dad says softly, brushing a tear from my cheek. "Adeline's here for you. Another friend, too. I can tell them to come back tomorrow, if you want."

I shake my head, and Dad nods and touches his forehead to mine. "Pancakes after practice tomorrow, baby girl."

There's a thrill in his voice as he tries to get me to smile, and a look on his face I haven't seen in forever.

What I wouldn't have given for this Dad that first week of practice. For his joy rather than his anger. And now I've tossed it away because boys are assholes. He'll be just as disappointed tomorrow when I tell him I'm not going to practice as he was last week, but for totally different reasons.

I am such a freaking letdown, no matter what I do.

Danielle gives my arm a squeeze before grabbing the beer bottles and disappearing into the house. "You really were super tonight."

As the storm door clicks shut and both of them disappear into the house, I pivot toward the street, mindful of my knee as I twist. Addie is standing there, and Nick takes up space behind her. He can't seem to look straight at me, eyes unfocused, almost as if he's ashamed. Good. If he knew what was going on, then he deserves to be ashamed.

"Is it true?" Addie asks, her voice unbelieving.

I close the distance between us. We're away from the house, down the driveway, Heather's favorite maple shading the streetlights and moon.

"What part?" I say, tears pricking my eyes again. "That I basically left the team? That Grey used me to get back at Stacey? Or that every single teammate *knew* what he was doing and no one thought to say something?" I shift my gaze to Nick and give him the exact same glare I gave his sister seconds before she hit me with a fastball.

Addie blinks and although the light is low, it's easy to spot the clear sheen of tears against her beautiful dark eyes. She lunges forward and wraps me in a vicious hug. I stifle a gasp, my sore muscles complaining, but wrench my arms around her anyway.

We stay like that for a good minute before Addie draws back, hands draped gently over my upper arms, her natural strength subdued.

"What do you need? What can I do?"

My gaze strays to Nick. Without a word, he disappears into the passenger side of Addie's Toyota. When he's gone, I sob-smile. "Get my Windsor Prep scholarship back?"

"Something more realistic?"

I chomp down on the inside of my cheek, willing the fresh tears to back off.

"Want me to talk to Grey?" she suggests.

I shake my head.

"How about Jake? Want me to talk to him?"

I shake my head.

"Stacey?" She throws a right cross into the shadows. "I can drive straight to Arizona and talk the hell out of that one. Or, you know, just deck her."

She says it to be funny and laughs a little with it, but instead, her words stick in my mind. I think of Grey running into that brawl and how worried I was that he might take a punch his brain couldn't handle. I shake my head to clear it, and force out the words. "She's actually here. She's the one who told me about her and Grey."

The tears start coming again.

"I've got my gloves in the car." Addie adds a one-two, hook-uppercut combo to shadow Stacey. That kickboxing class this summer really paid off in good form.

It's all so ridiculous that I laugh through the sob in my throat, words loosening. "How about you land one on my temple so I don't have to go to school Monday?"

"If your dad wouldn't kill me, I'd take you out of your misery, yes."

"You are *the* best friend." And she is. And I suck—again missing her games this week, because I'm *the worst*.

"Correction, I am Olive Rodinsky's best friend. And Olive Rodinsky is a damn good quarterback."

That just makes the tears fall harder. "The whole point

of football was to show what a team player I am, and I just basically *left* the team. Kitt is never going to see past that. Never."

Addie clutches my shoulders. "Then don't make it an issue." I blink at her, vision blurry. "She doesn't know the whole story. Were your coaches there? Did you say the words 'I quit' to Coach Lee?"

"Well, no—"

"Then go to practice tomorrow. Finish the season. In a few weeks, she'll be so impressed, you won't even need to try out."

"I can't," I say, voice shaking at a dangerous pitch.

"Yes, you can."

"No—you weren't there!" I hate my voice right now, every shaky syllable of it. All pitchy and raw. "Every single one of them knew about Grey and Stacey—how they dated for two years, how he totaled his car after she dumped him—all of it. Every single one of them knew how Grey was treating me. And every single one of them knew it was as fake as Stacey's new nose."

"So what! They're idiots. They used you? *Use them back*." She drives home the point with a playful jab, but her eyes are on fire. "Hold your head high and walk into practice tomorrow morning."

"I can't—"

"Yes, you can. You think this is hard? You think those boys are assholes? What if you *do* make the softball team?"

Tears roll down my cheeks. "What about playing on the same team as Kelly? The team you beat at the state semis before whooping up on its star player? You think that's going to be a freaking piece of Funfetti?"

"No, but I can't—"

"Did you break your leg tonight?" She taps each of my shins with the toes of her Nikes, like she's kicking the tires of a used car. "Nope? Okay, then walk into practice—"

"Weights. Saturday is weights."

"Weights—whatever. Walk in and show those assholes who's boss. They'll be so terrified of you there will be an inch-deep stream of piddle on the floor."

"But if I go back, then who am I?" My arms fling wide. "The girl who told them all to eff off because they were assholes and then came back for more? Isn't that the definition of a toxic relationship? Not feeling like you have the power to leave and staying where you're treated like garbage?"

"Not if you give it back." The wind kicks up and Addie's braids swirl into her face. "You *want* to be on the softball team. That's the end goal. Show up. Kick butt. Do what Kitt needs to see you do and then make the damn team."

She's right. I know she's right. But when I close my eyes, I see Grey's face in the parking lot. Angry. Unflinching. I see the remorse in Jake's one good eye and his teeth bare and flashing. I see the blank faces of the "friends" who never gave me a heads-up about this integral piece of Northland romantic history.

"I *can't.*" My eyes fly open. "I respect myself too much to go back there."

"You don't respect yourself at all if you let a group of stupid boys and an even stupider girl steal your dreams."

"They aren't—"

"You quit and yes they are."

"I'm quitting because I'm standing up for myself."

"Standing up for yourself doesn't mean walking away."

In my head, in this situation, it does. There's nothing much left to say. Addie knows it, too, and starts backing across the street toward her car.

"Show up to weights in the morning, Rodinsky."

I watch Addie drive away, Nick in the passenger seat. They're gone and I'm still standing here, her words swirling in my head.

32

AT SIX THIRTY, MY ALARM DETONATES AND THE SUN busts through my window all bright and cheery, like it's completely ignorant about last night.

My football gear is strewn all over the floor, a sweat-lined trail of disappointment. My phone's faceup, home screen lined with texts and missed calls. My head pounds, my knee throbs, and soreness roasts my muscles from the inside out. Even my *skin* seems to hurt.

Ughhhhhhhh.

Still, I pull myself to standing and head for the hall bathroom as silently as possible—Ryan's wedged under his pillow, sleeping off being a teenage boy.

The house is mostly quiet—Dad's snores replaced by clinking in the kitchen. Coffee before his morning jog. The case he was working really must be over. Mom's sleeping off her treatments in their room, and I hear Heather's voice coming from the back deck, running Danielle through sun salutations. Danielle's remarking—not *complaining*—that she's just not that damn flexible. Which is exactly why Heather wants her to do it.

And they all expect me to be gone in ten minutes.

Pancakes after practice tomorrow, baby girl.

Now Dad's over by the front door, probably stepping into his running shoes. *Humming.* Like he's freaking Mary Poppins and not a twenty-five-year cop crashing at his eldest daughter's house while the love of his life battles cancer.

Today, he's happy.

And last night was part of the reason.

I'm part of the reason.

That word flashes in my brain again—*can't.*

I can't tell him I quit. But I also can't go to practice. I can't look those assholes in the eye and lift weights like nothing happened.

I know why it's a good idea to go. I know I shouldn't let them get to me. I know that football is the path to my softball dreams. I know I shouldn't let that opportunity slip away, no matter how tough it is.

But I can't.

Can I?

I run a cold tap, scrub the last of my mascara onto the

towel, and pull my hair back into a ponytail. Look myself in the eye.

I can't go back. Not to last night. Not to that night in May.

But I can go forward.

~

I'm five minutes early, but when I walk into the weight room, everyone is there, save the coaches. The boys are hanging on benches, looking as shitty and rundown as I do, and when they see me, they go dead silent, like someone stole all the sound in the room.

Grey. Jake. Nick. Topps. Brady.

Everyone.

I simply find a seat right up front by the mirror and take a sip from my water bottle.

Addie was right.

These boys look like they just metaphorically peed their pants.

The coaches march in, Kelly with them. Her eyes bug out of her head at the sight of me, eyeliner sweeping into a big round O. But other than that, nothing happens. If Coach Lee knows what went down in the parking lot last night, he's not showing his cards, nor commenting on the fact that the room is very much everyone versus Liv. Instead, Coach Lee accepts a clipboard from Napolitano and starts naming off stations without a preamble.

"Squats—offensive line."

"Deads—defensive line."

"Pull-ups—secondary."

"Bench—quarterbacks and running backs."

Great. Fantastic. Ideal.

I keep my game face on, of course. Coach doesn't need to know how I feel about these boys. He just needs me to lift some goddamn weights.

On bench, we're supposed to pair off—one to spot, one to lift, then switch. But I'm not about to pick any of these people, so I go to the bench on the end and start racking my weights. Napolitano has written the set scheme on the mirror—ten reps, four sets for this station.

Grey starts in my direction, in his calm, relaxed way, and my eyes threaten to roll right out of my head, but then Jake appears and shoulders between Grey and my bench. They exchange a few whispered words... and then Grey starts racking weights two benches away. Brady partners with him, moving to the head of the bench, ready to spot.

And Jake joins me.

His swollen eye looks only marginally better than the night before, but the bruising is now so deep it's as if he painted Windsor Prep purple over the entire socket. The gash above it is covered with a bandage, a slice of white drawn sharply over his brow, the only visible signs of his mild concussion.

Still, even with the mess of his face, he looks… reserved? Nervous? I'm not sure what to call it, because I've never seen such a look on his face. Jake chews his bottom lip and takes a deep breath, which weirds me out even more. How hard did that Tetherman kid clock him?

Then he speaks.

"I know you don't want to talk to me, or anyone. And I don't blame you, but I have something I need you to hear." I slam the weights onto the rack. He's standing on the other side of the bench from me; less than a foot separates us. His back is to Grey, who is side-eyeing us as he runs through some dynamic warm-ups none of us ever take the time to do. "I'm glad you're here."

He looks relieved when I manage a smile back. "Thanks. Spot me?"

Then I lie down and flip my ponytail over the end of the bench so it won't jam me in the skull as I complete my set. Jake takes his place behind the bar.

And I lift.

"Can I come in?"

I knew this would happen.

Danielle has been keeping a close eye on me ever since I came home crying Friday night. Now it's Sunday after dinner and she's finally taking her chance.

Danielle never passes up an opportunity to dig in. Make progress. Needle at a sore spot until it goes butter-smooth.

I punch out a breath. "Yeah."

The door taps against the frame and Danielle crosses to my bed, stacking three notebooks and a giant copy of *Modern Physics* to make room before squeezing in next to me on the comforter.

"What's going on?"

My cheeks immediately pinking—traitors—I blink at her. The silence begins to stretch into the nether reaches of awkward, and I know she's not planning to save me from myself. Where in the hell do I even begin? I take a deep breath. "I—"

"She found out her boyfriend-slash-fellow-quarterback was using her to get back at his ex-girlfriend." Ryan fills the doorway, arms crossed, game-day glare pulled protectively across his brows.

"*Ryan*," I whine before flinging all six hundred pages of *Modern Physics* at him—going for the gut instead of his head, because I'd rather not know another teenage boy with a concussion.

Ever the soccer player, he deflects the book with his hip and it flops on the hardwood with a massive thud. "What? It's been all over school." Ryan holds up his phone, lit up with unread texts and Instagram notifications—all probably warning him of (or maybe just recounting) my parking lot meltdown. "It's not like everyone doesn't know already."

Danielle groans. "Well, *I* didn't know."

My gut twists and I so wish I had told her everything from day one. It all pours out as I recap everything except for Grey's concussion, and with each word, I realize more and more what Monday is going to look like for me. I felt like a badass staring down those boys in the locker room on Saturday, but tomorrow? At school? It's going to be brutal. Half the student body saw our fight—my heart and Grey's betrayal out there in the open in the fading Friday night lights.

Tears are welling in my eyes by the time I finish, the weight of it all slamming down.

It doesn't even matter that I showed up on Saturday. School is still going to be hell. And softball won't happen—not if a pissed-off Grey gets in Coach Kitt's ear.

For a split second, the worst part of me comes up for air. Because I know something about Grey that his mother doesn't.

It would be so easy to tell her about his concussion. To tell Coach Lee. Coach Shanks. The doc might clear him, but they'd still have to run tests. Hold him out of practice and games. At least until he's cleared—long enough to make it that much harder for him to get the full ride he wants.

It's all plausible. With just a few simple words, I could do that to him. And with a few simple words, he could steer Coach Kitt back into my corner.

But I can't.

I blink away the temptation and come back into myself, this room, this conversation.

Danielle's eyes are pure fury. "Is this why you were so upset Friday night? Grey? Why didn't you say anything?"

"It doesn't matter."

Danielle wraps me into a hug and the tears drop. "Of course it does. This is some major shit, Liv. Major. You shouldn't have to go through this by yourself."

I shove away from her. "Are you kidding? I've been suffering *alone* since May! All of you just stood by and nodded along with Dad as he pulled me from Windsor Prep and lectured me about learning my lesson. And now you want me to spill my guts and hope you'll want to listen? Why is this situation any more major than last summer?"

The words fall out of my mouth and I immediately know I've made it even worse. If only self-sabotage were an Olympic sport. I'd have a gold medal.

Danielle's mouth drops open. "That's not true! I've been here for you, I've—"

"Bullshit!" I say. Temper unsatisfied and stoked by sudden regret, I stalk across the room, scoop up the physics book, and chuck it again. It whacks off the wall and onto my bed with a *thud*.

"Liv!" Danielle grips anew, clutching my shoulders, dark eyes on fire. "Calm down! This is ridiculous! I've always supported you—I offered to pay your tuition, and

Mom and Dad *wouldn't let me.* You think I didn't want you on my team? You're my baby sister—I will always want you with me!"

I'm too stunned to speak—Danielle offered to pay my tuition to Windsor Prep? And I didn't know?

"What's going on?" Dad and Mom appear in the hall-way, concerned looks on their faces.

Ryan and Danielle both look to me. My spine stiff-ens and the tip of my chin tilts up, pointing straight at my parents. I take in Dad's planted feet and crossed arms; Mom's woozy stance, exhaustion trying to override her attention. I wouldn't blame Heather if she's hiding in the kitchen.

"Dad, you were right." I take a breath. "I was used. Used big-time. All of it came out Friday."

Mom immediately goes in to rub my arm while Dad asks, "Do I need to talk to Coach Lee?"

I shake my head, but a tear rolls down my cheek.

Dad licks his lips, the rest of him still and stunned. He's never seen me like this. "We need to talk about what happened—why didn't you say anything?"

Ryan scoffs. Like, literally scoffs. "After state you guys treated her like absolute shit—sorry, Mom—and then like a baby when she tried to make a rational decision. Finally, you're happy and proud? Come on, guys. That's total bullshit."

Ryan takes a swift step toward me, all anger swept

away as he pulls me into his chest and needles that pointy chin into my shoulder. I just yelled at him and this is what he does. I don't deserve him or Danielle. At all.

Through blurred eyes, I watch as Dad sighs. "Liv, do you want to leave the team?"

The question rolls into the air so easily that it's almost difficult to recall how impossible it was to convince him that I could make my own decisions—that I wasn't a child. That it didn't take nearly my whole family ganging up on him to let me stand by my choice. I don't feel like I've won anything other than another scar.

I shake my head. No. I want to finish this out. The end justifies the means.

Dad does his stoic cop nod. "Then that is the right decision."

Then he comes in and pulls Ryan and me into his chest. Danielle and Mom pile on for a hug, too. And, finally, I let myself breathe.

I need some air after all that. So while everyone disappears to watch the Chiefs' Sunday night game, I slip out the front door. The night is warm but crisp, a breeze bringing up goose bumps, even though I don't feel cold. I deliberately point myself away from the turn for Grey's house, instead walking in the direction of Northland.

"Liv, wait!" Half a block away, I turn around and see Danielle shuffle-sprinting my way in her adidas slides. I pause for her, though she's still so fast, even in those shoes, that she hardly needs it. She's next to me in a flash, the smell of jasmine perfume and fabric softener filling my nose.

"I'd hate to be sixteen again," she says without preamble.

A lump automatically forms in my throat, the hot threat of tears in my eyes—again. I swallow it all down to answer her, voice thick. "Why? You were a goddess at sixteen." I know her accomplishments as well as my own. "Softball captain, MVP of a state champion squad, junior prom queen."

A wry smile crosses her lips. "I was also a closeted lesbian at an all-girls school. Trust me, that was seven layers of hell."

Oh, yes, there was that. Pain and suffering that we didn't know existed until Danielle's senior year of college. That shit I heard from Stacey? Danielle has weathered that crap her whole life. And when she came out, being a softball player didn't help—stereotype city. Thankfully she'd found Heather by then to help her through when our family couldn't.

"Life gets better when you care a whole lot less about what other people think." She leans in, though we're alone on the sidewalk, the Chiefs game mumbling out of open windows and onto the street. "And judging by what went down Friday, you're probably pretty concerned with what kids are thinking right now, huh?"

I nod, a sob rising hot and fast in my throat. We halt on the sidewalk and Danielle hauls me in, her biceps and forearm curling against my back, pressing me into the hug I need more than anything—air, water, softball. Danielle holds me tight, fingers weaving together to keep me in, sister-durable chain link.

"Remember, high school doesn't last forever."

Too bad it lasts long enough.

When our hug ebbs, I pull away but keep both hands gripping her forearms. "Is it true? Did you really offer to pay my tuition?"

"I did. Got the paperwork ready and everything—10 percent employee discount! But without guardianship, Mom and Dad had to sign." She smiles sadly. "They were just doing what they thought was best, but damn if it wasn't the worst."

"You've got that right."

Danielle flips the grip on our embrace, taking my hands into hers. "Liv, why'd you punch Stacey?"

My breath catches. I don't want to tell her. It's not her fault that Stacey said those things or that I reacted the way I did. I never want her to think it could be. But I can't lie to her. Not again.

"She was trying to get under my skin the whole game. Talking about Jake..." I swallow, tears pressing hard against my lash line. "But what really did it was that she said something shitty about you."

Her brows draw together. "Me?" Danielle squeezes my fingers.

I force myself to meet her eyes. I know she's heard it all before, but I don't want her to hear anything else. I force the words out anyway. "She—she said something really homophobic and I couldn't let it go."

My sister draws in a deep breath. The reality of what happened and what I'm not saying flits across her face in the dying light in some sort of mixture of horror, frustration, and maybe a little pride, until her jaw is set and her eyes shine. The strength of her grip never lessens. My sister is a rock, brave and strong, and I love her more than anything.

"Liv, while I'm proud of you for standing up for me, and I realize you were trying to protect my feelings by not telling me about this, that wasn't the way to handle it." I nod, a tear finally rolling down my face. Because I know. Oh, I know. Danielle's thumb swipes at the tear. "Baby girl, you can't smack sense into a person like that. You need to use your words to tell them they're wrong, hope those words sink in, and if they don't, let karma do the rest."

I try and fail to smile at her, another tear snaking down, running into my mouth. "Am I an asshole if I hope karma's a total bitch to her?"

Danielle pulls me in close again. "No."

33

WALKING INTO SCHOOL MONDAY FEELS ALL WRONG.
Heavy. Exposed.

It is not an act I do alone.

Oh, I'm physically by myself. Ryan and Jesse took off like they always do—the girls they once chased now waiting for them next to the flagpole, books tucked coyly against their chests.

And so, I face down every set of eyes.

They watch me like I can't watch back. Like a tiger in a cage—unable to strike, no matter who's pressed against the glass with a steak in hand.

It's exactly what I pictured last night. I'm the villain. I'm the new girl who got in a public shouting match with a popular senior in front of half the school.

I'm the best gossip in town.

Head up, armor on, I push through. Through the junior-senior parking lot and over the orange paw prints. Through the stutter in my heart as I skip past the spot where Grey always waited—half smile at the ready, khakis pressed and perfect.

He's not there now, and both disappointment and relief catch at the base of my throat.

The hallway is full of more eyes. Faces I don't recognize but ones that know every inch of me. Staring without filter. Pity seeping into whispers.

I want to punch their pity in the face.

I enter Spanish and here, too, my presence is dissected by every student in the room—any remaining conversation becoming a distant remnant, lost to a new, shiny, O-Rod-shaped object.

I keep it neutral, keep it cool—no game-day scowling here. I blink and another set of eyes has joined the crowd: the pair belonging to Coach Kitt.

I expect her loyalty to her son to lay bare in her tawny features. Instead, there's the hint of a smile.

"Miss Rodinsky," she says. "Please stop by my office after the last bell."

There's no malice to the request. Nothing to indicate that I'm in trouble—her lips remain upturned, eyes clear. If anything, it's the warmest total expression she's ever aimed in my general vicinity. Still, my heart sinks and my blood pressure rises, my lungs suddenly sapped of air.

She must know what happened. That I accused her son of using me. And then softball will be over—no junior year for the scouts to see. Nothing. Nada.

Still, because my sister taught me well, I nod like I do any time I'm asked to do the impossible.

In a way, this day has been exactly like I expected my first day at Northland to be.

Quiet, awkward, cold.

Jake came late with a doctor's note and downturned posture, saying nothing to me—or anyone—during Spanish. Rather, he spent the entire class running a hand through his fresh buzz, head still ringing from that hit, his eye looking even worse than Saturday.

If Coach Kitt knew about the parking lot, she didn't show it. She just taught, like she wasn't Grey's mother. Like she wasn't the softball coach. Like she didn't call my butt to her office. Like she wasn't anything to me at all other than a vessel for the preterit of *ser*.

Lunch happened not in the bathroom of my summer daydreams but with my back pressed to a locker outside of Coach Lee's classroom. Not a single teacher who passed me said a word as I plowed through my turkey sandwich and mealy Red Delicious, though I'm sure eating in the hallway isn't technically allowed.

When the bell rings, I head to my seat for calc and wait.

Topps and Lily Jane appear first. As they approach, Topps looks away, cheeks blazing atop his man-beard. Coward. Lily Jane has far more balls than that. She doesn't just make eye contact, she *smiles* at me.

And when Topps drops into his chair, Lily Jane not only keeps upright but takes a few more steps until she's standing right in front of my desk, her impish face still split in two by a grin so fierce I can smell the strawberry soda she shared with Topps.

Five little fingers pat the meat of my forearm and squeeze as she leans down, gold tiger paw pendant swinging in front of my nose. Her voice is low and fast like she's about to be caught. And maybe she is.

"You're my hero, Liv. A goddamn hero. You were right to call those boys on their shit. All of them owe you an apology, even my Tobias."

"Um, thank you?" I say, blinking.

"Just wanted to make sure you knew that." She winks, but somehow it looks different from the one in Grey's arsenal. "And I would've given you a heads-up about Grey and Stacey that first day at lunch, but I thought you knew—I really did." With a hummingbird wave, she switches topics, clearly flustered at unintentionally keeping me in the dark. "Anyway. You're a badass. A hero-badass warrior princess."

One more squeeze of my forearm and she's gone.

And suddenly Grey is in her place.

There's not time to arrange my face or to analyze Lily Jane's suggestion that maybe not everyone—or just her, I suppose—thinks I'm a total loser.

Dark circles hug Grey's lower lashes and he looks exhausted for the first time since I met him. His eyes meet mine, their usual light snuffed out.

Still, he nods at me and settles into his desk, broad shoulders hunching in his polo, boat shoes crossed at the ankles. But there's a swooshy curve to his spine—as if every muscle in his body is fighting not to turn and sit sideways toward me the way he has every other day so that he can see both me and Coach Lee in the same sweep.

I realize that all the eyes are back on us, only Topps and Jake making an effort not to watch us fail to interact. Kelly, Lily Jane, and the others either blatantly stare or steal glances at us out of the sides of their eyes.

I wonder if it's been this way all day for Grey, too. Like you're literally the only thing on TV and there's nothing else for anyone to do but watch.

"I know we all love a good Shakespearean drama," Coach Lee's voice drawls out, and it's clearer than it was Saturday morning that he knows exactly what happened

Friday night. "But I'd appreciate it if you folks would at least *act* like you're paying attention to me right now."

Twenty heads snap toward the front.

Out of the spotlight, Grey's shoulders soften, and my earlier question is answered.

It *has* been this way all day for him, too.

Good.

34

I MAKE IT THROUGH CALC. I MAKE IT THROUGH THE
day.

Now, just two-hundred-plus more days until Grey's
and Jake's graduation and the reprieve of summer break.
Gotta survive and advance. It's like state, but life.

But first: Coach Kitt.

Her door is wide open, NPR whispering into the hallway. There's also the shuffle of papers and the fizzy pop
of a newly opened La Croix. In a word: comfortable. She's
comfortable even though she's about to see me.

Me—Hurricane Liv. Bringing the drama on one-
hundred-mile-per-hour winds to her team, then to her
school, then to her son.

Heart quickening, I tell myself she wants me here. She

invited me—with a smile. Last time, I was the one to invite myself in. It'll be different this time. Even if I have exactly zero defense for my attitude Friday night that wouldn't inadvertently throw her son under the bus.

"Coach?" The word feels thick and strange on my tongue, as if I haven't used it every day of my life.

Her eyes flash up and again, she smiles. "There you are—come in. I won't keep you long."

I sink into the chair opposite Coach Kitt. Her smile has vanished, something friendly but serious in its place.

"I know you have places to be, but I wanted to make sure you understand how much I appreciate the work you did Friday night in helping Kelly control her emotions."

WHUT.

It's only by the grace of Danielle's training that I manage to keep my features smooth.

"I know you might have thought about letting Kelly learn a lesson by allowing her to rush into that fight, where she might have gotten hurt, but you showed great maturity in making sure she didn't."

I suppose I did. But shock still zings up my spine that Coach Kitt noticed it. I figured she'd have been in the stands searching for Grey during the whole brawl.

"What you did showed incredible dedication to the Northland softball team," she continues. "And at the personal expense of the opportunity to defend someone important to you."

Grey. Jake. The team.

I watch Kitt's face for any sign of trepidation about the way I feel—how I *felt*—for her son, or for a hint that she'll bring up the yelling match in the parking lot. But there's none—she's already moved on.

"And though you aren't on the team yet, I really appreciated your thoughtfulness in the midst of the chaos."

Yet. She said yet. There's hope in that word.

I decide to stick with the simple truth. "I just did what I thought was right."

A single brisk nod from her and I know it's time to move on. "Yes, you did. And I wanted to let you know your actions didn't go unnoticed."

"Thanks, Coach."

The word feels a hundred times easier than when I entered her office. As I rise, she smiles again. I'm glad to see it, but it still feels weird to have that thing aimed at me.

So weird, in fact, that I feel the truth start to spill out onto my tongue. The truth about Grey's concussion. That he should see a doctor to be cleared. Just in case.

"Coach—" I start. But then the words die in my throat.

It's *his* future.

It's *his* decision.

It's *his* body.

Not mine.

He wants to play. So I just need to be good enough that he doesn't hit the field until I'm sure he's healed. And I do care about his safety, even if he's not exactly my favorite person right now.

Coach Kitt is looking at me and so I finish the thought with another truth.

"Grey's going to need to get another ride home after practice—I can't this week."

I run my prepractice laps with the other quarterbacks in complete silence—Grey in my periphery, setting the pace. His eyes keep flashing my direction, lashes shading them in a way that he thinks will keep me from noticing.

He wants to talk to me.

Maybe he wants to ask about the obvious hitch in my stride—stupid bruised knee. But mostly he wants to know if I'm going to rat on him. I purposely take a knee next to him after laps, just like old times. Grey's lips drop open to say something, but I hold up a hand to stop him. Then I lean in and whisper an inch from his ear.

"I was just alone with your mother and I didn't say a single thing about you-know-what. I'm not going to say anything to the coaches either, so you can stop looking at me like I'm radioactive." Then I turn away and refuse to look at him for the entirety of Coach's prepractice speech.

Grey gets the hint because we practice our routes in silence, Brady following our lead. After an hour, the receivers vanish and Coach Shanks pulls us over to one end zone, something in the lines of his face. He wasn't there for our argument Friday night but it's clear he's noticed something's off between us—or maybe he knows the whole story. Whatever. Raised as we were, Grey and I are both members of the "do the work" school of thought, so we've been professional for the last hour. But *professional* isn't much of a cover when we were basically glued at the hip for the past few weeks. Now Topps could easily fire off jumping jacks between us.

Coach reads our faces one final time—we're sweaty as hell, even with the threat of autumn creeping into the air. Humidity never really dies in Kansas. "Time for some three bar."

I have no idea what that is, but I know not to ask, either. Following Grey's lead, I hover around the ten-yard line and remove my helmet.

"Want to start us off with round one, Worthington?"

Grey shifts on his feet. "What are the stakes?"

"Frozen Snickers of Power to the last man or woman standing."

If there's chocolate involved, I am suddenly even more motivated to kick ass. These curves don't shape themselves.

Grey's lips pull up in his patented half smile—probably the first time I've seen it since Friday. And I wonder if this is what Coach thinks we need—to bond with a little friendly competition, the start not on the line. "Best out of three?"

Shanks nods and places three balls in the dead center of the five-yard line. "Right, left, center."

Grey takes a step back and drills the first ball straight into the right goalpost. In a single bend and step, he's scooped up the second ball and drilled it into the left post. Another step and scoop and he spirals the final ball into the exact middle of the lower bar that makes up the U shape of the upright.

I watch as Brady resets the balls and then fires in the same right, left, center pattern—missing the center target despite it being literally right in front of his face. His jaw tenses and he stomps heavily into the turf like a little kid.

I mean, I'm not surprised, but sheesh.

Grey shifts his eyes my way. I raise an eyebrow.

You're on, Worthington.

I collect the balls, having to jog past the field line to pick up Brady's miss. As I'm coming back, I catch Coach Lee watching from the opposite end of the field.

Fire right. Hit.

Fire left. Hit.

Fire center. Hit—directly where the post meets the bottom of the U, the dead center.

Grey shifts his weight and Brady's jaw tenses yet again. "Round one goes to Worthington and Rodinsky."

The angles of Grey's face go serious as he preps at the line. Within ten seconds, he's done—*bam, bam, bam*—perfection. Brady matches him and then it's my turn.

Right, left, center. Wham, bam, thank you, ma'am.

"Round two, draw. Worthington and Rodinsky still in the lead."

Grey lines up, all business. He wants more than the Snickers. He wants the start after our bye week. He knows Coach Lee is watching, too.

Predictably, he doesn't miss.

Brady stomps into the sod while lining up the balls for his turn, now sure there's absolutely no way he's getting a frosty postpractice treat unless he's paying for it himself. That knowledge, or maybe exhaustion, settles in because he misses two of the three bars, both end throws going wide before he carefully lines up for a parting shot.

Royally pissed off at himself, he takes his helmet and chucks it downfield.

Which Coach Shanks does not appreciate.

"Hey, now." Shanks's voice goes grumbly hard. "Go cool off, Mason. Ten laps. Now."

Brady scoops up his helmet and huffs off.

"Miss Rodinsky," Coach says by way of invitation.

I swallow and set up the balls, feeling more eyes on us. A quick glance confirms it—Jake and the other running backs are watching to my right. Kelly's standing next to Coach Lee.

Grey and I are a sideshow. Whatever. I can still do my job.

I swallow. Take a breath.

Right. Left. Center.

Hit. Hit. Hit.

Coach Shanks nods. "Good thing I stocked up on Snickers."

After our postpractice laps, Grey and I silently follow Shanks into his office, leaving Brady to sulk on his own.

Shanks's office is right next to Coach Lee's, and from the looks of it, he shares it with Napolitano. There are two desks shoved clown-car-style into an office built for one, a minifridge wedged into the minimal breathing room between.

Coach dumps his clipboard on the desk nearest the door, barely missing a half-dozen picture frames, all containing photos of two adorable little girls who are definitely in love with their dad.

The full photo-collage effect is as telling as Napolitano's completely bare desk. And when I say bare, I mean *spotless*. Coach Napolitano is clearly the kind of person who irons his jeans. Which is interesting, given he has the messy task of organizing a defensive effort.

Knees cracking, Shanks crouches down and pulls two Snickers ice-cream bars from the minifridge's freezer. He holds one in each hand. "I don't know what's going on with you two, but this better sweeten you both up."

We can't just take the chocolate in silence, so both of us say, nearly at the same time, "Thanks, Coach."

Shanks's eyes crinkle under his visor like he's trying to read the weight between us but can't quite get there. Finally, he relents and hands over the Snickers.

Grey turns and I start to follow, but Shanks calls me back. "O-Rod, a minute."

I halt and Shanks pulls his door shut.

"Liv, I don't know what happened with you and the boys on Friday, but I want to make sure you and I are clear on a few things." His dad voice is in full force. "It's imperative you understand this, especially in your current situation." He pauses and draws in a deep breath. "Teenage boys say really stupid shit to teenage girls."

I want to laugh, but his face is drawn up, tight and serious. So I don't. Okay, I still snort a little. Teachers don't cuss. We all know that. Just like they don't go to the bathroom or have bad handwriting. My mom *was* a teacher, my sister *is* a teacher, and I still believe that.

He doesn't register my laugh, just looks at me as serious as before. "I know this because I was one once. And I work with them every day. So I know that the stupid shit they say hasn't changed much in twenty years." Shanks tugs at his visor. "I'm going to tell you what I tell my daughters."

I can't help it, my eyes skip to the heart-shaped faces in the frames on his desk—kids who I hope, deep down, would like the fact that I'm playing for their dad.

"Boys say stupid things to girls because girls scare the crap out of them. The more they think about a girl, the faster their IQ numbers plummet. And you, my friend, are terrifying."

Thank God he's smiling as he says this.

"First of all, you're a girl with a pass to a sacred boyhood space—that's horror show material right off the bat. And then you come along playing almost as well as them with zero background. You work your tail off alongside them without a single complaint, and when you take off your helmet, they're reminded again and again that you are who you are."

This time I laugh for real but it's only because otherwise I might cry. Coach smiles.

"So whatever they said—remember that you're better than it. And I'll be sure to remind them they're better than whatever they said, too. And if any of them is idiotic enough not to listen to either of us, you tell me. It's not snitching—I need to know if they're up to something I won't tolerate. Understood?"

I suck in a breath, wincing as it shudders. Tears ping in my eyes, but I squint them off like the freaking pro I am. "You got it, Coach."

35

THE BYE WEEK ISN'T JUST A BREAK FROM HAVING A game, it's a break from our regular routine in general. We get out half an hour early on Monday night, and Tuesday night is more of the same, which means one thing: I can actually make it to one of Addie's volleyball games.

It's at Windsor Prep, but I love my Addie and damn if I won't be there.

I clean up as quickly as possible in the Northland locker room, baby-wiping the sweat from my body and spraying dry shampoo into my hair before brushing it into a fresh ponytail—clean enough for a life without Grey.

My heart is pounding as I park Helena in her old spot in

the student lot. Walk my old route to the gym. Open the Eagle-crested doors.

Sound pours out, the gym alive with the screechy euphoria of a volleyball game in full swing. I slip onto the nearest bench, finding a spot by the door and up a few rows—the place is packed with students, alumni, donors, and fans in Windsor Prep purple. There are a few scattered flecks of Wyandotte Rural powder blue dotting the pine, but most of it is swallowed by regal grape.

Not shockingly, Addie's dominating on the court—it's a fraction of a second after I sit before an Adeline McAndry kill crashes to the boards, icing the second set.

The bleachers erupt and so do I, hopping to my feet and screaming, enough to catch Addie's eye. My white shirt probably didn't hurt. Turning with her whole body, she waves, long fingers blurring in front of her mile-wide smile.

It's weird, but in that instant, my heart slows, my nerves fade, and my belly swells with the warmth of familiarity. I'm suddenly swept into the rhythm of all the home matches I attended last year. Huddling with the softball girls, passing around contraband Diet Coke (no food or drink in the gym!) and making up silly cheering chants in the front row.

I squint into the stands across the way and see that, yes, Christy, Mary Katherine, and Ava are there, tucked behind the Eagles bench, knees bouncing in matching pairs of running capris, probably as baby-wipe-clean as me after suffering through whatever "optional" (hardy har har) off-season workout Danielle programmed for today.

The three of them cheer as the Eagles line up for a Bobcats serve, and I wonder if they'll notice me, too, in my fluorescent white. I don't know if I should say hi or if we're even still cool after a few months apart and a rocky end to the season.

After the punch heard round the world, I basically ghosted on everyone who wasn't Addie or on my summer travel team. It was all just too royally embarrassing.

My heart thuds out a small ribbon of hope. Tiny enough that I wonder when I became so freaking timid. It's not in my DNA, yet it's been hanging around—

"Hey."

My head whips around at the familiar voice. Light blue eyes and ginger hair greet me, the scent of boy cologne so strong that I can't believe I didn't smell him before I saw him.

Thanks for the warning, nose.

Nick Cleary, in the flesh. Hair still wet, protein bar wrapper peeking out of his letter jacket's pocket. Here for Addie, straight from practice. Just like me—but showered.

I can't tell if I should melt from the cute (he came for

her!) or beat myself up for not realizing this would be a possibility.

"Hey," I parrot back, because other words won't come.

"How's our girl doing?"

"She's killin' it."

He grins and we both turn our attention to the court. I'm relieved after a minute when he pulls out his phone, aiming it toward the net, recording his girlfriend totally crushing it.

And she is.

Bump. Spike. Block. Kill.

She does it all with a graceful efficiency, pin-straight and wiry but panther-smooth. It's as beautiful as it is mesmerizing.

Nick and I don't speak during the final set of the sweep, watching in dull silence when we're not screaming into the noise of a Windsor Prep crowd.

And when it's over and the players are shaking hands, I'm surprised that Nick is the one who breaks our mutual hush. Even more so when I realize it's an invitation.

"I usually meet her on the floor after they leave the locker room."

Usually. He's done this before. Because of course he has. But I'm her best friend and this is the first match I've seen all season. Ugh.

We wait a few minutes, and as the locker room door

swings open, none of the players look twice at Nick, standing there, in full Northland gear. Nothing worth gawking about. Me, on the other hand... I stick out like the ghost of games past.

"OMG! Liv Rodinsky! Is that you?"

It's unclear which Eagle squeals it first, but they're on me in a flash—like they didn't just sprint across a gym for an hour. Whatever the reason for the surge, a dozen girls surround me, game-day glitter in their hair.

"Uh, hi." Their collective reaction is infectious, and I'm suddenly grinning.

"We miss you, Hot Roddy!" says Genevieve Suter, adding in deliberate *vroom* sounds that accompany the sometimes-nickname I inherited from Danielle.

"How's Northland?"

"We heard you're playing football!"

"Omigod, aren't the guys there ON FIRE? HI, NICK." Then, quieter yet somehow just as loud, "Do you have one for me?"

I laugh, not sure whom to answer first. So I answer them all. "I miss you guys, too! It's okay. I am. They are, but not enough to ruin my A average." (Insert hair flip.) I lean in to Barbie Villanueva, hopeful whisper-shouter. "And no, but I can be on the lookout."

Barbie clutches my wrist, eyes wide and lined in Eagles purple. "Good. I want a blond."

Wonder how good Brady's footwork would be with Adriana Lima's body double hustling after him. "I'll see what I can do."

"How about a star third baseman, can you headhunt one of those?"

It's said with a joking lilt, but a sour note halts the chatter, all of us staring, openmouthed, at the speaker: star catcher Christy Morris, who will probably be senior captain this year. Off to the side, leading the capri-tight gang of my former teammates.

Immediately, Addie appears. "With a mouth like that, you won't make captain, Morris. Not if I have anything to do with it."

Christy's bravado sinks, though her chin stays high. The other softball girls surround her, inspecting the gym floor, not willing to cross Addie.

"They need to clean the gym. Come on, Eagles," Coach Stevie shouts from crosscourt, already nearly to the gym doors, shoving a massive sack of volleyballs into the equipment closet. I'm grateful for the save.

The softball girls run out after her. The volleyball team lingers, the girls saying goodbye to me in pairs and triplets, slapping fives and stealing hugs in a barrage of smiles that warms me back up after that WTF sideswipe from Christy & Co.

I'm dying to ask Addie if that's how it's been all year at school, this stark divide between the softball team and the others. My absence felt by both types in completely different ways.

But for *far* too long—maybe since May—it's been all about me.

I pull Addie in for a bear hug as soon as the others leave, smooshing our faces together as much as they'll go with the four inches she has on me. She's freshly clean and smells 100 percent better than me. "You were amazing, McAndry! Freaking bloodbath."

Addie's laugh is loud and unforgiving, just like her performance. She shrugs. "They don't call them kills for nothing, O-Rod."

We giggle as Nick opens the door into the cooling night. "I wouldn't piss her off, Nick," I tell him. "Not if you value your life."

"He wouldn't," Addie says, beaming at him as we step outside. "Now I just have to teach him how to avoid pissing off my mama."

Oh. My. God. I don't know of a single boy who has made it far enough in Addie's life to meet Mrs. McAndry. Or Mr. McAndry, too, of course, but Trey McAndry has always deferred to his wife on literally everything. I stare wide-eyed at Nick. "When's your trial date, Cleary?"

He just smiles mildly, unafraid. "Saturday. But I've got this."

Addie plants one on his cheek. "Keep up that confidence, babe."

The cute is overwhelming and I know they need to say their goodbyes and it's probably best if it's not in front of me. I glide in for another hug.

"Great game, girl. See ya."

I leave them with a wave and step into the dark, the friendliest interaction I've had in days fading into the night.

36

THE POST-ADDIE SMILE FADES THE SECOND I GET A view of my car.

Grey's pushed up against Helena the Honda, hands stuffed in the pockets of his jeans, the cut of his jaw rivaling Captain America's in the security lighting. How does he always perfectly catch the light? *How?*

Behind him, a pickup lingers. It's either a forty-year-old man or Topps at the wheel, rolling up the driver's side window, cheeks red enough to give the International Space Station pause.

Memories of Nick messing with his phone at the match ping around in my brain—a whole conversation happening a foot away, leading to this moment. All around us engines rev and headlights flicker—no one at Windsor Prep is stopping to watch.

"Liv, I'm sorry."

His apology hangs in the almost-autumn air, and with those words I'm back in another parking lot, red-faced and yelling. I'm in Shanks's office, weathering fatherly advice. I'm back staring at Coach Kitt, Grey's secret welling inside me as I stuff it back down. Because even though he used me, I can't deny the flutter in my heart at seeing him standing here, hoping I'll hear him.

Grey's face is clear and honest. I believe him. He *is* sorry.

But everything still stings so badly that I want to twist the knob on his own pain and turn it up to eleven, up to where I've been at for days. I can feel my vocal cords tightening, tears pushing to the surface. "You lied about Stacey. You lied about what happened to you last summer. Why should I believe you when you say you're sorry?"

"I'm telling the truth."

"Prove it." My skin is damp against the night and though it's still warm, I start to shiver as the first tears fall. Still, I don't blink. "Before I walked out of that locker room, did you kiss Stacey?"

I tense, expecting him to snag my wrists, to yank me into his body to convince me he didn't. To try to dominate—he's a football player after all.

But what I forget is that he's also Grey.

That he's more akin to the friendly nudges of his shoulder than the sheer ferocity of the sport that made him, the sport that brought us together.

So instead, despite Topps totally watching from the shadows, despite the past week, despite the glare I'm giving him, he sweeps my face into his hands. Football-rough fingers spill across my cheeks and into my hair, the smooth sides of my ponytail bunching under his touch.

Gentle, strong, wanting—those hands make me match his gaze. Not because he's forcing me, but because there's so much tenderness pulsing through his skin that it is literally stunning.

He doesn't break eye contact. "No. I didn't kiss her." My heart lurches but I haul it back. That's not enough, and Grey seems to know it. "She broke up with me so she wouldn't be tied down in college. I hadn't even talked to her since that night over the summer. And then she hopped on me before I even saw her coming."

I don't move, my mind caught on that first day at the lunch table, when he echoed what I had said about her.

I'm fine with giving her the Voldemort treatment.

Me too.

"Why was she even here?" I ask.

"The softball team threw a surprise birthday party for Mom. I knew she'd be here for the weekend, just not that she'd be at our game."

Yet another reminder that I'm not part of that group—a club Stacey would always be a part of.

"These last few days have been hell," Grey says, eyes heavy with something that looks like remorse. "Not because of the stares in class or the shit at practice. It's been hell because I hurt you. I didn't mean to, but I did."

I cough out a sad laugh. "You definitely did. You could've told me about Stacey that very first day. Even if you didn't plan on using me as a way to get back at her, even if your motivations really were true, keeping something like that a secret still wasn't okay."

A prickly mix of gratification and shame drops in my stomach as he winces. But then he surprises me—God, I should've showered—letting his thumbs graze my temples. If anything, they're even more gentle. "How could I tell you? How could I introduce myself as this awesome starting quarterback and then tell you about my C team life—dumped, reckless, broken? I was already falling for you before I even got up the courage to talk to you."

I raise a brow. "You can tell me now."

Grey punches out a breath and gestures to the curb. "Sit down, this might take a while."

"I've got all night if it's actually the truth." But I can't keep from smiling.

He sinks to the concrete first, immediately and unsurprisingly manspreading, his bent knees frogging out. I find a square of curb out of their vicinity, extending my legs out front, crossing them tight, even though all they want to do is curve into him, to brush against the soft wash of his jeans, feel the warmth of his skin through the fabric.

"First things first," he says. "I dated Stacey because I'd

watched enough movies to know that's just what starting quarterbacks did—they date the head cheerleader.
No-brainer. Plus, she was a year older and wanted to go
out with me. Who says no to *that*?" He laughs at himself.
"I liked her well enough, but it wasn't like we had some
fantastic love story."

The breeze kicks up for a brief second, a few leaves
tumbling past.

"I should've told you that first day. If I'd been thinking
straight I would've seen the big picture, but honestly, I'd
never seen you up close before and I was sort of blindsided
by your face." A slow smile creeps across his lips. "Getting
socked in both the head and the heart clearly wasn't helpful for making good decisions."

His grin tells me *I'm* the heart part of the equation, not
Stacey dumping him at a party. Stupid butterflies rise from
the ashes lining my stomach once again.

Grey's fingers graze my elbow, not daring to do much
more. They're as soft as they were on my face, as gentle as the
next words are firm. "For the record, I don't regret recruiting
you, even if the whole thing turned out to be a disaster."

"A very public disaster."

"That's my fault. I should've let you go after the game. I
just—I couldn't let you walk away. Not like that." His eyes
reset and he sighs. "And it wasn't because I was worried
you'd rat me out for the concussion. I was worried I'd lose
you." His knee bops mine. "I wouldn't trade the time I've

had with you for anything, even if I wish it had turned out differently." A long finger circles slowly in the air. "Which brings me back around to the beginning." Half smile, no wink. "I'm sorry. I miss you. I made a mistake, a huge one."

His sweet face—as open as I've ever seen it—looms inches from mine. Close enough to kiss. But my vision is clouded by yet another replay of my fist connecting with Stacey's nose, my knuckles bruising with her cartilage.

I know all about mistakes.

We're quiet for a second, the clock approaching ten on a school night. I tap my watch. "Curfew's earlier on weeknights."

Weight lifted, a shade of the boy I met on the track that day comes clear, and his shoulder nudges mine. Briefly—we touch and then we don't. His next sentence is the same one he said when he appeared, but now there's so much more to it, the layers peeled back. Both our hearts exposed.

We're not back together but we're definitely in this together.

"Liv, I'm sorry."

I squeeze my eyes shut and force myself away from him, away from his body heat that calls to me, away from how easy it would be to curl into his chest in the shadows. I stand and pull out my keys.

"I know."

31

THE NEXT DAY, GREY AND I ORBIT EACH OTHER A LITTLE closer than we have in the past few days but still barely exchange a word. Which is fine. I'm not ready for more. Not yet. So when the end of Wednesday practice rolls around, I light out of the locker room as fast as possible yet again, this time with the immediate goal of proving my brother wrong.

Because I am finally going to make the *entirety* of a Northland varsity soccer game.

Even better: The soccer game is at home, just steps from the locker room. I manage to get there before it starts, but the soccer field is already freaking packed, the Northland orange outnumbering the South County yellow two to one. Bodies spill over into the grass on either side of both sets of bleachers, and it seems to take days for my eyes to finally settle on two pairs of waving arms. Danielle and Mom, holding spots three rows up.

I climb up to them, left knee protesting—the dull ache there as persistent as the one in my chest every time my mind skips to Grey. But when I reach them, all thoughts of Grey and my knee are driven from my mind.

Mom reaches over Danielle and squeezes my hand, her blue eyes on fire, chemo-downy hair haloing her cheekbones. "We think Ryan's going to start!"

At her thunder-whisper, Danielle rolls her eyes and stabs at a program I didn't see when I came in the gate. "Mom, Ry's already listed as a starter. It's not like the coach is going to change his mind."

"He might!" she clucks, and whacks Danielle on the thigh. "Don't ruin my moment."

Danielle smirks, shoots to her feet, cups her hands around her mouth, and aims at Ryan's back. "Hey, number eight! Lookin' good, STARTER!"

Ryan turns—as does half his team—and toasts us with blue Gatorade as Mom yanks Danielle butt-first back onto the bleachers. "You would have killed me if I did that to either one of you."

"She has a point, Dani." One of my favorite things about my family is that they aren't *completely* embarrassing spectators.

"Eh, he's the baby. He likes the attention."

"He would also tackle you for calling him a baby," I point out.

"Birth order, not a slight." Danielle waves me off and Mom chuckles, leaning back in her seat to avoid the impending cross fire.

"Says our *older* sister."

"With age comes its privileges."

"Like wrinkles?" Yeah, I do this all the time. I'm a total jerk.

"My skin is still flawless thanks to the fabulous genes of Ellen Rodinsky," Danielle says, rubbing Mom's shoulder. "And the fact that I'm only twenty-five."

The speakers crackle and we're asked to stand for the national anthem. The recording is mechanical and familiar, the pep band off doing something more important.

As the final strains of the song die out, the starters get to their feet, Ryan among them.

They don't announce the players. They don't say his name or number. But he's there, nervous legs bouncing in midfield as they line up for the draw, orange streaks chalked through his hair.

Number eight, Ryan Rodinsky, varsity starter as a freshman.

And I'm here to see it.

For the first time in weeks, I don't feel like a selfish sea monster, clouding the world with her own drama-spiked ink. I feel like a good friend, a good sister.

I feel like me.

We have weights and drills on Thursday, and by the end of it, I can't ignore my knee. The twinge has now revealed itself as an honest-to-God bruise—Windsor Prep purple—the tendons underneath puffy and inflamed.

It's nagged me all week, but I've managed to push through. I know exactly how to appear fine—the last thing you want is an opponent to know exactly where to take you out. I'm not paranoid, I'm experienced.

I last limped in a game when I was twelve. An ankle sprain had me stutter-stepping from third to home after Addie smashed a triple, and the next inning some asshole girl hooked her cleat right into my ankle when tagging third. Down I went, more injured than I was before.

So, yeah, I'm not about to let anyone know how much this hurts.

But I have to admit, after suffering through Napolitano's decision to superset front squats with walking lunges, it is literally all I can do not to fess up to the pain. Almost a full week of trying to hide it has only made it worse.

Still, I finish my weights—in capris, mind you, so that no one can see. I run through routes. I do my laps.

When I'm done, all I can think of is rest, but I'm not about to go home and sneak an ice pack out of the kitchen.

Because I know someone will notice, even if I hide down on the basement couch.

Someone will find me.

Someone will freak out.

So, instead, I wait until no one is looking and dump two handfuls of ice from the Gatorade jugs into my helmet and hightail it to the locker room. Yes, I've done this before. Softball is a game of many bruises.

Instead of showering, I swap my swampy clothes for fresh ones and then sit my butt on the locker room bench with wads of ice stuffed inside my gross jersey for a makeshift cold compress.

It feels so good that I'm almost too distracted to hear the locker room door swing open. Before I can get my stiff ass out of my current position, there's a swing of red ponytail in my periphery and I know I'm caught.

Kelly Cleary.

Shit.

"This isn't what it looks like," I say, sounding a lot like Grey the night I caught him with Stacey.

Kelly's cat eyes skip from my face to my knee and back again.

I expect a slight little smile from her. Something *mean girl* that is going to be trouble later. But, instead, all I get is a shrug. "You look like a football player."

Fishy. That smells fishy. "I'm totally fine. Just sore," I say. Which is true. I've just been sore for more than a week, and progressively more sore as that week went on. NBD.

Then, to my utter shock, Kelly sits down on the bench. She's chewing on her lip, heavily mascaraed eyes downcast and aimed at my iced knee.

"I'm jealous."

I gape at her. Whatever words I expected out of her mouth, those weren't them.

She's picking at her nails, painted in a gel black that's seen better days. "I'm jealous. Of how you've been able to join the team like it's nothing. How the guys accepted you. How...how Jake is with you." Her eyes flash up. "And I didn't know how to deal with it. I thought I had to be mean. And...that was immature."

I cannot believe this.

She stops biting her lip and frowns. "I let Stacey influence my opinion of you, and I should've learned from the boys and just made an opinion for myself."

Holy shit.

"I was the one who told Stacey you joined the team, about you and Grey, about everything."

Oh.

Stacey knew I'd meet Grey outside the locker room because Kelly had told her that's where I'd be. She knew she'd get a reaction out of me that would punish both Grey and myself.

Kelly lifts her eyes to mine. They really are the clearest of blues, shallow water on a hot day. "She wasn't my friend. Not really. The second she found out that Jake and I were going to homecoming together, she turned on me. In front of the team—all of our friends. In front of Coach Kitt on her birthday." She actually looks like she might cry. Kelly squeezes her eyes shut and there is wetness there, lapping at her eyeliner. I reach out and touch her shoulder. She doesn't move away. "It was something I should've seen coming."

I want to ask what happened, but I'm sure that will make it worse. And, God, she's already crying.

"If Stacey can't have someone, no one can." Her voice grows smaller. "Not even me."

"Kelly, that's shitty. I'm sorry."

She releases a shuttered sigh and just nods at me, spent. My hand on her shoulder suddenly doesn't feel right. "Can I hug you?" I ask, and I'm sort of surprised when Kelly consents. I wrap my arms around her and we stay like that for a solid minute. When we part, Kelly rubs her eyes, her thick liner mostly surviving.

She stands and what she says next absolutely knocks the wind out of me.

"I know what happened that day, you know. Walking

back from the mound. I heard exactly what she said that made you punch her. At the time, I thought maybe I didn't hear it right. That she said something else. But . . . that's the kind of person she is."

Then Kelly leaves me alone with my ice and disbelief.

38

FRIDAY NIGHT WITHOUT A FOOTBALL GAME FEELS weird. Really weird. Practice is short and sweet (my knee is *thrilled*) and, well, weird. I come home to fresh-out-of-the-oven pizza from Heather, who made both the pizza dough and mozzarella from scratch—?!?!?!?—and spend the next hour with Mom's head on my shoulder, watching *A League of Their Own* for the millionth time.

Not a bad way to be.

But around eight o'clock, Addie texts me. **Happy Cow?**

I'm surprised because I figured she'd be with Nick, running him through a mock cross-examination in preparation for his meeting of Mrs. McAndry. **Time?**

Ten minutes?

Deal.

I clear it with my parents and then hightail it to Happy Cow, cooling night air rushing in. Addie is already there, browsing the menu even though she always gets the Moookie Cookie concrete. *Always*.

I wrap my arm around her shoulders, catch the scooper's eye, and shove a twenty in his face, my allowance stash renewed after being free of Ryan's blackmail burgers for a few weeks. "Two large Mooo-kie Cookies, keep the change."

I spin her in the direction of a booth. "Nick asked you to homecoming, didn't he?" The timing of this frozen custard run is *so* suspect. Because typically a homecoming football game goes right along with a homecoming dance. My life is hell right now, but even in hell there are damn posters for that dance. Worse, the court was named this week and Grey, Jake, and Nick are on it. Which I'm sure Addie knows. "Subjecting Nick to your mother *and* randomly wanting to meet me for Mooo-kie Cookies the week before the dance? Secrets much?"

"It wasn't that I hadn't planned on telling you—it's that he asked me the night you tried to walk off the team." One perfectly white incisor bites her bottom lip. "I was pretty certain you didn't need a melty pile of Addie that night."

"I needed you that night any way I could have you." My fingers scrabble for hers. "And you came right away. Without hesitation." I wait for her to look up. "Tell me about it, please."

"Are you sure you want to—"

"Yes." And I mean it. This is my best friend.

Addie raises a brow, perfectly drawn winged liner lifting with it in a sweet swoop. "Okay, but you have to promise that if I get too melty, you have to make me stop."

"Deal."

The frozen custard dude sidles over and flips our twin Mooo-kie Cookies upside down, showing off their thick durability. The second he's gone, she launches into the story.

"That's why we weren't in the parking lot for, um, you know," Addie says, talking into her concrete instead of looking my way. The fight with Grey. "He had reservations for the back booth at Bruno's. The waiter dropped a white pizza in front of my face a minute after we sat down with 'H-o-m-e-c-o-m-i-n-g?' spelled out in olives."

"Omigod, no," I squeal, eyes wide. Fairly certain everyone in the place is staring at me, but I really don't care.

"*Yes*. Boy turned as pink as a strawberry waiting for me to say something."

"And you said...?"

"I said, 'You better meet my mother.'"

Her delivery is the perfect sort of dry, and I crack up. "Please tell me that pizza was better than our usual."

"I—well, I didn't get to eat it. Nick's phone started blowing up before we could start...."

I nod, understanding and guilt flooding my stomach. The Northland gossip tree at work.

Silence flies over and I force myself to ask a question I don't want to know the answer to, the custard I've ingested refreezing into something the size and shape of a bowling ball in my stomach. "So, who are you guys going with?"

Addie chews and chews. Finally, she swallows, everything moving at half speed—the opposite of normal Addie in every way. "Well, his sister, of course."

I'm actually surprised that I don't cringe at a mention of Kelly. "And Jake's her date."

Addie nods quickly but reaches across the table and grabs my hand. Her grip demands that I meet her eyes. "But I'd rather go with you." When I don't say anything, she squeezes my hand. "I'm serious. I think you should ask Grey to the dance."

My lips part and my heart is in my ears, *pound pound pounding* away.

She twists our hands over. "Nick is to Grey what you are to me. Which means Nick is who Grey calls when he's upset." Her eyes rise to mine. "Liv, this boy is devastated. Literally all he can do is talk in circles to Nick, walking through what he did wrong. What he should've done instead. Analyzing the shit out of the situation like the coach he'll probably be someday. Like the quarterback he is now."

I've seen those wheels turning at practice and in class.

"He came to find me after I saw you at the volleyball game. He apologized."

She nods. "I know. I told Nick that he shouldn't go—that he'd look like a stalker."

"Well, okay, valid concern."

We both laugh a little but then she resets her grip. Her eyes are just as insistent as her fingers wrapped around mine.

"He made a mistake. Lots of them, actually. And you called him on it. And you were right to. But I'm going to say it again: Standing up for yourself doesn't mean walking away. From that cute boy or those gross-ass shoulder pads." Her eyes flash to mine. "Go back to him. Try again."

There's a settling to the corner of her mouth and her focus sharpens, the same winner's smirk that slides in place as she steps into the batter's box, smashes a kill, or snags a rebound. It's at once beautiful and terrifying, the definition of badass.

Maybe it's that look of hers. Maybe it's the idea of Grey shrinking inside himself. Maybe it's that I needed her to say the words twice for them to really sink in—*Standing up for yourself doesn't mean walking away*—but my heart slows from frantic to confident, my vision clears, my breath and gut and blood all working in rhythmic synergy.

I can see Grey's face so clearly. The truth in it. The way he feels about me.

I made a mistake, a huge one.

His mistakes weren't any worse than mine. I lied by omission to people I care about, too, from day one.

In truth, we're both our own biggest hurdles. And forgiveness isn't something that comes easily to either of us.

But I can forgive him.

I know what I'm going to do: exactly what I would've done last year—stick my chin in the air and go after what I want.

And I want Grey.

Saturday morning, I arrive to weights early enough that the lights aren't even on yet. I flip on the fluorescents and sit on the first weight bench, my heart thumping in my throat as I stare through the propped-open door and into the dim hallway.

Boys begin to trickle in ten minutes later. Tate, Topps, Jake. But not Grey. Not yet.

As I wait, my heart thuds past my throat and into my ears, until it feels as if my heart is on the outside, pressing into the room, into the boys. Like it's so obvious that they all know what I'm going to do, but I don't care.

I'm going to do it anyway.

Grey appears like a vision in basketball shorts. He's in a fitted white T-shirt, the color perfectly outlining the cut and curve of his shoulders, chest, and upper arms. That half smile ticks up the corner of his mouth as he makes eye contact. Nick is at his shoulder, Kelly just behind him—clearly they carpooled.

Like everything else, I don't care. If I start getting distracted by them—by the possible embarrassment—I'll regret not listening to my heart, my head, my gut.

"I have a question for you," I say, my voice muffled in my ears by the pounding of my heart. I stand and take a step toward him. Grey stops and Nick skates around him, his hand around his sister's wrist, pulling her away. Kelly's head spins toward us anyway, along with everyone else's.

"Shoot." His grin stretches, the silence around us, too.

I take a step toward him, close enough that there's no way he can misread my expression. No crossed signals here. I want what I want and I'd prefer not to ask for it twice. "Homecoming dance. You and me."

There's a collective inhale from the crowd as surprise softens the angles of his face. "That wasn't a question, that was an order."

"Okay, it's an order. I am a quarterback, after all."

The grin widens. "You sure are."

I tilt my chin to him. "Are you going to answer me or not?"

Grey erases the final distance between us, close enough that his knees tap mine, our Nikes bumping together. Even with the eyes of our teammates on us, he dares to touch my face, his strong hands cupping my cheeks, rough thumbs dusting my mouth in the breath before his lips crash into mine. Immediately, I wrap my arms around his waist. The hard planes of his chest conform to my curves, the past days of frustration, awkwardness, sadness, and embarrassment spiraling up and away.

The wolf whistles start, some actual cheers, too, whooping coupled with a few musings I probably *really* don't want to hear.

But. I. Don't. Care.

It's only by sheer, indoctrinated willpower that I'm able to pull myself out of that kiss.

"I'll take that as a yes," I say.

Grey's fingers graze my forearm as if to keep me from pivoting away from him, moment over. His hand slides over my skin, coming to rest on my wrist, his head slightly bowed, his lips in my ear where the four dozen pairs of eyes surrounding us can't hear.

"Are you sure?" There's a hesitation in his voice like I've never heard from him before. "You trust me?"

There it is again. All that swagger and perfect hair and newscaster stoicism gone. The inner Grey laid bare.

I kiss him once more. When we part, I give him my serious, on-the-field face. "Take that as a yes. And you're my boyfriend again." I tilt my head toward the full weight room behind me. "You people can handle kissing in football, right?"

Around us, the boys nod in a chorus of yeahs, Jake's voice booming louder than others—a relief. Even Kelly chimes in. Good. They've already weathered our breakup and everything that came after—I believe them when they say they can survive us publicly liking each other.

I can't help but grin back. While adjusting my ponytail, which slipped when we kissed, the coaches appear at the door. Lee doesn't miss a thing—it's clear by the set of his jaw he knows something just went down. Shanks eyes the distance between Grey and myself, back to the few inches of practices pre–parking lot fight. Napolitano checks his clipboard. After a long, awkward pause, Lee addresses the room. "Do I even want to know?"

All the bravery has fled my body, my lips sealing themselves shut. Everyone is dead silent for a few beats. But then Grey clears his throat. Oh God.

"Your top two quarterbacks are dating," he says, grabbing my hand.

I want to dissolve into the padded floor. Somehow, him telling Coach both validates my love for Grey and makes me want to absolutely murder him. It's so much more embarrassing than what I forced myself to do just five minutes ago.

Coach Lee cocks a brow, dark eyes sliding from Grey's face to mine.

"That's a relief. I thought it'd be at least three more weeks before you two came to your damn senses." As my jaw drops, Coach Lee simply refers to his clipboard. "Quarterbacks and running backs at the squat racks, both lines at bench, secondary and special teams at the TRX..."

39

MONDAY AT PRACTICE, GREY IS WAITING FOR ME OUT-side the locker room. Brady, too, though I'm fairly certain that's just because he has nothing better to do. Or maybe he likes me now. Maybe I really should set him up with Barbie Villanueva back at Windsor Prep—he'd love me forever. Plus, she might distract him enough to clear his head of the attitude that's holding him back.

Grey bumps his shoulder to mine, our pads clicking at the contact. "Hey, babe." That's new, and I kind of like it. He grabs my hand and we walk like that to the practice field, with Brady as our silent third wheel.

It's all very obviously on display. And, damn, does it feel good.

Grey squeezes my fingers and then we separate, our feet picking up the pace into a run. Five laps in the falling temperatures, the sun suddenly something that won't be around much past the end of practice.

As we run, Grey dishes what he knows about our opponents this week, Jewell Academy, the reigning state champs. The all-boys sibling school to Windsor Prep. The team that ended Northland's season last year in substate.

"The Jewell linebackers are tough as nails and *fast*. We need you as mobile as possible. If the coaches want a simulation, you'll be seeing a lot of Cleary and Sanchez this week."

Oh, great, I love to be sat on.

"But you've got legs. Just keep moving and you'll be good."

My knee is better—the day off on Sunday helped immensely—but the ache's there, the bruise's placement wonky for how much running we have to do. I'm limping right now, the hitch in my stride impossible to hide. Something I know Grey's noticed, his eyes skirting down to my knee just like they did all last week, even when we weren't talking.

We finish our laps and drop to kneel—the sun low enough to slice straight into our eyeline. Nick drops in next to us, having survived Mrs. McAndry on Saturday night—Addie's texts on Sunday were epic enough that I think he should frame them, or maybe screenshot them for his college applications—Emma McAndry's endorsement will definitely go far.

Kelly's up by the coaches, finger bobbing as she tallies us all. Shanks and Lee are having a conversation up her way, talking with their clipboards fanned over their mouths like they would on the sidelines, discussing plays.

"Rodinsky!" Lee calls. My head swings his way; so do Grey's and Brady's. "Up here. Worthington, you, too."

Grey and I exchange a glance and jog up to where the coaches are huddled, leaving our helmets back on the turf with Brady.

"Coach?" I say, Grey echoing.

Lee glances between us, his lips thinned out. Shanks has his arms crossed over his barrel chest, his eyes hidden by his ever-present visor.

"Your knee," Lee says without inflection. Just a damning statement. "What's wrong with it?"

Shit. I nearly glance at Kelly, but her back is turned. Coward.

"Nothing, sir. It's fine." I don't break eye contact.

Lee purses his lips, not buying it. "Rodinsky, don't lie to me."

"I'm not lying, Coach. It's just bruised. Not injured."

Finally, Shanks makes eye contact. "How bruised?"

Shit. Shit. Shit.

I present my leg, pulling up the leggings and shifting around the padding so that the outer side of my knee is visible in the late-afternoon light. The bruise has lightened from purple to a dark green, making it look like the blip of a thunderstorm on the radar. A *big* blip. The thing is the size of my hand and wraps from the side of my knee just above the kneecap, all the way around to the base of my quad.

Shanks gets his nose down there to look, knee brace clicking as he sinks to the turf. Grey and Lee have eyes all over it, too.

"It really is just a bruise." I want to lie and say that I've had it checked out. That my LCL—I looked it up and that's the outside ligament—is just peachy. But I haven't. I mean, I think it's fine, but I really need to be done with the white lies.

Shanks asks, "May I touch it?" I nod, and though he's careful, I tense so much I know he can feel it, too. The initial damage was done more than a week ago, but continuing to practice has kept it ripe and tender. Shanks stretches to his full height before he speaks. "I believe you when you say it's just a bruise, but I'm still going to sit you on Friday."

Lee nods and turns his attention to Grey. "Worthington, the start is yours."

No.

I want to yell, to tell them that his head is way more important than my knee. But I can't. I can't. I *can't*. I can't do that to him. I can't sell him out.

So I turn. Grey's so stunned he just nods and turns away, too. No pithy comments. No nothing.

A hand is on my arm, nails coated in fresh gel polish—Kelly. When I look up, there's nothing brutal on her face. Just a calm, determined set to her jaw. Her voice is a whisper in my ringing ears.

"You can't risk making your knee worse. Sitting out is the best thing for you and the team."

But it's not the best thing for Grey.

Coach Lee is talking again. "Rodinsky, go with Coach Napolitano and get checked out."

I look to Grey and there's a mixture of confidence and relief in his eyes—he's trying to tell me that he's okay, that he wishes I weren't hurt, and that he's thankful I've kept his secret.

As I'm walking away, all I can think is that I may have gotten my boyfriend back, but I lost my chance to protect him.

A bruise to my LCL. Not a sprain, thank God, or I'd be out for two weeks. Napolitano sets me up with a soft knee brace and when I put it on under my uniform, the bottom of it pokes out, visibly marking me as injured. Dammit.

Still, I return to practice and move through the motions, alternating with Grey on the A team. I even run laps after practice in step with Grey, the brace definitely improving the hitch in my stride.

As the rest of the team stalks off to the showers, dinner on their minds, I tug Grey back, tucking him against the chain-link fence that separates the stadium from the alley of asphalt that leads to the locker rooms.

I twine his hands in mine and meet him with my game-day glare. "Tell me the truth. Are you really okay to play?"

Grey doesn't blink, the sweat on his face dried into fine white lines. His curls are matted down from his helmet, but they still look frustratingly perfect. "I'm fine. I promise."

A lump is in my throat and I know he can hear it when I ask, "You're sure?"

His hands come to my face, thumbs cradling my cheeks as if they're made of glass. "I promise. No more headaches."

My lips drop open, but before I can insist he tell me again, he's turned the tables on me. "And your knee? When were you going to tell me about that?"

"It's nothing," I say, though he's no dummy to the brace or my diagnosis. "I know what a real injury feels like. It's not a big deal."

His little half smile kicks up and his gray eyes flash in the dying light. "So you *weren't* going to tell me."

"No," I admit. "But you would've found out Saturday night, anyway." I lean in to him, our lips close enough I can feel his breath. Our pads click together, numbers sixteen and thirteen becoming one. "My homecoming dress does have a pretty good slit in it." I can't afford a new dress, so I'm wearing Addie's from last year, and, yeah, it's epic.

"Oh, it does, does it?" His face breaks into a real smile, everything about him softening. "I can't wait."

And then he kisses me.

40

AT THE END OF THE WEEK, THE STADIUM IS PACKED—brimming with Northland orange, Styrofoam cups of hot cocoa, and vats of popcorn, M&Ms spilling to the bleachers in tragic numbers. A contingent wrapped in shimmering Jewell Academy gold with slick black accents has no problem equally filling the other side of the stadium; a win is that much more satisfying on a competitor's homecoming night. On our side, Dad, Mom, Ryan, Danielle, Heather, and Addie are scrunched into the northeast corner. This time, they are ALL wearing orange, even Addie and Danielle.

Down on the field, the electricity of it all, sparking from the stadium bodies as much as from the Friday night lights, crackles across the loop of exposed skin at my wrists, the scoop of my neck, my face. The current drills through the fabric, pads and bones and straight to my heart.

And my heart can barely take it.

I'm standing next to Grey, fighting the urge not to tie him to the fence lining the infield and track—far from where he can get hurt.

He's his own person. He's making his own decision.

My dad trusted me to do the same, and I can't ask Grey to do differently.

I respect Grey's choice—but...

But it still makes the walls of my heart deflate.

The team stands together along the sideline, all facing Coach Lee, who's hopped onto one of the aluminum benches, eyes glittering under the lights. I'm in the very center of the circle, crowded in next to Grey, our shoulders kissing. I make a grab for his hand, pinkie and ring fingers hauling his hand into mine.

"Hello, Tigers."

"Hello, Coach," the team yells back, enthusiastic as ever.

"We're playing the defending state champs—that's worth as much weight as any words of encouragement I could spit out at you. So, I'll leave it at this." There's a pause the size of Topps's truck. "This is a damn good football team, and whatever happens tonight won't change that."

Coach Lee uses words in a more meaningful way than almost anyone I've ever met. And yet the way he crafted that sentence is almost like he's giving us an out. A pre-emptive strike.

Almost like he expects us to lose.

The circle is silent, Coach's words coiling inside each of the jerseyed bodies rather than evaporating into the cool night air.

Grey's game face tightens—all his warm, happy cat energy evaporated. Still, he squeezes my hand before reaching up to put on his helmet. Jake appears at his side—my past and my present so close, the edges of my shadow blur into theirs, a trick of the blazing overheads, making us one.

We stand that way, watching the defense take the field after Jewell wins the coin toss and decides to receive the kickoff. One play later and they've scored, their kicker coming out to make it 7–0.

Thirty seconds off the clock and we're down.

With that, Jake taps out a fist bump and Grey checks my shoulder, breaking his game face just long enough to toss me a half smile.

And then they're gone.

At the half, we're tied; 21–all.

We squeeze into the locker room, and the bodies give just enough that I can huddle in next to Grey. Grass stains and flecks of sod ruin the perfect white of his pants, his orange jersey smeared along the backside. Sweat clings to the angles of his jawline and cheekbones. He's done a stellar job, already past the hundred-yard mark passing on the day, spry in the pocket, avoiding the sack. He's been knocked down once or twice, sure, but it's been nothing terrible, thank God. He and Jake have worked perfectly in tandem to keep up with Jewell, like the pros they are. Like the college players they want to be.

Both of their faces are hard with hope. Eyes set on Coach Lee. Waiting for some confirmation that he was wrong before kickoff. That we don't need an out. That we can get the win.

"Tigers," Coach starts, "you're fighting. Fighting hard. And it shows. But—"

I swallow, stomach dropping though I haven't taken a snap.

"But running stride for stride won't win us this game. Winning means we can't just *match* Jewell, we must *best* Jewell."

Coach glances at Nick and the other linebackers. "Trample Jewell."

At Jake and the receivers flanking him. "Outsprint Jewell."

At Grey, and by extension, me. "Sail above Jewell."

He lets that sink in, challenge given and clear.

We do have a chance.

But only if we work for it.

We're ushered back out of the locker room to announcements from the stands about tomorrow night's dance, and I'm glad I'm not expected to play this half because all of a sudden, visions of Grey in a suit have me just a tad distracted.

We hit the sidelines to warm back up, Grey drilling it to both Brady and myself at different distances for three minutes tops before Shanks snags him and Jake to talk specific scenarios. We're starting the half receiving the kickoff, and against Jewell Academy, that means score first or be crushed.

"O-Rod! Brady!" Shanks's big arm motions us to come over.

Brady's final pass lands in my outstretched fingertips and we jog over, Grey shifting to make room. The circle also includes both tight ends and the secondary, plus Topps for good measure.

"Okay, team, the ground game is still our best bet, but they were plugging the holes at the end of the half—gotta start adding in the pass." We all nod and Shanks begins circling certain plays with a dry-erase marker on the laminated cheat sheet. "Worthington, let's start with your best Joe Montana impression and go from there."

Translated, that means short passes that lead to big runs—the hallmark of Montana's 49ers days. It's basically what we do on a normal basis, but Shanks has eliminated passes that go deeper than ten yards. Which is fine with me—the less amount of time Grey has the ball in his hands, the better, because he's less likely to be drilled.

The drums start and a line of golden uniforms stretches the field. Our receivers, Gonzalez and Chow, are deep, awaiting the ball, bouncing on their toes, speed sparking at their cleats.

The ball is up and high, rocketing toward the end zone. Gonzalez is there, waiting for it to drop at the ten-yard line. He catches it and loops right, snaking down the sideline.

There's a whistle. A waving of hands. Lots of pointing, the refs saying he stepped out.

I call bullshit because Jaden Gonzalez is a senior and pretty much a professional tightrope walker. But all the Jewell players and coaches are pointing to the spot, down at our fifteen. And the refs are corroborating it.

A golden cheer floats into the night as the Northland bench peters into a frustrated grumble. We now have to get it eighty-five yards downfield on this drive, when Gonzalez was in position to make it all the way down past midfield, well into Jewell territory.

If Grey is daunted, it doesn't register. He gives me a grin and a piece of a three-way QB fist bump and trots out onto the turf, gathering the offense into a huddle.

Jake gets the first play, snagging it from Grey on a roll-out and pushing for four yards when the hole closes on top of him. The next play is a Montana-style dump, barely over the heads of the line, but the target, Tate, falls backward on the plant.

Losing at least a yard.

Meaning we need a yard on the next two plays to keep it moving.

Predictably, Jake gets the next call, barely gaining the needed yard, and audibly chewing out the line for not making room.

Still, the chains move.

But the next two plays aren't as lucky. Jake gets stuffed both times. Grey goes for another Montana-style dump, but Tate is pushed out of position and the whole thing ends up a fingertip away from an interception.

Grey pulls the offense back into the huddle, and the punter stays on the sidelines, which sort of scares the shit out of me because if we miss the next play, Jewell gains possession inside the thirty. Which means they'll score in less than a minute—I'd bet every Snickers in Shanks's freezer.

But Grey holds firm, shouting out White Forty-Two.

A play that is most definitely not on the approved list.

My lungs stutter to a halt as I watch him palm Topps's snap and rocket back into the pocket, gaining a better view.

Grey's arm swings back, target in sight: Chow, fifty yards downfield.

Chow dodges his defender and manages to get open. Grey launches the ball toward him, the arc perfect.

But I don't see if the pass connects.

I don't see if it's intercepted.

All I see is Grey being swallowed by gold two seconds after he releases the ball.

The ground seems to shake under my feet as they hit the sod in a tangle, numbers fifty-five and ninety-two landing so hard on top of Grey that they bounce on impact, revealing a flash of orange and white for a split second before devouring him once more.

They lay there in a pile, the only movement a Northland helmet rolling free across the turf.

"Grey!" I've never yelled so loudly in my life, but his name is still drowned by the crowd. Helmetless and stiff knee balking, I sprint onto the field, both running toward him and waving my arms, trying to get any ref's attention for this insane roughing-the-passer bullshit.

But the refs aren't looking. They're at the other end, officiating whatever happened with the ball, the brutality of the unnecessary hit completely swallowed in sound.

"GREY!" I reach the pile and start yanking at number fifty-five. "Get off him, you ass!"

Cleary and Sanchez join me, the linebackers much more effective at peeling a combined five hundred pounds off my boyfriend.

The second I see Grey's face, time screeches to a halt.

His eyes are closed, temple to the ground, stripes of turf running the length of his forehead and into his hair.

In my mind, all I can think of is what I know about a grade three concussion: loss of consciousness.

Two of those just months apart and...I—I don't know. But it can't be good.

My hands hover above his body, trembling at the thought of making it worse. Because it seems safest, I grab his right hand with both of mine and squeeze. "You're going to be okay. You're going to be okay. You're going to be okay...."

Next to me, Nick yells back at the sideline: "We need a medic!"

Khaki rushes the field. Napolitano, trailed by Shanks and Lee. They kneel down, hands braver than mine touching Grey's head, touching his cheeks. Napolitano's voice crackles into a radio, requesting the on-site EMT.

"No, stop...." We all stop and stare as Grey's voice ghosts into the night, followed by the fluttering appearance of his eyes. "I'm fine."

"Grey!" I'm not sure what I expect, but my heart surges as he blinks, grasping at focus. I flash four fingers in front of his eyes, just because I've seen it in so many movies. "How many fingers am I holding up?"

"Enough to block your face. Don't do that." He's still speaking slowly, but I barely have enough time to move my hand before his hands cup the back of my head, pulling me into a kiss. Inches from our coaches, right in the middle of the field.

It's quick, and probably not all that obvious from the stands, but it means everything to me.

Grey releases me, attempting to sit up just as the medic crashes to the turf with his pack of gear.

"No movement until I run through the concussion protocol," the medic warns, forcing Grey to lie back down before flashing lights in his eyes and barking orders. This was something I couldn't see when Jake went down, and now it makes way more sense why he was on the ground for so long.

"I lost consciousness," Grey says, and looks to me and Nick to confirm how long—we were the first ones there and he was awake by the time the EMT arrived.

"He was out maybe five to ten seconds," I say, and Nick nods in agreement.

The EMT takes that in with the efficiency of most health-care professionals. "Any recent head trauma?"

Yes. Yes. Yes.

I look to Grey and then to the medic and back to Grey. I open my mouth because this is the exact situation where it can't stay secret anymore. Screw college football, Grey's head is worth more than just a scholarship. Feeling my panic, my coming words, Grey squeezes my hand. At first I think it might be to beg for my silence, but then he simply says, "I hit my head in a car wreck this summer."

The air in my chest won't come as I watch the coaches for a reaction. Grey's done hiding.

Coach Lee looks like he's swallowed a vat of soot. *"Excuse me?"*

Grey's eyes slide his way and they actually look relieved. "I was never diagnosed with anything, but it's relevant. I lost consciousness. I'm sure of it. Just like I did now."

The medic simply takes in that information without a word, but Coach is sputtering—anger, frustration, and maybe a prickle of humiliation at not suspecting it himself coming out in puffed cheeks and a shaking head.

"You're a smart kid, Worthington—what the hell were you doing not telling us?"

"Being an idiot," Grey says as the medic again begins to shine a light into his eyes.

That's when the shoving starts downfield. The excitement on the other end of the field—a Northland touchdown, as it happens—turning into anger about our laid-out quarterback. The whole crowd notices the action, too, a rumbling silence falling over the stadium.

Which only makes the ensuing fight louder.

Shanks, Napolitano, Cleary, and Sanchez begin herding Tigers back to the sidelines, the Jewell Academy coaches slow to do the same. But a core group continues to snipe at each other despite the distance, the refs playing force field.

Left with me, Coach Lee doesn't flinch at the noise, patiently watching the medic do his work, but my body aches to run, muscles tense and ready to hurry Grey back to the relative safety of the sidelines.

After forever and a day, the medic gives the official word—probable grade three concussion.

Out comes Napolitano with the cart. Grey's parents arrive, too.

I want to cry, but I actually feel so much better knowing that he's okay. That he's getting medical help. That the truth is out there and it's going to be okay.

Though, man, if Grey isn't going to have to run a bazillion extra laps for this.

As he's loaded onto the cart, Grey's hand lands on my thigh as I try to climb on, too. To stop me. To get my attention. To bring me out of girlfriend mode and into player mode.

"Better grab Brady and get warm. The rest of this game is yours."

I'm in command.

I lean down and give him one more kiss—quick and gentle.

And then the cart, with Grey's parents and the medic in the back, drives away. The crowd erupts as Grey raises a hand and flashes that smile of his toward the stands.

41

JEWELL SCORES QUICKLY ON THE NEXT DRIVE, AGAIN proving why they're the defending state champs. After the extra point flies in, we're again tied up, 28–all. The ensuing kick drives us to the enemy forty-nine; it's not great, but better than on the other side of midfield.

Time to go.

My heart thumps, a cold trickle of fear behind it. My knee is injured, yes, but I can do this. I *can*. I can do it and I can do it without making it worse.

I hope.

A raucous cheer goes up as I jog onto the turf with the offense, the whole stadium—not just my family, not just my friends—lighting up. The thunder and crackle of the undertone clear: The girl quarterback is on the field.

I let the sound stream through my bones. Let it infuse any possible extra strength to my muscles. It's oh so powerful.

For extra measure, my eyes shoot to the stands. My parents, Danielle, Ryan, Heather, and Addie—all together in a row. Their presence gives me an extra spring in my step.

I can do this.

The huddle is silent, all eyes on me. There's no dissent, no questioning glances at my knee, though it's still in its neoprene sleeve—just a hungry look on each face. I know that look well. The one of feeling like you're down even though you're actually tied, even though it's your night, all because you have to work so much harder than your opponent.

I know that look, but I also know we've got this.

"They're going to expect me to throw—new quarterback, showing off." I glance to Jake. "So we run."

Jake's face breaks into a wolf's smile. "White Three?"

It's the perfect play for turbo Jake. "Exactly."

"Break!" My voice rings into the night and we face the golden line. Fifty-five, one of the linebackers who downed Grey, does all he can to force me to recognize the evil grin on his face.

Suck it, fifty-five. You aren't taking me out.

"WHITE THREE! WHITE THREE! HUT-HUT!"

Topps snaps the ball and I shoot back, Jake snagging

the ball before my arm goes up and back. I bomb through the motion as number thirty-two turns the line, breaking into the open. A defender finally wises up and is on him, Jake's arm propped out in the Heisman pose—

A beefy arm slams into my sternum, the wind and thought knocked out of me as my body plunges to the turf.

The shriek of a whistle; the whizz of a flag in my periphery.

"Football isn't for girls," a rough voice informs me when I'm finally on the ground, face to the grass. Something, a hand, maybe, presses me deeper into the sod for good measure.

I roll over, golden jersey stalking away, his number stuttering out in triplicate across my vision.

Fifty-five. Fifty-five. Fifty-five.

He did get me.

Dammit.

But as I rise to my knees, I realize he's been punished— for both the late hit and unnecessary roughness.

Meaning we gain another fifteen yards and a first down on the play.

Topps lends a hand and I take it, using the solid anchor of two hundred fifty pounds to stand. My knee doesn't hitch, and for that, I'm thankful. I take a step, and though the bruise is still there, it's unbothered, the tight sleeve adding support. I don't even have to pretend not to limp.

"You okay, O-Rod?"

I give him my best smile. "We just made it to the twenty-five. I'm great."

Topps doesn't seem convinced, but isn't stupid enough to harp on the fact that I've got a clod of turf lodged in the front of my helmet and a glorious green streak down the length of my number thirteen. I find my dad's eyes in the stands yet again and he raises a fist.

I can do this.

The boys huddle back up and I confirm Shanks's call from the sidelines.

"Orange Nine." Tate's eyes flash. Our favorite. "Break!"

I make sure number fifty-five gets a good look at the calm on my face. Just so he knows there's no way in hell he's affected me now, even if I'll surely be aching tomorrow.

"ORANGE NINE! ORANGE NINE! HUT-HUT!"

The ball is gone a second later, Tate in the perfect position.

He slams into the defender but holds fast, and the Jewell player goes down, allowing him to break loose. Tate dodges to the sideline and tightropes it all the way down before being shoved out at the one.

A single yard at the end zone is the most difficult yard in football.

But I've got Jake.

We don't even need a huddle.

"WHITE NINETEEN! WHITE NINETEEN! HUT-HUT!"

I twist my shoulders to expose the ball to Jake, who squeezes it into the three and two on his chest before vaulting over the line and somersaulting into the end zone.

He stands and spikes it, arms out wide as Tate greets him in a chest bump.

Tigers: back on top.

~

The minutes tick down and we've still traded scores.

But, incredibly, even that's not good enough *because we're losing*.

On its last possession, Jewell Academy went for two, rather than the extra point. With precision and what I would say was a huge-ass amount of swagger, the golden guild coolly went up one.

So, Jewell's up 43–42 with exactly a minute left on the clock.

Goddammit.

Every bone in my body is weary as I cough down one last swig of Gatorade. My knee's been much better than I hoped, but it aches more than the rest of me if I'm being honest. Lee and Shanks loom above my spot on the bleachers. I'm missing Grey, who's still somewhere with the medic, and I'm wishing he were here, shoulder-knocking the jitters out of me.

"Plenty of time, plenty of time," Lee says, almost as a mantra. I force myself to look Coach in the eye, but all I can see is him addressing us during my first practice, sharing his hopes and dreams for us—for his final season.

Lose this one and getting to state becomes nearly impossible. Not totally, but reality takes a detour into the Candy Land of statistics and scenarios.

I have to win. I can't be the gamble who led the offense in the two losses in Coach Lee's final year. I can't.

"Rodinsky, you listening?" I nod and his voice drops twenty decibels, zeroing in on me. "Look, I know I give you a hard time. You're not the second coming of Peyton Manning, but you're not half-bad. Know that." *Sheesh, thanks.* "Keep those feet moving and follow your instincts. You know better than those boys out there how to win."

I don't know that I do, especially compared to "those boys" on the Jewell side, but something about Coach Lee's voice makes me believe. Maybe because he's never said anything so damn nice to me in regard to my football playing.

Lee pats me on the helmet and peels off, visor pointed toward the ensuing kickoff.

Shanks squats down in his place—his dark face looming level with my eyes.

"No matter what happens here, you Orange Nine to Tate. Next White Nine to Jake. We'll call it from there."

The drums begin, another kickoff imminent. My mind swims with images of that final-second loss to Central. I shake my head, ponytail a ratty ball of tangles. Those memories have no place in the now.

Champions don't dwell on past mistakes.

Champions don't dwell on things they can't control.

Champions only look forward, they never look back.

I could go on all day with the pearls of wisdom Danielle stole from some book and then sprinkled throughout my sweat-stained childhood.

"Liv!"

My head whirls around to the sound of Grey's voice. He's walking as fast as possible, the medic behind him, yelling after him not to break into a run.

But *I* can run to him. I get to my feet and sprint his way before stopping on a dime—not wanting to crash into him and do more damage.

"You came back," I say, thrilled.

"As soon as they'd let me." Grey wraps an arm around my shoulders as the crowd thunders in the background, cheering on our guys as they sprint the kickoff back down the field.

The whistle blows. The ball down at our forty. A sixty-yard march in less than sixty seconds, coming up.

"You've got this, Liv," he says, squeezing me into his body.

I'm programmed to nod, so I do. He doesn't buy it.

"No, look at me." My eyes fly up from the middle distance to his. "You've got this. You will find a way to win. You will make it happen. Because you're Liv Rodinsky and you're absolute magic."

I just kiss him. Quick and hard.

In goes the mouth guard. On goes the helmet.

I start yelling the second I'm on the field, not wanting to waste any time with a huddle.

"ORANGE NINE! ORANGE NINE!"

I curl in behind Topps. "HUT-HUT!"

I launch back five steps, spot Tate slightly off route and readjust, aiming to split his numbers. Some asshole in gold is tailing him, but I know Zach Tate's got this and I release the ball as planned.

Tate catches it and tucks the ball into his elbow as his cleats make contact with the turf, legs churning as he dodges left. The Jewell player goes down in his dust. A linebacker rushes over to help, tripping up Tate at the knees. But he's made it to the Jewell forty-one—a nineteen-yard gain and a first down.

We step up to the line, the seconds ticking toward a half minute remaining. No huddle, just my voice and our collective muscle memory.

"WHITE NINE! WHITE NINE! HUT-HUT!"

The handoff to Jake isn't the smoothest, both of us eager to do our jobs, the ball bobbling in his fingertips. But he's Jake effing Rogers and he's done this a million times. The ball is safe and sound in a fraction of a second and then number thirty-two is on the move.

Jake loops out along the sideline and, as the second defender closes in, he smartly steps out of bounds— stopping the clock.

Nineteen seconds and twenty-five yards remain.

I look to Shanks, not missing our kicker warming up on the sidelines, ready for the winning field goal. I half expect the coaches to call in special teams right now, but they decide to give it one more try for a better position.

White Fifteen. It's a play he hasn't called all night. Jewell definitely won't know what hit them.

I glance at Jake and he nods. *Ready.*

Again, we rush the line, the Jewell defense clearly unsettled with our lack of huddle. Gotta use that to our advantage one last time.

"WHITE FIFTEEN! WHITE FIFTEEN! HUT-HUT!"

I take the ball and shoot back, Topps holding the pocket.

But Jake's run into trouble—number fifty-five glued to his back.

Dammit.

Still, in front of me, there's an opening. A *huge* opening.

For a split second, I consider dumping the ball to the sideline like I should to stop the clock again, but I know what's best, what will end the game at this very moment. Coach is right, my instincts *can* win this game—even if they don't involve my throwing arm.

Tucking the ball, I plow through the parted bodies and into the open. I'm certain Grey's voice rises above the crowd, the clash of bodies, my breath thundering in my ears.

"Run, O-Rod!"

My feet automatically coast left when I realize there's a body at my side, but it's Topps, who somehow shook his assignment and sprinted fast enough to block for me.

The end zone looms ahead, the goalposts the whole of my vision. I can't feel my knee—I can't feel anything except the tight thrill of tunnel vision, single-mindedness the whole of my being.

Another body zooms into my periphery—another flash of orange.

"Liv! Go!"

Jake.

Now I've got guys on either side, protecting me. And Grey in my head, telling me I've got this.

Five yards.

Four yards.

Three.

Two.

One.

My cleats hit the end zone with three seconds to spare. Arms raised, I spike the ball and turn to the crowd, inhaling the thunder and love.

"Ooooooo-ROOOOOODDDDD!" Topps hooks me under the shoulders and hoists me into the air, Jake in step with us. I spot Danielle in the crowd first, her hands in the air, screaming—Dad, Mom, Ryan, Heather, and Addie high-fiving. Jake's wide grin is the next thing I see as Topps returns me safely to the turf, and we slap hands.

Coach Lee lets the time run out, extra point unneeded. The refs don't even seem pissed when the entire Tigers bench floods the field, the end zone and night ours. Grey shoves his way through the bodies to me, picking me up and twirling me like I'm freaking Ginger Rogers, not a sweaty girl in a jersey and pads. The moment my cleats hit solid ground, he pulls me into a deep kiss.

And it might just be my imagination, but the crowd seems to get even louder.

When we part, the band starts into the Northland fight song, our whole side swaying as one, homecoming spirit times a million.

Jewell players hang their golden heads, the assistants already packing up because even champions—especially defending state champions—never dwell on a loss.

Even when they get their asses handed to them by a girl.

Epilogue

IT'S THE BOTTOM OF THE SEVENTH. THE BASES LOADED. Two out.

The crowd is still—orange and purple cleaved together in silence, all eyes pinned to the long-legged strut of the next batter.

The player with the most hits in the state championship game—this year, and maybe ever.

The player who has batted in every run the de facto home team has so far tonight.

The player who is my best friend.

Addie settles into her too-straight stance, always a praying mantis in cleats. From first base—my new, albeit strange home, the position the only one open on an already solid team—I've got a great view of the determination on her face. The set of her mouth is deadly, rigid. She's led Windsor Prep all year with that grit and hauled the Eagles to the final game in May. To the championship against a team they split games with in the regular season—the revamped Northland Tigers.

She's the star player and she's not planning to fail. A home run and she'd walk off a winner—beating us 6–5. Anything less and there would still be work to do. An out and it would be over, Windsor Prep a runner-up for the second year in a row.

Cleats scratching, I bounce in the dirt, my knee not even complaining. Training with Napolitano in the weight room all fall and winter, making sure it healed properly, paid off. My eyes are on the Eagle next to me, Ava, who is ready to run the second Addie makes fair contact.

From the mound, Kelly's cat eyes check the bases, red ponytail whipping across her shoulders. Rodinsky at first—a replacement for the graduated Sanderson—Janecki at second, Cortez at third. All of us holding strong.

The situation is so similar to last year that my heart starts to pound, bittersweet in the back of my throat.

The same teams.

The same polite cheering from my family and rowdy rumble from football-jersey-clad boys in orange.

The same best friend up to bat, the bases loaded, the win in her hands as Addie stares down Kelly at the mound.

But so much is different—not just my uniform. Not just my family's custom shirts, displaying both purple and orange, split down the middle, a house's interests divided. Not just the game, one better than last year.

There's been no smack talk on base tonight, only mutual respect and admiration. There's not been a single slur. Not a single punch thrown.

Addie's prehit ritual over with, her hips sink slightly lower in the batter's box. Kelly's arm windmills through the motion, plant leg sliding under the force. The ball rockets through the bottom right corner of the strike zone, whizzing past Addie's knees.

Strike one.

Addie stands and readjusts her gloves, Velcro cracking into the night. Danielle's voice shoots out of the Eagles dugout as the team claps and hugs the rail. "Good look, McAndry. Good look. Wait for it. Wait for it."

Addie nods as Coach Kitt counters from the steps of the Tigers' side. "Close it out, Cleary. *Close. It. Out.*"

Behind her, in the stands, a line of boys with boulders for shoulders screams Kelly's name. Jake, Topps, Brady, the receivers, and tight ends, all cupping their hands around their mouths—*Cleary, Cleary, Cleary!* All but the boy who shares the name, too divided in this situation to do much more than just stand there, not sure whom to root for. Like during football, like the rest of the softball season, Grey's voice hits my ears harder than any of the others.

"Lookin' alive, O-Rod! Lookin' good!"

There's his patented half smile in the sound, along with the confidence that comes with being a reigning state champion himself. He started every game of the postseason, his experience and talent catching the eyes of several schools. But he chose to go to KU—less than an hour's drive away from home. Away from me.

Of course, if he's a state champ in football, so am I. And Addie knows that feeling well, having picked up her own trophy in volleyball. Yes, fall was good to us.

But none of that matters on this field. In this moment. In this sport.

Just like last year doesn't matter.

The slate's wiped clean—for our teams. For me. All thanks to the least likely of sources. In the end, it wasn't public compliments from my teammates, Grey's good word, or my hours practicing in the batting cages that finally moved the chains on my softball dreams.

It was Kelly.

Kelly, waltzing into Kitt's office just before Halloween, a story on her lips. A story of what she'd overheard walking from the mound to the dugout two seconds before Stacey was on the ground, blood spurting from her nose.

Kitt called me in soon after and asked for all the answers I'd never offered up. The past skewed through a different lens in five minutes flat. I know it wouldn't have been that easy if I'd told the tale on my own. Kelly's confirmation provided exactly the verification I needed.

Now, Kelly checks each base as all three runners—Ava, Rosemary, and Christy—inch off again, angling for the maximum possible advantage. Her arm windmills through in a blur, a perfect fastball, straight through the heart of the strike zone.

It's a dare.

Hit me with your best shot.

And Addie can't resist.

She swings hard, bat aimed at the fences, legs powering through. But the ball connects high on the shaft, clipping up and out, fair but losing steam quick.

The runners take off and Kelly stutter-steps off the mound, positioning herself right under the ball as it descends straight in her glove.

The third out.

The orange side of the crowd erupts, cheers falling onto the diamond like snow as the outfield storms in, greeting Kelly and the rest of the infield in one hopping, cheering, index-finger-pointing huddle.

We've won.

I'll join them in a second, but first I have to take care of some important business.

We come at each other like magnets and we hug each

other deeply. Addie's heart drums against the EAGLES looping across her button-up.

"You rocked it, McAndry."

She nods into my shoulder, besting my squeeze by a mile, always the strongest person I know. Behind her, I see Danielle in front of the dugout, greeting the Eagles as they stumble off the field, pulling them in for hugs before sending each girl to the postgame handshake line.

"Go celebrate," Addie says when she pushes away, disappointed tears already welling—though she doesn't crumble, brave face on for me. I squeeze her once more and do what she says. It'll only hurt more if I linger.

As I jog to the mound, I'm caught from behind. Forearms tan from baseball season haul me in, offset nicely by his bright orange Northland football jersey. I twist into Grey and wrap my arms around his neck, squeezing him as hard as possible into a hug. Jake streaks past us, on his way to Kelly. Over Grey's shoulder, I spy Nick taking Addie into his arms by the Windsor Prep dugout.

"Touchdown, champ!" Grey says, pride thick in his voice.

I plant a kiss on his cheek and whisper in his ear, "Wouldn't be here without you, teammate."

Grey jostles his grip until I'm on my tiptoes, looking into his steel-gray eyes.

"Are you kidding me? You would've gotten here anyway.

Our road was just much more fun." He kisses me, hard and hungry. "Now, go up there with your team."

I flash a smile back at him and run up to the mound, which is all noise and bouncing girls, with Kelly somewhere in the center. I hop in, fingers raised to the sky, hair ribbons catching the light in flickers of orange. We jump and scream for ages, no one escaping a hug, no one at a loss for love.

Our team huddle unfurls into a flock of girls thundering toward Coach Kitt. Even with Gatorade dumped and dripping over her back, Kitt directs traffic toward the handshake finale, the Windsor Prep players waiting politely in a line, tears smudging eye black.

I make it a point to say every girl's name as we pass, a flip-book of my old life gaining speed with each stop and face. And when I hit the end of the line, there's Danielle, her arms thrown wide. When I fall into them, they feel like home.

"I'm so proud of you, *champ*." And now *I'm* crying, tears bracketing the grin I can't lose. My sister is the first person I always want to impress, and nothing will ever change that. We'll always be a team, even if we aren't on the same side. "You're totally going to rub this in for the next 365 days, aren't you?"

I laugh as we unfold just enough—arms across each other's backs, hands landing on outside hips—that we can both face Mom and Dad, calling for a picture. Mom is looking good, her cheeks almost full, hair thickening up. Behind them, Ryan has his hands up, grin a mile wide, while Heather gives him a deep hug.

"Eh, winning isn't everything."

Acknowledgments

Like Liv, I am privileged to have a bunch of amazing humans on my team—and even better that I get a chance to thank them now. Books are extra great in that way.

First, a major thank you to my wonderful editing team of Hannah Milton and Pam Gruber—I would dump Gatorade on you if it wouldn't make a mess of the very nice Little, Brown offices. Your love and enthusiasm for Liv and her story is so tangible, I often feel like I could present it with a hug and a plate of warm cookies. Thank you so much for your guidance and care. I owe you a lifetime supply of doughnuts—Krispy Kreme, if you prefer.

And to the rest of the team at Hachette, Poppy, Little, Brown Books for Young Readers, and The Novl, thank you for your belief in my romantic girl-power football book. You got what we were trying to do and never batted an eye. And to our adorable cover models, Renee and Dylan, know that we're all shipping you. Sorry/not sorry—you were perfect as Liv and Grey!

Thank you to my head cheerleader, Whitney Ross, agent extraordinaire, who grabbed the baton from the lovely Rachel Ekstrom Courage, and made sure Liv and Grey saw the light of day. You immediately understood exactly what I hoped for this book and my readers, and it wouldn't be successful without you. And thank you to Rachel, who worked so hard to see this one through.

Thank you to my authenticity readers, who took such care in examining the relationships and characters detailed on the page. And to Randy Shemanski, who backed me up with his own knowledge of the sports we both love. Also, a last-minute shout-out to Jennifer Iacopelli, whose keen eye in the ARC stage caught one thing we all missed. If readers find fault in the depiction of the characters or the athletics in this book, that is my shortcoming, not of these early readers and their thoughtful consideration.

Thank you to the people who keep me rolling along day to day with a smile on my face. To the Kansas Writers crew, most especially for this particular book, Rebecca Coffindaffer, who provided excellent early feedback. To my Madcap writing retreat buddies who cheered me on as I hacked twenty thousand words from this baby in the Texas hill country. To my far-flung troop of author friends, I'm so lucky to have you book after book. And to my non-writer-ly buddies, who are extremely good at listening to me babble about writer-ly things. To my parents, Mary and Craig Warren, who always encouraged my love of athletics—Dad, all those Sundays watching the Chiefs totally paved the way for this book. To my husband, Justin, who lets me hog the TV when gymnastics is on and puts up with the fact that I only like post-season baseball (Go, Royals!). And to Nate, Amalia, and Emmie—follow your dreams but don't lie to us about it, mmmkay?

And finally—I've always felt that sports create the best stories because the stakes are immediate, the drama is intense, and the conflict is built-in. Those little five-minute vignette reels detailing how hard an athlete worked when no one was looking—the struggles no one saw to earn the glory that might be front-page news? Almost better than chocolate (*almost*). My love of sports stories translated into working in sports journalism for the majority of my newspaper career. Therefore, I owe a huge thank you to those who I worked with over the years on the sports desk and in the press box. I learned valuable lessons, not just about sports and storytelling from you, but also about life. A special shout-out in particular to the women who filled these spaces with me—Lydia, Mel, Jenny, Jenn, Lindsay, and all the rest, plus the trailblazing ladies of the Association of Women in Sports Media (AWSM).